THE
COLLECTOR

JOHN FOWLES

THE COLLECTOR

BARNES & NOBLE *Modern Classics*

que fors aus ne le sot riens nee

1

WHEN SHE WAS HOME FROM HER BOARDING-SCHOOL I used to see her almost every day sometimes, because their house was right opposite the Town Hall Annexe. She and her younger sister used to go in and out a lot, often with young men, which of course I didn't like. When I had a free moment from the files and ledgers I stood by the window and used to look down over the road over the frosting and sometimes I'd see her. In the evening I marked it in my observations diary, at first with X, and then when I knew her name with M. I saw her several times outside too. I stood right behind her once in a queue at the public library down Crossfield Street. She didn't look once at me, but I watched the back of her head and her hair in a long pigtail. It was very pale, silky, like Burnet cocoons. All in one pigtail coming down almost to her waist, sometimes in front, sometimes at the back. Sometimes she wore it up. Only once, before she came to be my guest here, did I have the privilege to see her with it loose, and it took my breath away it was so beautiful, like a mermaid.

Another time one Saturday off when I went up to the Natural History Museum I came back on the same train. She sat three seats down and sideways to me, and read a book, so I could watch her for thirty-five minutes. Seeing her always made me feel like I was catching a rarity, going up to it very careful, heart-in-mouth as they say. A Pale Clouded Yellow, for instance. I always thought of her like that, I mean words like elusive and sporadic, and very refined—not like the other ones, even the pretty ones. More for the real connoisseur.

The year she was still at school I didn't know who she was,

only how her father was Doctor Grey and some talk I overheard once at a Bug Section meeting about how her mother drank. I heard her mother speak once in a shop, she had a la-di-da voice and you could see she was the type to drink, too much make-up, etcetera.

Well, then there was the bit in the local paper about the scholarship she'd won and how clever she was, and her name as beautiful as herself, Miranda. So I knew she was up in London studying art. It really made a difference, that newspaper article. It seemed like we became more intimate, although of course we still did not know each other in the ordinary way.

I can't say what it was, the very first time I saw her, I knew she was the only one. Of course I am not mad, I knew it was just a dream and it always would have been if it hadn't been for the money. I used to have daydreams about her, I used to think of stories where I met her, did things she admired, married her and all that. Nothing nasty, that was never until what I'll explain later.

She drew pictures and I looked after my collection (in my dreams). It was always she loving me and my collection, drawing and colouring them; working together in a beautiful modern house in a big room with one of those huge glass windows; meetings there of the Bug Section, where instead of saying almost nothing in case I made mistakes we were the popular host and hostess. She all pretty with her pale blonde hair and grey eyes and of course the other men all green round the gills.

The only times I didn't have nice dreams about her being when I saw her with a certain young man, a loud noisy public-school type who had a sports car. I stood beside him once in Barclays waiting to pay in and I heard him say, I'll have it in fivers; the joke being it was only a cheque for ten pounds. They all behave like that. Well, I saw her climb in his car sometimes, or them out together in the town in it, and those days I was very short with the others in the office, and I didn't use to mark the X in my entomological observations diary (all this was before she went to London, she dropped him then). Those were days I let myself have the bad dreams. She cried or usually knelt. Once I let myself dream I hit her across the face as I saw it done once by a chap in a telly play. Perhaps that was when it all started.

My father was killed driving. I was two. That was in 1937. He was drunk, but Aunt Annie always said it was my mother that drove him to drink. They never told me what really happened, but she went off soon after and left me with Aunt Annie, she only wanted an easy time. My cousin Mabel once told me (when we were kids, in a quarrel) she was a woman of the streets who went off with a foreigner. I was stupid, I went straight and asked Aunt Annie and if there was any covering-up to do, of course she did it. I don't care now, if she is still alive, I don't want to meet her, I've got no interest. Aunt Annie's always said good riddance in so many words, and I agree.

So I was brought up by Aunt Annie and Uncle Dick with their daughter Mabel. Aunt Annie was my father's elder sister.

Uncle Dick died when I was fifteen. That was 1950. We went up to Tring Reservoir to fish, as usual I went off with my net and stuff. When I got hungry and came back to where I left him, there were a knot of people. I thought he'd caught a whopper. But he'd had a stroke. They got him home, but he never said another word or properly recognized any of us again.

The days we spent together, not together exactly, because I always went off collecting and he'd sit by his rods, though we always had dinner together and the journey there and home, those days (after the ones I'm going to say about) are definitely the best

I have ever had. Aunt Annie and Mabel used to despise my butterflies when I was a boy, but Uncle Dick would always stick up for me. He always admired a good bit of setting. He felt the same as I did about a new imago and would sit and watch the wings stretch and dry out and the gentle way they try them, and he also let me have room in his shed for my caterpillar jars. When I won a hobby prize for a case of Fritillaries he gave me a pound on condition I didn't tell Aunt Annie. Well, I won't go on, he was as good as a father to me. When I held the pools cheque in my hands, he was the person, besides Miranda of course, I thought of. I would have given him the best rods and tackle and anything else he wanted. But it was not to be.

I did the pools from the week I was twenty-one. Every week I did the same five-bob perm. Old Tom and Crutchley, who were in Rates with me, and some of the girls clubbed together and did a big one and they were always going at me to join in, but I stayed the lone wolf. I never liked old Tom or Crutchley. Old Tom is slimy, always going on about local government and buttering up to Mr. Williams, the Borough Treasurer. Crutchley's got a dirty mind and he is a sadist, he never let an opportunity go of making fun of my interest, especially if there were girls around. "Fred's looking tired—he's been having a dirty weekend with a Cabbage White," he used to say, and, "Who was that Painted Lady I saw you with last night?" Old Tom would snigger, and Jane, Crutchley's girl from Sanitation, she was always in our office, would giggle. She was all Miranda wasn't. I always hated vulgar women, especially girls. So I did my own entry, like I said.

The cheque was for £73,091 and some odd shillings and pence. I rang up Mr. Williams as soon as the pools people confirmed the

Tuesday that all was well. I could tell he was angry that I left like that, although he said at first he was pleased, he was sure they were all pleased, which of course I know they weren't. He even suggested I might invest in the Council 5% Loan! Some of them at Town Hall lose all sense of proportion.

I did what the pools people suggested, moved straight up to London with Aunt Annie and Mabel till the fuss died down. I sent old Tom a cheque for £500 and asked him to share with Crutchley and the others. I didn't answer their thank-you letters. You could see they thought I was mean.

The only fly in the ointment was Miranda. She was at home at the time of winning, on holidays from her art school, and I saw her only the Saturday morning of the great day. All the time we were up in London spending and spending I was thinking I wasn't going to see her any more; then that I was rich, a good spec as a husband now; then again I knew it was ridiculous, people only married for love, especially girls like Miranda. There were even times I thought I would forget her. But forgetting's not something you do, it happens to you. Only it didn't happen to me.

If you are on the grab and immoral like most nowadays, I suppose you can have a good time with a lot of money when it comes to you. But I may say I have never been like that, I was never once punished at school. Aunt Annie is a Nonconformist, she never forced me to go to chapel or such like, but I was brought up in the atmosphere, though Uncle Dick used to go to the pub on the q.t. sometimes. Aunt Annie let me smoke cigarettes after a lot of rows when I came out of the army, but she never liked it. Even with all that money, she had to keep on saying spending it was against her principles. But Mabel went at her behind the scenes, I heard her doing it one day, and anyway I said it was my money and my conscience, she was welcome to all she wanted and none if she didn't, and there was nothing about accepting gifts in Nonconformism.

What this is all leading to is I got a bit drunk once or twice when I was in the Pay Corps, especially in Germany, but I never had anything to do with women. I never thought about women much before Miranda. I know I don't have what it is girls look for; I know chaps like Crutchley who just seem plain coarse to me get on well with them. Some of the girls in the Annexe, it was really disgusting, the looks they'd give him. It's some crude animal thing I was born without. (And I'm glad I was, if more people were like me, in my opinion, the world would be better.)

When you don't have money, you always think things will be very different after. I didn't want more than my due, nothing excessive, but we could see straight away at the hotel that of course they were respectful on the surface, but that was all, they really despised us for having all that money and not knowing what to do with it. They still treated me behind the scenes for what I was—a clerk. It was no good throwing money around. As soon as we spoke or did something we gave the game away. You could see them saying, don't kid us, we know what you are, why don't you go back where you came from.

I remember a night we went out and had supper at a posh restaurant. It was on a list the pools people gave us. It was good food, we ate it but I didn't hardly taste it because of the way people looked at us and the way the slimy foreign waiters and everybody treated us, and how everything in the room seemed to look down at us because we weren't brought up their way. I read the other day an article about class going—I could tell them things about that. If you ask me, London's all arranged for the people who can act like public schoolboys, and you don't get anywhere if you don't have the manner born and the right la-di-da voice—I mean rich people's London, the West End, of course.

One evening—it was after the posh restaurant, I was feeling depressed—I told Aunt Annie I felt like a walk, which I did. I walked and I suddenly felt I'd like to have a woman, I mean to be able to know I'd had a woman, so I rang up a telephone number a chap at the cheque-giving ceremony gave me. If you want a bit of you-know-what, he said.

A woman said, "I'm engaged." I asked if she knew any other number, and she gave me two. Well, I took a taxi round to the second one's address. I won't say what happened, except that I was no good. I was too nervous, I tried to be as if I knew all about it and of course she saw, she was old and she was horrible, horrible. I mean, both the filthy way she behaved and in looks. She was worn, common. Like a specimen you'd turn away from, out collecting. I thought of Miranda seeing me there like that. As I said, I tried to do it but it was no good and I didn't try hardly.

I'm not the crude pushing sort, I never have been, I always had higher aspirations, as they say. Crutchley used to say you had to push nowadays to get anywhere, and he used to say, look at old Tom, look where being slimy's got him. Crutchley used to be very familiar, much too so in yours truly's opinion, as I said. Though he knew when to be slimy when it paid; to Mr. Williams, for instance. A bit more life, Clegg, Mr. Williams once said to me, when I was on Inquiries. The public like a smile or a small joke once in a while, he said, we aren't all born with a gift for it, like Crutchley, but we can try, you know. That really riled me. I can say I was sick to death with the Annexe, and I was going to leave anyhow.

*   *   *

I was not different, I can prove it, one reason I got fed up with
Aunt Annie was I started to get interested with some of the books
you can buy at shops in Soho, books of stark women and all that.
I could hide the magazines, but there were books I wanted to buy
and I couldn't in case she tumbled. I always wanted to do photography, I got a camera at once of course, a Leica, the best, telephoto
lens, the lot; the main idea was to take butterflies living like the famous Mr. S. Beaufoy; but also often before I used to come on
things out collecting, you'd be surprised the things couples get up
to in places you think they would know better than to do it in, so
I had that too.

Of course the business with the woman upset me though, on
top of all the other things. For instance Aunt Annie had set her
heart on going on a sea-cruise to Australia to see her son Bob and
Uncle Steve her other younger brother and his family, and she
wanted me to go too, but like I say I didn't want to be any more
with Aunt Annie and Mabel. It was not that I hated them, but you
could see what they were at once, even more than me. What they
were was obvious; I mean small people who'd never left home. For
instance, they always expected me to do everything with them and
tell them what I'd done if by any chance I had an hour off on my
own. The day after the above-mentioned I told them flat I wasn't
going to Australia. They took it not too bad, I suppose they had
time to reckon it was my money after all.

The first time I went to look for Miranda it was a few days after I
went down to Southampton to see off Aunt Annie; May 10th, to
be exact. I was back in London. I hadn't got any real plan, and I
told Aunt Annie and Mabel I might go abroad, but I didn't truly
know. Aunt Annie was scared, really, the night before they went
she had a solemn talk with me about how I wasn't to marry, she

hoped—that is, without her meeting the bride. She said a lot about it being my money and my life and how generous I was and all that, but I could see she was really scared I might marry some girl and they'd lose all the money they were so ashamed of, anyway. I don't blame her, it was natural, especially with a daughter who's a cripple. I think people like Mabel should be put out painlessly, but that's beside the point.

What I thought I would do (I already, in preparation, bought the best equipment in London) was to go to some of the localities where there were rare species and aberrations and get proper series. I mean turn up and stay somewhere for as long as I liked, and go out and collect and photograph. I had driving lessons before they went and I got a special van. There were a lot of species I wanted—the Swallowtail for instance, the Black Hairstreak and the Large Blue, rare Fritillaries like the Heath and the Glanville. Things most collectors only get a go at once a lifetime. There were moths too. I thought I might take them up.

What I'm trying to say is that having her as my guest happened suddenly, it wasn't something I planned the moment the money came.

Well, of course with Aunt Annie and Mabel out of the way I bought all the books I wanted, some of them I didn't know such things existed, as a matter of fact I was disgusted, I thought here I am stuck in a hotel room with this stuff and it's a lot different from what I used to dream of about Miranda and me. Suddenly I saw I'd thought myself into thinking her completely gone out of my life, as if we didn't live within a few miles of each other (I was moved into the hotel in Paddington then) and I hadn't anyhow got all the time in the world to find out where she lived. It was easy, I looked up the Slade School of Art in the telephone directory, and I waited outside one morning in the van. The van was the one

really big luxury I gave myself. It had a special fitting in the back
compartment, a camp bed you could let down and sleep in; I
bought it to carry all my equipment for when I moved round the
country, and also I thought if I got a van I wouldn't always have
to be taking Aunt Annie and Mabel around when they came back.
I didn't buy it for the reason I did use it for. The whole idea was
sudden, like a stroke of genius almost.

The first morning I didn't see her, but the next day at last I did.
She came out with a lot of other students, mostly young men. My
heart beat very fast and I felt sick. I had the camera all ready, but
I couldn't dare use it. She was just the same; she had a light way of
walking and she always wore flat heels so she didn't have that
mince like most girls. She didn't think at all about the men when
she moved. Like a bird. All the time she was talking to a young
man with black hair, cut very short with a little fringe, very
artistic-looking. There were six of them, but then she and the
young man crossed the street. I got out of the van and followed
them. They didn't go far, into a coffee-bar.

I went into that coffee-bar, suddenly, I don't know why, like I
was drawn in by something else, against my will almost. It was full
of people, students and artists and such-like; they mostly had that
beatnik look. I remember there were weird faces and things on the
walls. It was supposed to be African, I think.

There were so many people and the noise and I felt so nervous I didn't see her at first. She was sitting in a second room at
the back. I sat on a stool at the counter where I could watch. I
didn't dare look very often and the light in the other room wasn't
very good.

Then she was standing right next me. I was pretending to read
a newspaper so I didn't see her get up. I felt my face was red, I
stared at the words but I couldn't read, I daren't look the smallest

look—she was there almost touching me. She was in a check dress, dark blue and white it was, her arms brown and bare, her hair all loose down her back.

She said, "Jenny, we're absolutely broke, be an angel and let us have two cigarettes." The girl behind the counter said, "Not again," or something, and she said, "Tomorrow, I swear," and then, "Bless you," when the girl gave her two. It was all over in five seconds, she was back with the young man, but hearing her voice turned her from a sort of dream person to a real one. I can't say what was special in her voice. Of course it was very educated, but it wasn't la-di-da, it wasn't slimy, she didn't beg the cigarettes or like demand them, she just asked for them in an easy way and you didn't have any class feeling. She spoke like she walked, as you might say.

I paid as quick as possible and went back to the van and the Cremorne and my room. I was really upset. It was partly that she had to borrow cigarettes because she had no money and I had sixty thousand pounds (I gave Aunt Annie ten) ready to lay at her feet—because that is how I felt. I felt I would do anything to know her, to please her, to be her friend, to be able to watch her openly, not spy on her. To show how I was, I put five five-pound notes I had on me in an envelope and addressed it to Miss Miranda Grey, the Slade School of Art . . . only of course I didn't post it. I would have if I could have seen her face when she opened it.

That was the day I first gave myself the dream that came true. It began where she was being attacked by a man and I ran up and rescued her. Then somehow I was the man that attacked her, only I didn't hurt her; I captured her and drove her off in the van to a remote house and there I kept her captive in a nice way. Gradually she came to know me and like me and the dream grew into the one about our living in a nice modern house, married, with kids and everything.

It haunted me. It kept me awake at nights, it made me forget what I was doing during the day. I stayed on and on at the Cremorne. It stopped being a dream, it began to be what I pretended was really going to happen (of course, I thought it was only pretending) so I thought of ways and means—all the things I would have to arrange and think about and how I'd do it and all. I thought, I can't ever get to know her in the ordinary way, but if she's with me, she'll see my good points, she'll understand. There was always the idea she would understand.

Another thing I began to do was read the classy newspapers, for the same reason I went to the National Gallery and the Tate Gallery. I didn't enjoy them much, it was like the cabinets of foreign species in the Entomology Room at the Natural History Museum, you could see they were beautiful but you didn't know them, I mean I didn't know them like I knew the British. But I went so as I could talk to her, so I wouldn't seem ignorant.

In one of the Sunday papers I saw an advert in capitals in a page of houses for sale. I wasn't looking for them, this just seemed to catch my eye as I was turning the page. "FAR FROM THE MADDING CROWD?" it said. Just like that. Then it went on:

> Old cottage, charming secluded situation, large garden, 1 hr.
> by car London, two miles from nearest village . . .

—and so on. The next morning I was driving down to see it. I phoned the estate agent in Lewes and arranged to meet someone at the cottage. I bought a map of Sussex. That's the thing about money. There are no obstacles.

I expected something broken-down. It looked old all right, black beams and white outside and old stone tiles. It stood right on its own. The estate agent came out when I drove up. I thought he would be older, he was my age, but the public schoolboy type, full of silly remarks that are meant to be funny, as if it was below him to sell anything and there was some difference between selling houses and something in a shop. He put me off straight away because he was inquisitive. Still, I thought I better look round, having come all that way. The rooms were not much, but it was well fitted out with all mod cons, electricity, telephone and all. Some retired navy admiral or somebody had had it and died, and then the next buyer died unexpectedly as well and so it was on the market.

I still say I didn't go down there with the intention of seeing whether there was anywhere to have a secret guest. I can't really say what intention I had.

I just don't know. What you do blurs over what you did before.

The chap wanted to know if it was just for myself. I said it was for an aunt. I told the truth, I said I wanted it to be a surprise for her, when she came back from Australia and so on.

How about their figure, he wanted to know.

I've just come into a lot of money, I said, to squash him. We were just coming downstairs when he said that, having seen everything, I thought. I was even going on to say it wasn't what I wanted, not big enough, to squash him more, when he said, well, that's the lot, bar the cellars.

You had to go out through the back where there was a door beside the back door. He took the key from under a flowerpot. Of course the electricity was off, but he had a torch. It was cold out of the sun, damp, nasty. There were stone steps down. At the bottom he shone his torch round. Someone had whitewashed the walls, but it was a long time ago, and pieces had come off so that the walls looked mottled.

Runs the whole length, he said, and there's this too. He shone the torch and I saw a doorway in the corner of the wall facing us as we came down the stairs. It was another large cellar, four big steps down from the first one, but this time with a lower roof and a bit arched, like the rooms you see underneath churches sometimes. The steps came down diagonally in one corner so the room ran away, so to speak.

Just the thing for orgies, he said.

What was it for? I asked, ignoring his silly facetiousness.

He said they thought it might be because the cottage was so on its own. They'd have to store a lot of food. Or it might have been a secret Roman Catholic chapel. One of the electricians later said it was a smugglers' place when they used to be going to London from Newhaven.

Well, we went back upstairs and out. When he locked the door and put the key back under a flowerpot, it was like down there didn't exist. It was two worlds. It's always been like that. Some days I've woken up and it's all been like a dream, till I went down again.

He looked at his watch.

I'm interested, I said. Very interested. I was so nervous he looked at me surprised and I said, I think I'll have it. Just like that. I really surprised myself. Because before I always wanted something up to date, what they call contemporary. Not an old place stuck away.

He stood there looking all gormless, surprised that I was so interested, surprised I had money, I suppose, like most of them.

He went away back to Lewes then. He had to fetch someone else interested, so I said I would stay in the garden and think things over before a final decision.

It was a nice garden, it runs back to a field which had lucerne then, lovely stuff for butterflies. The field goes up to a hill (that is north). East there are woods on both sides of the road running up from the valley towards Lewes. West there are fields. There is a farmhouse about three-quarters of a mile away down the hill, the nearest house. South you have a fine view, except it was blocked by the front hedge and some trees. Also a good garage.

I went back to the house and got the key out and went down into the cellars again. The inner one must have been five or six feet under the earth. It was damp, the walls like wet wood in winter, I couldn't see very well because I only had my lighter. It was a bit frightening, but I am not the superstitious type.

Some might say I was lucky to find the place first go, however I would have found somewhere else sooner or later. I had the money. I had the will. Funny, what Crutchley called "push." I didn't push at the Annexe, it didn't suit me. But I would like to see Crutchley organize what I organized last summer and carry it through. I am not going to blow my own trumpet, but it was no small thing.

I read in the paper the other day (Saying of the Day)— "What Water is to the Body, Purpose is to the Mind." That is very true, in my humble opinion. When Miranda became the purpose of my life I should say I was at least as good as the next man, as it turned out.

I had to give five hundred more than they asked in the advert, others were after it, everyone fleeced me. The surveyor, the builder, the decorators, the furniture people in Lewes I got to furnish it. I didn't care, why should I, money was no object. I got long letters

from Aunt Annie, which I wrote back to, giving her figures half
what I really paid.

I got the electricians to run a power cable down to the cellar,
and the plumbers water and a sink. I made out I wanted to do carpentry and photography and that would be my workroom. It
wasn't a lie, there was carpentry to do all right. And I was already
taking some photographs I couldn't have developed in a shop.
Nothing nasty. Just couples.

At the end of August, the men moved out and I moved in. To
begin with, I felt like in a dream. But that soon wore off. I wasn't
left alone as much as I expected. A man came and wanted to do the
garden, he'd always done it, and he got very nasty when I sent him
away. Then the vicar from the village came and I had to be rude
with him. I said I wanted to be left alone, I was Nonconformist, I
wanted nothing to do with the village, and he went off la-di-da in
a huff. Then there were several people with van-shops and I had
to put them off. I said I bought all my goods in Lewes.

I had the telephone disconnected, too.

I soon got in the habit of locking the front gate, it was only a
grille, but had a lock. Once or twice I saw tradesmen looking
through, but people soon seemed to get the point. I was left alone,
and could get on with my work.

I worked for a month or more getting my plans ready. I was alone
all the time; not having any real friends was lucky. (You couldn't
call the Annexe people friends, I didn't miss them, they didn't
miss me.)

I used to do odd jobs for Aunt Annie, Uncle Dick taught me. I
wasn't bad at carpentering and so on, and I fitted out the room
very nicely, though I say it myself. After I got it dried out I put
several layers of insulating felt and then a nice bright orange car-

pet (cheerful) fitting the walls (which were whitewashed). I got in a bed and a chest of drawers. Table, armchair, etcetera. I fixed up a screen in one corner and behind it a wash-table and a camper's lavatory and all the etceteras—it was like a separate little room almost. I got other things, cases and a lot of art books and some novels to make it look homely, which it finally did. I didn't risk pictures, I knew she might have advanced taste.

One problem of course was doors and noise. There was a good old oak frame in the door through to her room but no door, so I had to make one to fit, and that was my hardest job. The first one I made didn't work, but the second one was better. Even a man couldn't have bust it down, let alone a little thing like her. It was two-inch seasoned wood with sheet metal on the inside so she couldn't get at the wood. It weighed a ton and it was no joke getting it hung, but I did it. I fixed ten-inch bolts outside. Then I did something very clever. I made what looked like a bookcase, only for tools and things, out of some old wood and fitted it with wooden latches in the doorway, so that if you gave a casual look it just seemed that it was just an old recess fitted up with shelves. You lifted it out and there was the door through. It also stopped any noise getting out. I also fitted a bolt on the inner side of the door which had a lock too down to the cellar so I couldn't be disturbed. Also a burglar alarm. Only a simple one, for the night.

What I did in the first cellar was I put in a small cooker and all the other facilities. I didn't know there wouldn't be snoopers and it would look funny if I was always carrying trays of food up and down. But being at the back of the house I didn't worry much, seeing there was only fields and woods. Two sides of the garden there is a wall, anyhow, and the rest is hedge you can't see through. It was nearly ideal. I did think of having a stair run down from inside, but the expense was high and I didn't want risk of suspicions. You can't trust workmen now, they want to know everything.

All this time I never thought it was serious. I know that must sound very strange, but it was so. I used to say, of course, I'll never do it, this is only pretending. And I wouldn't have pretended even like that if I hadn't had all the time and money I wanted. In my opinion a lot of people who may seem happy now would do what I did or similar things if they had the money and the time. I mean, to give way to what they pretend now they shouldn't. Power corrupts, a teacher I had always said. And Money is Power.

Another thing I did, I bought a lot of clothes for her at a store in London. What I did was, in one I saw an assistant just her size and I gave the colours I always saw Miranda wear and I got everything there they said a girl would need. I told a story about a girlfriend from the North who'd had all her luggage stolen and I wanted it to be a surprise, etcetera. I don't think she believed me in the store, but it was a good sale—I paid out nearly ninety pounds that morning.

I could go on all night about the precautions. I used to go and sit in her room and work out what she could do to escape. I thought she might know about electricity, you never know with girls these days, so I always wore rubber heels, I never touched a switch without a good look first. I got a special incinerator to burn all her rubbish. I knew nothing of hers must ever leave the house. No laundry. There could always be something.

Well, at last I went back up to London to the Cremorne Hotel. For several days I watched for her but I didn't see her. It was a very anxious time, but I kept on. I didn't take the camera, I knew it was too risky, I was after bigger game than just a street shot. I went twice to the coffee-bar. One day I spent nearly two hours there pretending to read a book, but she didn't come. I began to get wild ideas, perhaps she'd died, perhaps she wasn't doing art there any more. Then one day (I didn't want the van to get too familiar) as I was getting off the Underground at Warren Street, I saw her. She was getting off a train coming from the north on the other platform. It was easy. I followed her out of the station, and saw her go off towards the College. The next days I watched the tube station. Perhaps she didn't always use the tube to go home, I didn't see her for two days, but then the third day I saw her cross the road and go into the station. That's how I found out where she came from. It was Hampstead. I did the same thing there. I waited for her to come out the next day and she did and I followed her about ten minutes through a lot of little streets to where she lived. I walked on past the house she went into and found out the number and then at the end of the road the name of it.

It was a good day's work.

I booked out of the Cremorne three days before, and every night I moved into a new hotel and booked out the next morning so that I couldn't be traced. In the van I had the bed ready and the straps and scarves. I was going to use chloroform, I used it once in the killing-bottle. A chap in Public Analysis let me have it. It doesn't go weak but just to make sure I decided to mix in a bit of carbon tetrachloride, what they call CTC and you can buy anywhere.

I drove round the Hampstead district and learnt the A to Z for that part off and how to get quickly away down to Fosters. Everything was ready. So now I could watch and when I saw the chance, do it. I was really peculiar those days, I thought of everything, just like I'd been doing it all my life. Like I'd been a secret agent or a detective.

*   *   *

It finally ten days later happened as it sometimes does with butterflies. I mean you go to a place where you know you may see
something rare and you don't, but the next time not looking for it
you see it on a flower right in front of you, handed to you on a
plate, as they say.

This night I was outside the tube as usual with the van up a
side street. It had been a fine day but close; and it came on to
thunder and rain. I was standing in the doorway of a shop opposite the exit, and I saw her come up the steps just as it was teem-
ing. I saw she had no raincoat, only a jumper. Soon she ran round
the corner into the main part of the station. I crossed, there were
a mass of people milling about. She was in a telephone box. Then
she came out and instead of going up the hill like she usually did
she went along another street. I followed her, I thought it was no
good, I couldn't understand what she was doing. Then she suddenly shot up a side road and there was a cinema and she went in.
I saw what it was, she had rung up where she lived to say it was
raining hard and she was going in the cinema to wait for it to clear
up. I knew it was my chance, unless someone came to meet her.
When she had gone in, I went and saw how long the programme
lasted. It was two hours. I took a risk, perhaps I wanted to give
fate a chance to stop me. I went into a café and had my supper.
Then I went to my van and parked where I could see the cinema.
I didn't know what to expect, perhaps she was meeting a friend. I
mean I felt I was swept on, like down rapids, I might hit something, I might get through.

She came out alone, exactly two hours later, it had stopped
raining more or less and it was almost dark, the sky overcast. I
watched her go back the usual way up the hill. Then I drove off
past her to a place I knew she must pass. It was where the road she

lived in curved up away from another one. There was trees and bushes on one side, on the other a whopping big house in big grounds. I think it was empty. Higher up there were the other houses, all big. The first part of her walk was in bright-lit streets.

There was just this one place.

I had a special plastic bag sewn in my mac pocket, in which I put some of the chloroform and CTC and the pad so it was soaked and fresh. I kept the flap down, so the smell kept in, then in a second I could get it out when needed.

Two old women with umbrellas (it began to spot with rain again) appeared and came up the road towards me. It was just what I didn't want, I knew she was due, and I nearly gave up then and there. But I bent right down, they passed talking nineteen to the dozen, I don't think they even saw me or the van. There were cars parked everywhere in that district. A minute passed. I got out and opened the back. It was all planned. And then she was near. She'd come up and round without me seeing, only twenty yards away, walking quickly. If it had been a clear night I don't know what I'd have done. But there was this wind in the trees. Gusty. I could see there was no one behind her. Then she was right beside me, coming up the pavement. Funny, singing to herself.

I said, excuse me, do you know anything about dogs?

She stopped, surprised. "Why?" she said.

It's awful, I've just run one over, I said. It dashed out. I don't know what to do with it. It's not dead. I looked into the back, very worried.

"Oh the poor thing," she said.

She came towards me, to look in. Just as I hoped.

There's no blood, I said, but it can't move.

Then she came round the end of the open back door, and I stood back as if to let her see. She bent forward to peer in, I flashed a look down the road, no one, and then I got her. She didn't make a sound, she seemed so surprised, I got the pad I'd been holding in my pocket right across her mouth and nose, I caught her to me, I could smell the fumes, she struggled like the dickens, but she wasn't strong, smaller even than I'd thought. She made a sort of gurgling. I looked down the road again, I was thinking this is it, she'll fight and I shall have to hurt her or run away. I was ready to bolt for it. And then suddenly she went limp, I was holding her up instead of holding her quiet. I got her half into the van, then I jerked open the other door, got in and pulled her after me, then shut the doors quietly to. I rolled and lifted her on to the bed. She was mine, I felt suddenly very excited, I knew I'd done it. I put the gag on first, then I strapped her down, no hurry, no panic, like I planned. Then I scrambled into the driving seat. It all took not a minute. I drove up the road, not fast, slow and quiet, and turned to a place I'd noticed on Hampstead Heath. There I got into the back again, and did the tying up properly, with the scarves and everything, so that she wouldn't be hurt, and so she couldn't scream or bang the sides or anything. She was still unconscious, but she was breathing, I could hear her, as if she had catarrh, so I knew she was all right.

Near Redhill I drove off the main road as planned and up a lonely side road and then got in the back to look at her. I laid a torch where it gave a bit of light and I could see. She was awake. Her eyes seemed very big, they didn't seem frightened, they seemed proud almost, as if she'd decided not to be frightened, not at any price.

I said, don't be alarmed, I'm not going to hurt you. She remained staring at me.

It was embarrassing, I didn't know what to say. I said, are you all right, do you want anything, but it sounded silly. I really meant did she want to go outside.

She began to shake her head. I could see she meant the gag was hurting.

I said, we're miles in the country, it's no good screaming, if you do, I'll put the gag straight back, do you understand?

She nodded, so I undid the scarf. Before I could do anything she reached up as high as she could and sideways and she was sick. It was horrible. I could smell the chloroform and the sick. She didn't say anything. She just groaned. I lost my head, I didn't know what to do. I suddenly felt we had to get home as quick as possible, so I put the gag on again. She struggled, I heard her say under the cloth, no, no, it was horrible, but I made myself do it because I knew it was for the best in the end. Then I got into the driving-seat and on we went.

We got here just after half past ten. I drove into the garage, went and looked about to make sure nothing had happened in my absence, not that I expected anything. But I didn't want to spoil the ship for the little bit of tar. I went down to her room, everything was all right, not too stuffy because I'd left the door open. I slept in it one night before to see if there was enough air and there was. There were all the doings to make tea with and so on. It looked very snug and cosy.

Well, at last the great moment was come. I went up to the garage and opened the back of the van. Like the rest of the operation it went according to plan. I got the straps off her, made her sit up, her legs and feet still bound of course. She kicked about for a moment, I was obliged to say that if she did not keep quiet I would have to resort to more of the chloro and CTC (which I showed), but that if she kept still I wouldn't hurt her. That did the trick. I lifted her, she was not so heavy as I thought; I got her down quite easily; we did have a bit of a struggle at the door of her room, but there wasn't much she could do then. I put her on the bed. It was done.

Her face was white, some of the sick had gone on her navy jumper, she was a real sight; but her eyes weren't afraid. It was funny. She just stared at me, waiting.

I said, this is your room. If you do what I say, you won't be hurt. It's no good shouting. You can't be heard outside and anyway there's never anyone to hear. I'm going to leave you now, there's some biscuits and sandwiches (I bought some in Hampstead) and if you want to make tea or cocoa. I'll come back tomorrow morning, I said.

I could see she wanted me to take the gag off, but I wouldn't do it. What I did was I undid her arms and then immediately went back out; she struggled to get the gag off, but I got the door closed first and the bolts in. I heard her cry, come back! Then again but not loud. Then she tried the door, but not very hard. Then she began to bang on the door with something hard. I think it was the hairbrush. It didn't sound much, anyhow I put the false shelf in and knew you wouldn't hear anything outside. I stayed an hour in the outer cellar, just in case. It wasn't necessary, there was nothing in her room she could have broken the door down with even if she had the strength, I bought all plastic cups and saucers and aluminium teapot and cutlery, etcetera.

Eventually I went up and went to bed. She was my guest at last and that was all I cared about. I lay awake a long time, thinking about things. I felt a bit unsure the van would be traced, but there were hundreds of vans like that, and the only people I really worried about were those two women who passed.

Well, I lay there thinking of her below, lying awake too. I had nice dreams, dreams where I went down and comforted her; I was excited, perhaps I went a bit far in what I gave myself to dream, but I wasn't really worried, I knew my love was worthy of her. Then I went to sleep.

After, she was telling me what a bad thing I did and how I ought to try and realize it more. I can only say that evening I was very happy, as I said, and it was more like I had done something very daring, like climbing Everest or doing something in enemy territory. My feelings were very happy because my intentions were of the best. It was what she never understood.

    To sum up, that night was the best thing I ever did in my life (bar winning the pools in the first place). It was like catching the Mazarine Blue again or a Queen of Spain Fritillary. I mean it was like something you only do once in a lifetime and even then often not; something you dream about more than you ever expect to see come true, in fact.

I didn't need the alarm, I was up before. I went down, locking the cellar door behind me. I'd planned everything, I knocked on her door and shouted please get up, and waited ten minutes and then drew the bolts and went in. I had her bag with me which I had searched, of course. There was nothing she could use except a nail-file and a razor-blade cutter which I removed.

    The light was on, she was standing by the armchair. She'd got all her clothes on and she stared at me again, no sign of fear, bold as brass she was. It's funny, she didn't look quite like I'd always remembered her. Of course I'd never seen her so close before.

    I said, I hope you slept well.

    "Where is this, who are you, why have you brought me here?" She said it very coldly, not at all violent.

I can't tell you.

She said, "I demand to be released at once. This is monstrous."

We just stood staring at each other.

"Get out of the way. I'm going to leave." And she came straight towards me, towards the door. But I didn't budge. I thought for a minute she was going to attack me, but she must have seen it was silly. I was determined, she couldn't have won. She stopped right up close to me and said, "Get out of the way."

I said, you can't go yet. Please don't oblige me to use force again.

She gave me a fierce cold look, then she turned away. "I don't know who you think I am. If you think I'm somebody rich's daughter and you're going to get a huge ransom, you've got a shock coming."

I know who you are, I said. It's not money.

I didn't know what to say, I was so excited, her there at last in the flesh. So nervous. I wanted to look at her face, at her lovely hair, all of her all small and pretty, but I couldn't, she stared so at me. There was a funny pause.

Suddenly she said accusing like, "And don't I know who you are?"

I began to go red, I couldn't help it, I never planned for that, I never thought she would know me.

She said slowly, "Town Hall Annexe."

I said, I don't know what you mean.

"You've got a moustache," she said.

I still don't know how she knew. She saw me a few times in the town, I suppose, perhaps she saw me out of the windows of their house sometimes, I hadn't thought of that, my mind was all in a whirl.

She said, "Your photo was in the paper."

I've always hated to be found out, I don't know why, I've always tried to explain, I mean invent stories to explain. Suddenly I saw a way out.

I said, I'm only obeying orders.

"Orders," she said. "Whose orders?"

I can't tell you.

She would keep staring at me. Keeping her distance, too. I suppose she thought I would attack her.

"Whose orders?" she said again.

I tried to think of someone. I don't know why, the only name I could think of she might know was Mr. Singleton. He was the manager of the Barclays. I knew her father banked there. I saw him several times in there when I was, and talking with Mr. Singleton.

Mr. Singleton's orders, I said.

She looked really amazed, so I went on quick. I'm not meant to tell you, I said, he'd kill me if he knew.

"Mr. Singleton?" she said, as if she wasn't hearing properly.

He's not what you think, I said.

Suddenly she sat down on the arm of the armchair, like it was all too much for her. "You mean Mr. Singleton ordered you to kidnap me?"

I nodded.

"But I know his daughter. He's . . . oh, it's mad," she said.

Do you remember the girl in Penhurst Road?

"What girl in Penhurst Road?"

The one that disappeared three years ago.

It was something I invented. My mind was really quick that morning. So I thought.

"I was probably away at school. What happened to her?"

I don't know. Except he did it.

"Did what?"

I don't know. I don't know what happened to her. But he did it, whatever it was. She's never been heard of since.

Suddenly she said, "Have you got a cigarette?"

I was all awkward, I got a packet out of my pocket and my lighter and went and passed them to her. I didn't know if I ought to light her cigarette, but it seemed silly.

I said, you haven't eaten anything.

She held the cigarette, very ladylike, between her fingers. She'd cleaned the jumper up. The air was stuffy.

She took no notice. It was funny. I knew she knew I was lying.

"You're telling me that Mr. Singleton is a sex maniac and he kidnaps girls and you help him?"

I said, I have to. I stole some money from the bank, I'd go to prison if they found out, he holds it over me, you see.

All the time she was staring at me. She had great big clear eyes, very curious, always wanting to find out. (Not snoopy, of course.)

"You won a lot of money, didn't you?"

I knew what I said was confused. I felt all hot and bothered.

"Why didn't you pay back the money then? What was it—seventy thousand pounds? You didn't steal all that? Or perhaps you just help him for the fun of it?"

There's other things I can't tell you. I'm in his power.

She stood up with her hands in her skirt pockets. She stared at herself in the mirror (metal, of course, not glass) for a change.

"What's he going to do to me?"

I don't know.

"Where is he now?"

He'll be coming. I expect.

She said nothing for a minute. Then she suddenly looked as if she'd thought of something nasty, what I said might be true sort of thing.

"Of course. This must be his house in Suffolk."

Yes, I said, thinking I was clever.

"He hasn't got a house in Suffolk," she said, all cold.

You don't know, I said. But it sounded feeble.

She was going to speak but I felt I had to stop her questions, I didn't know she was so sharp. Not like normal people.

I came to ask you what you'd like for breakfast, there's cereal, eggs, etcetera.

"I don't want any breakfast," she said. "This horrid little room. And that anaesthetic. What was it?"

I didn't know it would make you sick. Really.

"Mr. Singleton should have told you." You could see she didn't believe it about him. She was being sarcastic.

I said in a hurry, would you like tea or coffee and she said coffee, if you drink some first, so with that I left her and went out to the outer cellar. Just before I shut the door she said, "You've forgotten your lighter."

I've got another. (I hadn't.)

"Thank you," she said. It was funny, she almost smiled.

I made the Nescafé and I took it in and she watched me drink some and then she drank some. All the time she asked questions, no, all the time I felt she might ask a question, she'd come out quickly with a question to try and catch me. About how long she had to stay, why I was being so kind to her. I made up answers, but I knew they sounded feeble, it wasn't easy to invent quickly with her. In the end I said I was going into the shops and she was to tell me what she wanted. I said I'd buy anything she wanted.

"Anything?" she said.

In reason, I said.

"Mr. Singleton told you to?"

No. This is from me.

"I just want to be set free," she said. I couldn't get her to say anything more. It was horrible, she suddenly wouldn't speak, so I had to leave her.

She wouldn't speak again at lunch. I cooked the lunch in the outer cellar and took it in. But hardly any of it was eaten. She tried to bluff her way out again, cold as ice she was, but I wasn't having any.

That evening after her supper, which she likewise didn't eat much, I went and sat by the door. For some time she sat smoking, with her eyes shut, as if the sight of me tired her eyes.

"I've been thinking. All you've told me about Mr. Singleton is a story. I don't believe it. He's just not that sort of man, for one thing. And if he was, he wouldn't have you working for him. He wouldn't have made all these fantastic preparations."

I didn't say anything, I couldn't look at her.

"You've gone to a lot of trouble. All those clothes in there, all these art books. I added up their cost this afternoon. Forty-three pounds." It was like she was talking to herself. "I'm your prisoner, but you want me to be a happy prisoner. So there are two possibilities: you're holding me to ransom, you're in a gang or something."

I'm not. I told you.

"You know who I am. You must know my father's not rich or anything. So it can't be ransom."

It was uncanny, hearing her think it out.

"The only other thing is sex. You want to do something to me." She was watching me.

It was a question. It shocked me.

It's not that at all. I shall have all proper respect. I'm not that sort. I sounded quite curt.

"Then you must be mad," she said. "In a nice kind way, of course."

"You admit that the Mr. Singleton story is not true?"

I wanted to break it gently, I said.

"Break what?" she asked. "Rape? Murder?"

I never said that, I answered. She always seemed to get me on the defensive. In my dreams it was always the other way round.

"Why am I here?"

I want you to be my guest.

"Your guest!"

She stood up and walked round the armchair and leant against the back, eyes on me all the time. She'd taken her blue jumper off, she stood there in a dark green tartan dress, like a schoolgirl tunic, with a white blouse open at the throat. Her hair swept back into the pigtail. Her lovely face. She looked brave. I don't know why, I thought of her sitting on my knees, very still, with me stroking her soft blonde hair, all out loose as I saw it after.

Suddenly I said, I love you. It's driven me mad.

She said, "I see," in a queer grave voice.

She didn't look at me any more then.

I know it's old-fashioned to say you love a woman, I never meant to do it then. In my dreams it was always we looked into each other's eyes one day and then we kissed and nothing was said until after. A chap called Nobby in R.A.P.C. who knew all about women, always said you shouldn't ever tell a woman you loved her. Even if you did. If you had to say "I love you," you said it joking—he said that way it kept them after you. You had to play hard to get. The silly thing was I told myself a dozen times before I mustn't tell her I loved her, but let it come naturally on both sides. But when I had her there my head went round and I often said things I didn't mean to.

I don't mean I told her everything. I told her about working in the Annexe and seeing her and thinking about her and the way she behaved and walked and all she'd meant to me and then having money and knowing she'd never look at me in spite of it and being lonely. When I stopped she was sitting on the bed looking at the carpet. We didn't speak for what seemed a long time. There was just the whir of the fan in the outer cellar.

I felt ashamed. All red.

"Do you think you'll make me love you by keeping me prisoner?"

I want you to get to know me.

"As long as I'm here you'll just be a kidnapper to me. You know that?"

I got up. I didn't want to be with her any more.

"Wait," she said, coming towards me, "I'll make a promise. I understand. Really. Let me go. I'll tell no one, and nothing will happen."

It was the first time she'd given me a kind look. She was saying, trust me, plain as words. A little smile round her eyes, looking up at me. All eager.

"You could. We could be friends. I could help you."

Looking up at me there.

"It's not too late."

I couldn't say what I felt, I just had to leave her; she was really hurting me. So I closed the door and left her. I didn't even say good night.

No one will understand, they will think I was just after her for the obvious. Sometimes when I looked at the books before she came, it was what I thought, or I didn't know. Only when she came it was all different, I didn't think about the books or about her posing, things like that disgusted me, it was because I knew they would disgust her too. There was something so nice about her you had to be nice too, you could see she sort of expected it. I mean having her real made other things seem nasty. She was not like some woman you don't respect so you don't care what you do, you respected her and you had to be very careful.

I didn't sleep much that night, because I was shocked the way things had gone, my telling her so much the very first day and how she made me seem a fool. There were moments when I thought I'd have to go down and drive her back to London like she wanted. I could go abroad. But then I thought of her face and the way her pigtail hung down a bit sideways and twisted and how she stood and walked and her lovely clear eyes. I knew I couldn't do it.

After breakfast—that morning she ate a bit of cereal and had some coffee, when we didn't speak at all—she was up and dressed, but the bed had been made differently from at first so she must have slept in it. Anyhow she stopped me when I was going out.

"I'd like to talk with you." I stopped.

"Sit down," she said. I sat down on the chair by the steps down.

"Look, this is mad. If you love me in any real sense of the word love you can't want to keep me here. You can see I'm miserable. The air, I can't breathe at nights, I've woken up with a headache. I should die if you kept me here long." She looked really concerned.

It won't be very long. I promise.

She got up and stood by the chest of drawers, and stared at me.

"What's your name?" she said.

Clegg, I answered.

"Your first name?"

Ferdinand.

She gave me a quick sharp look.

"That's not true," she said. I remembered I had my wallet in my coat with my initials in gold I'd bought and I showed it. She wasn't to know F stood for Frederick. I've always liked Ferdinand, it's funny, even before I knew her. There's something foreign and distinguished about it. Uncle Dick used to call me it sometimes, joking. Lord Ferdinand Clegg, Marquis of Bugs, he used to say.

It's just a coincidence, I said.

"I suppose people call you Ferdie. Or Ferd."

Always Ferdinand.

"Look, Ferdinand, I don't know what you see in me. I don't know why you're in love with me. Perhaps I could fall in love with you somewhere else. I . . ." she didn't seem to know what to say, which was unusual ". . . I *do* like gentle, kind men. But I couldn't possibly fall in love with you in this room, I couldn't fall in love with anyone here. Ever."

I answered, I just want to get to know you.

All the time she was sitting on the chest of drawers, watching me to see what effect the things she said had. So I was suspicious. I knew it was a test.

"But you can't kidnap people just to get to know them!"

I want to know you very much. I wouldn't have a chance in London. I'm not clever and all that. Not your class. You wouldn't be seen dead with me in London.

"That's not fair. I'm not a snob. I hate snobs. I don't prejudge people."

I'm not blaming *you,* I said.

"I hate snobbism." She was quite violent. She had a way of saying some words very strong, very emphatic. "Some of my best friends in London are—well, what some people call working class. In origin. We just don't think about it."

Like Peter Catesby, I said. (That was the young man with the sports car's name.)

"Him! I haven't seen him for months. He's just a middle-class suburban oaf."

I could still see her climbing into his flashy M.G. I didn't know whether to trust her.

"I suppose it's in all the papers."

I haven't looked.

"You might go to prison for years."

Be worth it. Be worth going for life, I said.

"I promise, I swear that if you let me go I will not tell anyone. I'll tell them all some story. I will arrange to meet you as often as you like, as often as I can when I'm not working. Nobody will ever know about this except us."

I can't, I said. Not now. I felt like a cruel king, her appealing like she did.

"If you let me go now I shall begin to admire you. I shall think, he had me at his mercy, but he was chivalrous, he behaved like a real gentleman."

I can't, I said. Don't ask. Please don't ask.

"I should think, someone like that must be worth knowing." She sat perched there, watching me.

I've got to go now, I said. I went out so fast I fell over the top step. She got off the drawers and stood looking up at me in the door with a strange expression.

"Please," she said. Very gently and nicely. It was difficult to resist.

It was like not having a net and catching a specimen you wanted in your first and second fingers (I was always very clever at that), coming up slowly behind and you had it, but you had to nip the thorax, and it would be quivering there. It wasn't easy like it was with a killing-bottle. And it was twice as difficult with her, because I didn't want to kill her, that was the last thing I wanted.

She often went on about how she hated class distinction, but she never took me in. It's the way people speak that gives them away, not what they say. You only had to see her dainty ways to see how she was brought up. She wasn't la-di-da, like many, but it was there all the same. You could see it when she got sarcastic and impatient with me because I couldn't explain myself or I did things wrong. Stop thinking about class, she'd say. Like a rich man telling a poor man to stop thinking about money.

I don't hold it against her, she probably said and did some of the shocking things she did to show me she wasn't really refined, but she was. When she was angry she could get right up on her high horse and come it over me with the best of them.

There was always class between us.

I went into Lewes that morning. Partly I wanted to see the papers, I bought the lot. All of them had something. Some of the tripe papers had quite a lot, two had photographs. It was funny, reading the reports. There were things I didn't know before.

Longhaired blonde, art-student Miranda Grey, 20, who last year won a major scholarship to London's top Slade School of Art, is missing. She lived in term-time at 29 Hamnet Rd., N.W.3, with her aunt, Miss C. Vanbrugh-Jones, who late yesterday night alerted the police.

After class on Tuesday Miranda phoned to say she was going to a cinema and would be home soon after eight.

That was the last time she was seen.

There was a big photo of her and beside it it said: *Have You Seen This Girl?*

Another paper gave me a good laugh.

> Hampstead residents have been increasingly concerned in recent months about prowling "wolves" in cars. Piers Broughton, a fellow-student and close friend of Miranda, told me in the coffee-bar he often took Miranda to, that she seemed perfectly happy the day of her disappearance and had arranged to go to an exhibition with him only today. He said, "Miranda knows what London is like. She's the last person to take a lift from a stranger or anything like that. I'm most terribly worried about all this."
>
> A spokesman for the Slade School said, "She is one of our most promising second-year students. We are sure that there is some quite harmless explanation for her disappearance. Artistic young people have their whims."
>
> There the mystery rests.
>
> The police are asking anyone who saw Miranda on Tuesday evening, or who heard or noticed anything suspicious in the Hampstead area, to get in touch with them.

They said what clothes she was wearing and so on and there was a photo. Another paper said the police were going to drag the ponds on Hampstead Heath. One talked about Piers Broughton and how he and she were unofficially engaged. I wondered if he was the beatnik I saw her with. Another said, "She is one of the most popular students, always willing to help." They all said she was pretty. There were photos. If she was ugly it would all have been two lines on the back page.

I sat in the van on the road verge on the way back and read all the papers said. It gave me a feeling of power, I don't know why. All those people searching and me knowing the answer. When I drove on I decided definitely I'd say nothing to her.

As it happened, the first thing she asked me about when I got back was newspapers. Was there anything about her? I said I hadn't looked and I wasn't going to look. I said I wasn't interested in the papers, all they printed was a lot of tripe. She didn't insist.

I never let her see papers. I never let her have a radio or television. It happened one day before ever she came I was reading a book called *Secrets of the Gestapo*—all about the tortures and so on they had to do in the war, and how one of the first things to put up with if you were a prisoner was the not knowing what was going on outside the prison. I mean they didn't let the prisoners know anything, they didn't even let them talk to each other, so they were cut off from their old world. And that broke them down. Of course, I didn't want to break her down as the Gestapo wanted to break their prisoners down. But I thought it would be better if she was cut off from the outside world, she'd have to think about me more. So in spite of many attempts on her part to make me get her the papers and a radio I wouldn't ever let her have them. The first days I didn't want her to read about all the police were doing, and so on, because it would have only upset her. It was almost a kindness, as you might say.

That night I cooked her a supper of fresh frozen peas and frozen chicken in white sauce and she ate it and seemed to like it. After, I said, can I stay a bit?

"If you want," she said. She was sitting on the bed, with the blanket folded at her back like a cushion, against the wall, her feet folded under her. For a time she just smoked and looked at one of the art picture books I'd bought her.

"Do you know anything about art?" she asked.

Nothing you'd call knowledge.

"I knew you didn't. You wouldn't imprison an innocent person if you did."

I don't see the connection, I said.

She closed the book. "Tell me about yourself. Tell me what you do in your free time."

I'm an entomologist. I collect butterflies.

"Of course," she said. "I remember they said so in the paper. Now you've collected me."

She seemed to think it was funny, so I said, in a manner of speaking.

"No, not in a manner of speaking. Literally. You've pinned me in this little room and you can come and gloat over me."

I don't think of it like that at all.

"Do you know I'm a Buddhist? I hate anything that takes life. Even insects' lives."

You ate the chicken, I said. I caught her that time.

"But I despise myself. If I was a better person I'd be a vegetarian."

I said, if you asked me to stop collecting butterflies, I'd do it. I'd do anything you asked me.

"Except let me fly away."

I'd rather not talk about that. It doesn't get us anywhere.

"Anyway, I couldn't respect anyone, and especially a man, who did things just to please me. I'd want him to do them because he believed they were right." All the time she used to get at me, you'd think we were talking about something quite innocent, and suddenly she'd be digging at me. I didn't speak.

"How long shall I be here?"

I don't know, I said. It depends.

"On what?"

I didn't say anything. I couldn't.

"On my falling in love with you?"

It was like nagging.

"Because if it does, I shall be here until I die."

I didn't answer that.

"Go away," she said. "Go away and think it over."

The next morning she made the first attempt to escape. She didn't catch me off guard, exactly, but it taught me a lesson. She had her breakfast and then she told me her bed was loose, it was the far back leg, right up in the corner. I thought it was going to collapse, she said, there's a nut loose. Like a mutt I went to help her hold it and suddenly she gave me a heavy push, just as I was off balance, and ran past me. She was at the steps and up them like lightning. I had allowed for it, there was a safety hook holding the door back open and a wedge she was trying to kick away when I came after her. Well, she turned and ran, screaming help, help, help, and up the steps to the outer door, which was of course locked. She pulled at it and banged it and went screaming on, but I got her then. I hated doing it, but action was necessary. I got her round the waist and one hand over her mouth and dragged her down back. She kicked and struggled, but of course she was too small and I may not be Mr. Atlas but I am not a weakling either. In the end she went limp and I let her go. She stood a moment, then she suddenly jumped and hit me across the face. It didn't really hurt but the shock of it was most nasty, coming when I least expected it and after I'd been so reasonable when others might have lost their heads. Then she went into the room slamming the door behind her. I felt like going in and having it out with her, but I knew she was angry. There was real hatred in her looks. So I bolted the door and put up the false door.

*   *   *

The next thing was she wouldn't talk. That next lunch she said not a word when I spoke to her and said I was ready to let bygones be bygones. She just gave me a big look of contempt. It was the same that evening. When I came to clear, she handed me the tray and turned away. She made it very plain she didn't want me to stay. I thought she'd get over it, but the next day it was worse. Not only she didn't speak, she didn't eat.

Please don't do this, I said. It's no good.

But she wouldn't say a word, wouldn't even look at me.

The next day it was the same. She wouldn't eat, she wouldn't speak. I'd been waiting for her to wear some of the clothes I'd bought, but she kept on wearing the white blouse and the green tartan tunic. I began to get really worried, I didn't know how long people could go without food, she seemed pale and weak to me. She spent all the time sitting against the wall on her bed, her back turned, looking so miserable I didn't know what to do.

The next day I took in coffee for breakfast and some nice toast and cereal and marmalade. I let it wait a bit so she could smell it.

Then I said, I don't expect you to understand me, I don't expect you to love me like most people, I just want you to try and understand me as much as you can and like me a little if you can.

She didn't move.

I said, I'll make a bargain. I'll tell you when you can go away, but only on certain conditions.

I don't know why I said it. I knew really I could never let her go away. It wasn't just a barefaced lie, though. Often I did think she would go away when we agreed, a promise was a promise, etcetera. Other times I knew I couldn't let her do it.

She turned then and stared at me. It was the first sign of life she'd shown for three days.

I said, my conditions are that you eat food and you talk to me like you did at the beginning and don't try to escape like that.

"I can never agree to the last."

What about the first two, I said. (I thought even if she did promise not to escape, I'd still have to take precautions, so it was pointless, that condition.)

"You haven't said when," she said.

In six weeks, I said.

She just turned away again.

Five weeks then, I said after a bit.

"I'll stay here a week and not a day more."

Well, I said I couldn't agree to that and she turned away again. Then she was crying. I could see her shoulders moving, I wanted to go up to her, I did near the bed but she turned so sharp I think she thought I was going to attack her. Full of tears her eyes were. Cheeks wet. It really upset me to see her like that.

Please be reasonable. You know what you are to me now; can't you see I haven't made all these arrangements just so you'd stay a week more?

"I hate you, I hate you."

I'll give you my word, I said. When the time's up you can go as soon as you like.

She wouldn't have it. It was funny, she sat there crying and staring at me, her face was all pink. I thought she was going to come at me again, she looked as if she wanted to. But then she began to dry her eyes. Then she lit a cigarette. And then she said, "Two weeks."

I said, you say two, I say five. I'll agree to a month. That'd be November the fourteenth.

There was a pause, and she said, "Four weeks is November the eleventh."

I was worried about her, I wanted to clinch it, so I said, I meant a calendar month, but make it twenty-eight days. I'll give you the odd three days, I said.

"Thank you very much." Sarcastic, of course.

I handed her a cup of coffee, which she took.

"I've some conditions too," she said before she drunk it. "I can't live all the time down here. I must have some fresh air and light. I must have a bath sometimes. I must have some drawing materials. I must have a radio or a record-player. I need things from the chemist. I must have fresh fruit and salads. I must have some sort of exercise."

If I let you go outside, you'll escape, I said.

She sat up. She must have been acting it up a bit before, she changed so quickly. "Do you know what on parole means?"

I replied yes.

"You could let me out on parole. I'd promise not to shout or try to escape."

I said, have your breakfast and I'll think about it.

"No! It's not much to ask. If this house really is lonely, it's no risk."

It's lonely all right, I said. But I couldn't decide.

"I'm going on hunger strike again." She turned round, she was really putting on the pressure, as they say.

Of course you can have drawing materials, I said. You only had to ask anyhow. And a gramophone. Any records you want. Books. The same with food. I told you you need only ask. Anything like that.

"Fresh air?" She still had her back turned.

It's too dangerous.

Well, there was a silence, she spoke as plain as words, though, and in the end I gave in.

Perhaps at night. I'll see.

"When?" She turned then.

I'll have to think. I'd have to tie you up.

"But I'd be on parole."

Take it or leave it, I said.

"The bath?"

I could fix up something, I said.

"I want a proper bath in a proper bath. There must be one upstairs."

Something I thought a lot about was how I would like her to see my house and all the furnishings! It was partly I wanted to see her there in it, naturally when I had dreams she was upstairs with me, not down in the cellar. I'm like that, I act on impulse sometimes, taking risks others wouldn't.

I'll see, I said. I'd have to make arrangements.

"If I gave you my word, I wouldn't break it."

I'm sure, I said.

So that was that.

It seemed to clear the air, so to speak. I respected her and she respected me more afterwards. The first thing she did was write out a list of things she wanted. I had to find an artshop in Lewes and buy special paper and all sorts of pencils and things: sepia and Chinese ink and brushes, special hair and sizes and makes. Then there were things from the chemist: smell-removers and so on. It was a danger getting ladies' things I couldn't want for myself, but I took the risk. Then she wrote down food to buy, she had to have fresh coffee, and a lot of fruit and vegetables and greens—she was very particular about that. Anyway after she used to write down almost every day what we had to buy, she used to tell me how to cook it too, it was just like having a wife, an invalid one you had to do shopping for. I was careful in Lewes, I never went to the same shop twice running so that they wouldn't think I was buying a lot for one person. Somehow I always thought people could tell I lived on my own.

That first day I bought a gramophone too. Only a small one, but I must say she looked very pleased, I didn't want her to know I didn't know anything about music but I saw a record with some orchestra music by Mozart so I bought that. It was a good buy, she liked it and so me for buying it. One day much later when we were hearing it, she was crying. I mean, her eyes were wet. After, she said he was dying when he wrote it and he knew he was dying. It just sounded like all the rest to me but of course she was musical.

Well, the next day she brought up the business about having a bath and fresh air again. I didn't know what to do; I went up to the bathroom to think about it without promising anything. The bathroom window was over the porch round the cellar door. Out the back, which was safer. In the end I got up some wood and boarded across the frame, three-inch screws, so she couldn't signal with the light or climb out. Not that there was anyone likely to be out the back late at night.

That took care of the bathroom.

What I did next was I pretended she was with me and walked up from below to see where the danger spots would be. The downstairs rooms had wooden inside shutters, it was easy to draw them across and lock them (later I got padlocks) so she couldn't attract attention through a window and no snoopers could be looking in and seeing things. In the kitchen I made sure all knives etcetera were well out of harm's way. I thought of everything she could do to try and escape and in the end I felt it was safe.

Well, after supper she was on to me again about the bath and I

let her begin to go sulky again and then I said, all right, I will take
the risk, but if you break your promise, you stay here.

"I never break promises."

Will you give me your parole of honour?

"I give you my word of honour that I shall not try to escape."

Or signal.

"Or signal."

I'm going to tie you up.

"But that's insulting."

I wouldn't blame you if you broke your word, I said.

"But I . . ." she didn't finish, she just shrugged and turned and
held her hands behind her. I had a scarf ready to take the pressure
of the cord, I did it real tight but not so as to hurt, then I was going
to gag her, but first she had me collect up the wash-things she
needed and (I was very glad to see) she had chosen some of the
clothes I had bought.

I carried her things and went first, up the steps in the outer cellar and she waited till I unlocked the door and came up when I ordered, having first listened to make sure no one was about.

It was very dark of course, but clear, you could see some stars.
I took her arm tight and let her stand there for five minutes. I
could hear her breathing deep. It was very romantic, her head
came just up to my shoulder.

You can hear it's a long way from anywhere, I said.

When the time was up (I had to pull her) we went in through
the kitchen and dining-room and into the hall and up the stairs to
the bathroom.

There's no lock on the door, I said, you can't shut it even, I've
nailed a block in, but I shall respect your every privacy providing
you keep your word. I shall be here.

I had a chair on the landing outside.

I am now going to take your hand-cords off if you give me your word you will keep the gag on. Nod your head.

Well, she did, so I untied her hands. She rubbed them a bit, just to get at me, I suppose, then went in the bathroom.

All went off without trouble, I heard her have her bath, splashing etcetera, quite natural, but I got a shock when she came out. She hadn't got the gag on. That was one shock. The other was the way she was changed with the new clothes and her hair washed, it hung all wet and loose on her shoulders. It seemed to make her softer, even younger; not that she was ever hard or ugly. I must have looked stupid, looking angry because of the gag, and then not being able to be it because she looked so lovely.

She spoke very quick.

"Look, it began to hurt horribly. I've given you my word. I give it to you again. You can put this back on if you like—here. But I would have screamed by now if I'd wanted to."

She handed me the gag and there was something in her look, I couldn't put it on again. I said, the hands will do. She had on her green tunic, but with one of the shirts I bought and I guessed she had on the new underclothes underneath.

I did up her hands behind her back.

I'm sorry I'm so suspicious, I said. It's just that you're all I've got that makes life worth living. It was the wrong moment to say a thing like that, I know, but having her standing there like that, it was too much.

I said, if you went, I think I'd do myself in.

"You need a doctor."

I just made a noise.

"I'd like to help you."

You think I'm mad because of what I've done. I'm not mad.

It's just, well, I've got no one else. There's never been anyone but you I've ever wanted to know.

"That's the worst kind of illness," she said. She turned round then, all this was while I was tying. She looked down. "I feel sorry for you."

Then she changed, she said, "What about washing? I've washed some things. Can I hang them out? Or is there a laundry?"

I said, I'll dry them in the kitchen. You can't send anything to the laundry.

"What now?"

And she looked round. There was something mischievous about her sometimes, you could see she was looking for trouble, in a nice way. Teasing like.

"Aren't you going to show me your house?"

She had a real smile on, the first I ever saw; I couldn't do anything but smile back.

It's late, I said.

"How old is it?" She spoke as if she didn't hear me.

There's a stone says 1621 over the door.

"This is the wrong-coloured carpet. You ought to have rush matting or something. And those pictures—horrible!"

She moved along the landing to see them. Cunning.

They cost enough, I said.

"It's not money you go by."

I can't say how strange it was, us standing there. Her making criticisms like a typical woman.

"Can I look in the rooms?"

I wasn't myself, I couldn't resist the pleasure, so I stood with her in the doorways and showed them, the one ready for Aunt Annie, and Mabel's, if they ever came, and mine. Miranda looked very close round each one. Of course the curtains were drawn, and I watched right next to her to see she didn't try any funny business.

I got a firm to do it all, I said, when we were at the door of mine.

"You're very neat."

She saw some old pictures of butterflies I bought in an antique shop. I chose them, I said.

"They're the only decent things here."

Well, there we were, she was making compliments and I admit I was pleased.

Then she said, "How quiet it is. I've been listening for cars. I think it must be North Essex." I knew it was a test, she was watching me.

You've guessed right, I said. Acting surprised.

Suddenly she said, "It's funny, I should be shivering with fear. But I feel safe with you."

I'll never hurt you. Unless you force me to.

It was suddenly as I always hoped, we were getting to know each other, she was beginning to see me for what I really was.

She said, "That air was wonderful. You can't imagine. Even this air. It's free. It's everything I'm not."

And she walked away, so I had to follow her downstairs. At the bottom in the hall she said, "Can I look in here?" Hung for a sheep as well as a lamb, I thought, anyway the shutters were across and the curtains. She went in the lounge and looked round it, touring round and looking at everything with her hands behind her back, it was comic, really.

"It's a lovely room. It's wicked to fill it with all this shoddy stuff. Such muck!" She actually kicked one of the chairs. I suppose I looked like I felt (offended) because she said, "But you must see it's wrong! Those terrible chichi wall-lamps and"—she suddenly caught sight of them—"not china wild duck!" She looked at me with real anger, then back at the ducks.

"My arms ache. Would you mind tying my hands in front of me for a change?"

I didn't want to spoil the mood, as they say, I couldn't see any harm, as soon as I had the cords off her hands (I was all ready for trouble) she turned and held her hands out in front for me to tie, which I did. Then she shocked me. She went up to the fireplace where the wild duck were, there were three hung up, thirty-bob each and before you could say Jack Knife she had them off the hook and bang crash on the hearth. In smithereens.

Thank you very much, I said, very sarcastic.

"A house as old as this has a soul. And you can't do things like that to beautiful things like this old, old room so many people have lived in. Can't you feel that?"

I haven't any experience in furnishing, I said.

She just gave me a funny look and went past me into the room opposite, what I called the dining-room, though the furniture people called it the dual-purpose room, it was half fitted out for me to work in. There were my three cabinets, which she saw at once.

"Aren't you going to show me my fellow-victims?"

Of course I wanted nothing better. I pulled out one or two of the most attractive drawers—members of the same genus drawers, nothing serious, just for show, really.

"Did you buy them?"

Of course not, I said. All caught or bred by me and set and arranged by me. The lot.

"They're beautifully done."

I showed her a drawer of Chalkhill and Adonis Blues, I have a beautiful var. *ceroneus* Adonis and some var. *tithonus* Chalkhills,

THE COLLECTOR

and I pointed them out. The var. *ceroneus* is better than any they
got in the N.H. Museum. I was proud to be able to tell her something. She had never heard of aberrations.

"They're beautiful. But sad."

Everything's sad if you make it so, I said.

"But it's you who make it so!" She was staring at me across the
drawer. "How many butterflies have you killed?"

You can see.

"No, I can't. I'm thinking of all the butterflies that would have
come from these if you'd let them live. I'm thinking of all the living beauty you've ended."

You can't tell.

"You don't even share it. Who sees these? You're like a miser,
you hoard up all the beauty in these drawers."

I was really very disappointed, I thought all her talk was very
silly. What difference would a dozen specimens make to a species?

"I hate scientists," she said. "I hate people who collect things,
and classify things and give them names and then forget all about
them. That's what people are always doing in art. They call a
painter an impressionist or a cubist or something and then they put
him in a drawer and don't see him as a living individual painter
any more. But I can see they're beautifully arranged."

She was trying to be nice again.

The next thing I said was, I do photography too.

I had some pictures of the woods behind the house, and some
of the sea coming over the wall at Seaford, really nice ones, I en-
larged them myself. I put them out on the table where she could
see them.

She looked at them, she didn't say anything.

They're not much, I said. I haven't been doing it long.

"They're dead." She gave me a funny look sideways. "Not

these particularly. All photos. When you draw something it lives and when you photograph it it dies."

It's like a record, I said.

"Yes. All dry and dead." Well I was going to argue, but she went on, she said, "These are clever. They're good photographs as photographs go."

After a bit I said, I'd like to take some pictures of you.

"Why?"

You're what they call photogenic.

She looked down, then she looked up at me and said, "All right. If you want to. Tomorrow."

That gave me a real thrill. Things were really changed.

I decided about then it was time she went down. She didn't hardly object, just shrugged, let me tie the gag, and all went well as before.

Well, when we were down, she wanted a cup of tea (some special China she made me buy). I took the gag off and she came out in the outer cellar (her hands still bound) and looked at where I cooked her meals and all that. We didn't say anything, it was nice. The kettle boiling and her there. Of course I kept a sharp eye on her. When it was made, I said, shall I be mother?

"That's a *horrid* expression."

What's wrong with it?

"It's like those wild duck. It's suburban, it's stale, it's dead, it's . . . oh, everything square that ever was. You know?"

I think you'd better be mother, I said.

Then it was strange, she smiled just like she was going to laugh, and then she stopped and turned and went into her room, where I followed with the tray. She poured out the tea, but something had made her angry, you could see. She wouldn't look at me.

I didn't mean to offend you, I said.

"I suddenly thought of my family. They won't be laughing over jolly cups of tea this evening."

Four weeks, I said.

"Don't remind me of it!"

She was just like a woman. Unpredictable. Smiling one minute and spiteful the next.

She said, "You're loathsome. And you make me loathsome."

It won't be long.

Then she said something I've never heard a woman say before. It really shocked me.

I said, I don't like words like that. It's disgusting.

Then she said it again, really screamed it at me.

I couldn't follow all her moods sometimes.

She was all right the next morning, though she did not apologize. Also, the two vases in her room were broken on the steps when I went in. As always, she was up and waiting for me when I came in with her breakfast.

Well, the first thing she wanted to know was whether I as going to allow her to see daylight. I told her it was raining.

"Why couldn't I go out into the other cellar and walk up and down? I want exercise."

We had a good old argument about that. In the end the arrangement was if she wanted to walk there in daytime she would have to have the gag on. I couldn't risk someone chancing to be round the back—not that it was likely, of course, the front gate and garage gate were locked always. But at night just the hands would do. I said I wouldn't promise more than one bath a week. And nothing about daylight. I thought for a moment she would go into one of her sulks again, but she began to understand about that time sulks didn't get her anywhere, so she accepted my rules.

*   *   *

Perhaps I was overstrict, I erred on the strict side. But you had to be careful. For instance, at week-ends there was a lot more traffic about. Fine Sundays there were cars passing every five minutes. Often they would slow as they passed Fosters, some would reverse back to have another look, some even had the cheek to push their cameras through the front gate and take photos. So on week-ends I never let her leave her room.

One day I was just driving out to go down to Lewes and a man in a car stopped me. Was I the owner? He was one of those ever-so-cultured types with a plum in their throat. The I'm-a-friend-of-the-boss type. He talked a lot of stuff about the house and how he was writing some article for a magazine and would I let him look round and take photographs, he especially wanted to have a look at the priest's chapel.

There's no chapel here, I said.

But my dear man, that's fantastic, he said, it's mentioned in the County History. In dozens of books.

You mean that old place in the cellar, I said, as if I had just cottoned on. That's blocked up. Been bricked in.

But this is a scheduled building. You can't do things like that.

I said, well it's still there. It's just you can't see anything. It was done before I came.

Then he wanted to look indoors. I said I was in a hurry, I couldn't wait. He'd come back—"Just tell me a day." I wouldn't have it. I said I got a lot of requests. He went on nosing, he even started threatening me with an order to view, the Ancient Monuments people (whoever they are) would back him up, really offensive, and slimy at the same time. In the end he just drove off. It was all bluff on his part, but that was the sort of thing I had to think about.

*   *   *

I took the photos that evening. Just ordinary, of her sitting reading. They came out quite well.

One day about then she did a picture of me, like returned the compliment. I had to sit in a chair and look at the corner of the room. After half an hour she tore up the drawing before I could stop her. (She often tore up. Artistic temperament, I suppose.)

I'd have liked it, I said. But she didn't even reply to that, she just said, don't move.

From time to time she talked. Mostly personal remarks.

"You're very difficult to get. You're so featureless. Everything's nondescript. I'm thinking of you as an object, not as a person."

Later she said, "You're not ugly, but your face has all sorts of ugly habits. Your underlip is worst. It betrays you." I looked in the mirror upstairs, but I couldn't see what she meant.

Sometimes she'd come out of the blue with funny questions.

"Do you believe in God?" was one.

Not much, I answered.

"It must be yes or no."

I don't think about it. Don't see that it matters.

"You're the one imprisoned in a cellar," she said.

Do you believe, I asked.

"Of course I do. I'm a human being."

She said, stop talking, when I was going on.

She complained about the light. "It's this artificial light. I can never draw by it. It lies."

I knew what she was getting at, so I kept my mouth shut.

Then again—it may not have been that first morning she drew me, I can't remember which day it was—she suddenly came out

with, "You're lucky having no parents. Mine have only kept together because of my sister and me."

How do you know, I said.

"Because my mother's told me," she said. "And my father. My
mother's a bitch. A nasty ambitious middle-class bitch. She drinks."

I heard, I said.

"I could never have friends to stay."

I'm sorry, I said. She gave me a sharp look, but I wasn't being
sarcastic. I told her about my father drinking, and my mother.

"My father's weak, though I love him very much. Do you
know what he said to me one day? He said, I don't know how two
such bad parents can have produced two such good daughters. He
was thinking of my sister, really. She's the really clever one."

You're the really clever one. You won a big scholarship.

"I'm a good draughtsman," she said. "I might become a very
clever artist, but I shan't ever be a great one. At least I don't think so."

You can't tell, I said.

"I'm not egocentric enough. I'm a woman. I have to lean on
something." I don't know why but she suddenly changed the subject and said, "Are you a queer?"

Certainly not, I said. I blushed, of course.

"It's nothing to be ashamed of. Lots of good men are." Then
she said, "You want to lean on me. I can feel it. I expect it's your
mother. You're looking for your mother."

I don't believe in all that stuff, I said.

"We'd never be any good together. We both want to lean."

You could lean on me financially, I said.

"And you on me for everything else? God forbid."

Then, here, she said and held out the drawing. It was really
good, it really amazed me, the likeness. It seemed to make me
more dignified, better-looking than I really was.

Would you consider selling this, I asked?

"I hadn't, but I will. Two hundred guineas?"

All right, I said.

She gave me another sharp look.

"You'd give me two hundred guineas for that?"

Yes, I said. Because you did it.

"Give it to me." I handed it back and before I knew what, she was tearing it across.

Please don't, I said. She stopped, but it was torn half across.

"But it's bad, bad, bad." Then suddenly she sort of threw it at me. "Here you are. Put it in a drawer with the butterflies."

The next time I was in Lewes I bought her some more records, all I could find by Mozart, because she liked him, it seemed.

Another day she drew a bowl of fruit. She drew them about ten times, and then she pinned them all up on the screen and asked me to pick the best. I said they were all beautiful but she insisted so I plumped for one.

"That's the worst," she said. "That's a clever little art student's picture." She said, "One of them is good. I know it is good. It is worth all the rest a hundred times over. If you can pick it in three guesses you can have it for nothing when I go. If I go. If you don't, you must give me ten guineas for it."

Well, ignoring her dig I had three guesses, they were all wrong. The one that was so good only looked half-finished to me, you could hardly tell what the fruit were and it was all lop-sided.

"There I'm just on the threshold of saying something about the fruit. I don't actually say it, but you get the idea that I might. Do you feel that?"

I said I didn't actually.

She went and got a book of pictures by Cézanne.

"There," she said, pointing to a coloured one of a plate of apples. "He's not only saying everything there is about the apples, but everything about all apples and all form and colour."

I take your word for it, I said. All your pictures are nice, I said. She just looked at me.

"Ferdinand," she said. "They should have called you Caliban."

One day three or four after her first bath she was very restless. She walked up and down in the outer cellar after supper, sat on the bed, got up. I was looking at drawings she'd done that afternoon. All copies of pictures from the art-books, very clever, I thought, and very like.

Suddenly she said, "Couldn't we go for a walk? On parole?"

But it's wet, I said. And cold. It was the second week in October.

"I'm going mad cooped up in here. Couldn't we just walk round the garden?"

She came right up close to me, a thing she usually avoided and held out her wrists. She'd taken to wearing her hair long, tied up with a dark blue ribbon that was one of the things she wrote down for me to buy. Her hair was always beautiful. I never saw more beautiful hair. Often I had an itch to touch it. Just to stroke it, to feel it. It gave me a chance when I put the gag on.

So we went out. It was a funny night, there was a moon behind the cloud, and the cloud was moving, but down below there was hardly any wind. When we came out she spent a few moments just taking deep breaths. Then I took her arm respectfully and led her up the path between the wall that ran up one side and the lawn. We passed the privet hedge and went into the vegetable garden at the top with the fruit trees. As I said, I never had any nasty desire to take advantage of the situation, I was always perfectly respectful towards her (until she did what she did) but perhaps it was the darkness, us walking there and feeling her arm through her sleeve, I really would have liked to take her in my arms and kiss her, as a matter of fact I was trembling. I had to say something or I'd have lost my head.

You wouldn't believe me if I told you I was very happy, would you, I said. Of course she couldn't answer.

Because you think I don't feel anything properly, you don't know I have deep feelings but I can't express them like you can, I said.

Just because you can't express your feelings it doesn't mean they're not deep. All the time we were walking on under the dark branches.

All I'm asking, I said, is that you understand how much I love you, how much I need you, how deep it is.

It's an effort, I said, sometimes. I didn't like to boast, but I meant her to think for a moment of what other men might have done, if they'd had her in their power.

We'd come to the lawn on the other side again, and then to the house. A car sounded and grew close and went on down the lane beyond the house. I had a tight hold on her.

We came to the cellar door. I said, do you want to go round again?

To my surprise, she shook her head.

Naturally I took her back down. When I got the gag and cords off she said, "I'd like some tea. Please go and make some. Lock the door. I'll stay here."

I made the tea. As soon as I took it in and poured it, she spoke.

"I want to say something," she said. "It's got to be said."

I was listening.

"You wanted to kiss me out there, didn't you?"

I'm sorry, I said. As usual I started to blush.

"First of all I should like to thank you for not doing so, because I don't want you to kiss me. I realize I'm at your mercy, I realize I'm very lucky you're so decent about this particular thing."

It won't happen again, I said.

"That's what I wanted to say. If it does happen again—and worse. And you have to give way to it. I want you to promise something."

It won't happen again.

"Not to do it in a mean way. I mean don't knock me unconscious or chloroform me again or anything. I shan't struggle, I'll let you do what you like."

It won't happen again, I said. I forgot myself. I can't explain.

"The only thing is, if you ever do anything like that I shall never never respect you, I shall never, never speak to you again. You understand?"

I wouldn't expect anything else, I said. I was red as a beet-root by then.

She held out her hand. I shook it. I don't know how I got out of the room. She had me all at sixes and sevens that evening.

Well, every day it was the same: I went down between eight and nine, I got her breakfast, emptied the buckets, sometimes we talked a bit, she gave me any shopping she wanted done (sometimes I stayed home but I went out most days on account of the fresh vegetables and milk she liked), most mornings I cleaned up the house after I got back from Lewes, then her lunch, then usually we sat and talked for a bit or she played the records I brought back or I sat and watched her draw; she got her own tea, I don't know why, we sort of came to an agreement not to be together then. Then there was supper and after supper we often talked a bit more. Sometimes she made me welcome, she usually wanted her

walk in the outer cellar. Sometimes she made me go away as soon
as supper was over.

I took photos whenever she would let me. She took some of
me. I got her in a lot of poses, all nice ones, of course. I wanted
her to wear special clothes, but I didn't like to ask. I don't know
why you want all these photos, she always said. You can see me
every day.

So nothing happened really. There were just all those evenings
we sat together and it doesn't seem possible that it will never be
again. It was like we were the only two people in the world. No
one will ever understand how happy we were—just me, really, but
there were times when I consider she didn't mind in spite of what
she said, if she thought about it. I could sit there all night watching her, just the shape of her head and the way the hair fell from it
with a special curve, so graceful it was, like the shape of a swallowtail. It was like a veil or a cloud, it would lie like silk strands all
untidy and loose but lovely over her shoulders. I wish I had words
to describe it like a poet would or an artist. She had a way of
throwing it back when it had fallen too much forward, it was just
a simple natural movement. Sometimes I wanted to say to her,
please do it again, please let your hair fall forward to toss it back.
Only of course it would have been stupid. Everything she did was
delicate like that. Just turning a page. Standing up or sitting down,
drinking, smoking, anything. Even when she did things considered ugly, like yawning or stretching, she made it seem pretty. The
truth was she couldn't do ugly things. She was too beautiful.

She was always so clean, too. She never smelt anything but
sweet and fresh, unlike some women I could mention. She hated
dirt as much as I do, although she used to laugh at me about it. She
told me once it was a sign of madness to want everything clean. If
that is so, then we must both have been mad.

Of course it wasn't all peace and light, several times she tried to escape, which just showed. Luckily I was always on the look-out.

One day she nearly had me. She was dead cunning, when I went in she was being sick, and she looked a real mess. I kept on saying what's wrong, what's wrong, but she just lay there like she was in pain.

"It's appendicitis," she got out in the end.

How do you know, I asked.

"I thought I'd die in the night," she said. She spoke like she hardly could.

I said it could be other things.

But she just turned her face to the wall and said, Oh, God.

Well, when I got over the shock, I saw it might be just her game.

The next thing was she was all doubled up like in a spasm and then she sat up and looked at me and said she would promise anything but she must have a doctor. Or go to hospital, she said.

It's the end for me, I said. You'd tell them.

"I promise, I promise," she said. Really convincing. She could certainly act.

I'll make you a cup of tea, I said. I wanted time to think. But she doubled up again.

There was all the sick on the floor. I remembered Aunt Annie said with appendicitis it could kill, only a year back the boy next door got it, and she said then they waited too long—Aunt Annie knew all the time, and it was a wonder he never died. So I had to do something.

I said, there's a house with a telephone down the lane. I'll run down.

"Take me to hospital," she said. "It's safer for you."

What's it matter, I said, like I was really in despair. It's the end. It's goodbye, I said. Until the police court. I could act too.

Then I rushed out like I was very upset. I left the door open, and the outer door, and I just waited there.

And out she came, in a minute. No more ill than I was. No trouble, she just gave me one look and went on back down. I looked nasty just to give her a scare.

She had moods that changed so quick that I often got left behind. She liked to get me stumbling after her (as she said one day—poor Caliban, always stumbling after Miranda, she said), sometimes she would call me Caliban, sometimes Ferdinand. Sometimes she would be nasty and cutting. She would sneer at me and mimic me and make me desperate and ask me questions I couldn't answer. Then other times she would be really sympathetic, I felt she understood me like no one since Uncle Dick, and I could put up with everything.

I remember a lot of little things.

One day, she was sitting showing me the secrets of some paintings—secrets were the things you had to think about to see, the secrets of proportion and harmony she called them. We sat with the book between us and she talked about the pictures. We sat on the bed (she made me get cushions and a rug on it for the day), close but not touching. I made sure of that after the events in the garden. But one evening she said, don't be so stiff, I shan't kill you if your sleeve touches mine.

All right, I said, but I didn't move.

Then she moved, so our arms touched, our shoulders. All the time she went on talking and talking about the picture we were looking at, I thought she wasn't thinking about the touching but a few pages later she suddenly looked at me.

"You're not listening."

Yes, I am, I said.

"No, you're not. You're thinking about touching me. You're all stiff. Relax."

It was no good, she'd got me all tense. She stood up. She was wearing a narrow blue skirt I bought her and a big black jumper and a white blouse, the colours really suited her. She stood in front of me and after a bit she said, Oh, God.

Then she went and beat her fist against the wall. She used to do that sometimes.

"I've got a friend who kisses me every time he sees me and he doesn't mean anything—his kisses are meaningless. He kisses everybody. He's the other side of you. You don't have any contact with anybody and he has it with everybody. You're both equally sick."

I was smiling, I used to smile when she attacked me as a sort of defence.

"Don't put on that ghastly smile."

There's not much else I can do. You're always right.

"But I don't want always to be right. Tell me I'm wrong!"

Oh, you're right, I said. You know you're right.

"Oh, Ferdinand!" she said. And then twice more, Ferdinand, Ferdinand, and she sort of prayed to heaven and acted someone in great pain, so I had to laugh, but suddenly she was all serious, or pretending it.

"It's not a little thing. It's terrible that you can't treat me as a friend. Forget my sex. Just relax."

I'll try, I said. But then she wouldn't sit by me again. She leant against the wall reading another book.

Another day, it was downstairs, she just screamed. For no reason at all, I was fixing up a painting she'd done and wanted to see up on the wall and suddenly sitting on the bed she screamed, bloodcurdling it was and I jumped round and dropped the tape and she just laughed.

What's up, I said.

"I just felt like a good scream," she said.

She was unpredictable.

She was always criticizing my way of speaking. One day I remember she said, "You know what you do? You know how rain takes the colour out of everything? That's what you do to the English language. You blur it every time you open your mouth."

That is just one sample of many, of the way she treated me.

Another day she got round me on the subject of her parents. She'd been on for days about how they would be sick with worry and how mean I was not letting them know. I said I couldn't take the risk. But one day after supper she said, I'll tell you how to do it, without any risk. You wear gloves. You buy paper and some envelopes from Woolworth's. You dictate a letter to me to write. You go to the nearest big town and post it. You can't be traced. It might be any Woolworth's in the country.

Well, she kept on at me so about it that one day I did what she suggested and bought some paper and envelopes. That evening I gave her a sheet and told her to write.

"I am safe and not in danger," I said.

She wrote it, saying, "That's filthy English, but never mind."

You write what I say, I answered, and went on, "Do not try to find me, it is impossible."

"Nothing's impossible," she said. Cheeky as usual.

"I am being well looked after by a friend," I went on. Then I said, that's all, just put your name.

"Can't I say, Mr. Clegg sends his regards?"

Very funny, I said. She wrote something more and handed me the sheet of paper. It said, See you soon, love, Nanda, at the bottom.

What's this? I asked.

"My baby name. They'll know it's me."

I prefer Miranda, I said. It was the most beautiful for me. When she had written the envelope I put the sheet in and then luckily I looked inside. At the bottom of the envelope there was a piece of paper no bigger than half a cigarette paper. I don't know how but she must have had it ready and slipped it in. I opened it out and looked at her. She was bold as brass. She just leant back in the chair and stared at me. She'd written very very small with a sharp pencil, but the letters were clear. It wasn't like her other note, it said:

> D.M. Kidnapped by madman. F. Clegg. Clerk
> from Annexe who won pool. Prisoner in cellar
> lonely timbered cottage date outside 1621 hilly
> country two hours London. So far safe.
> Frightened.
>
>   M.

I was really angry and shocked, I didn't know what to do. In the end I said, are you frightened? She didn't say anything, she just nodded.

But what have I done? I asked.

"Nothing. That's why I'm frightened."

I don't understand.

She looked down.

"I'm waiting for you to do something."

I've promised and I'll promise again, I said. You get all high and mighty because I don't take your word, I don't know why it's different for me.

"I'm sorry."

I trusted you, I said. I thought you realized I was being kind. Well, I'm not going to be used. I don't care about your letter.

I put it in my pocket.

There was a long silence, I knew she was looking at me, but I wouldn't look at her. Then suddenly she got up and stood in front of me and put her hands on my shoulders so that I had to look at her, she made me look down into her eyes. I can't explain it, when she was sincere she could draw the soul out of me, I was wax in her hands.

She said, "Now you're behaving like a little boy. You forget that you are keeping me here by force. I admit it is quite a gentle force, but it is frightening."

As long as you keep your word, I'll keep mine, I said. I had gone red, of course.

"But I've not given you my word not to try and escape, have I?"

All you live for is the day you see the last of me, I said. I'm just a nobody still, aren't I?

She turned half away. "I want to see the last of this house. Not of you."

And mad, I said. Do you think a madman would have treated you the way I have? I'll tell you what a madman would have done. He'd have killed you by now. Like that fellow Christie, I suppose you think I'm going for you with a carving-knife or something. (I was really fed up with her that day.) How daft can you get? All right, you think I'm not normal keeping you here like this. Perhaps I'm not. But I can tell you there'd be a blooming lot more of this if more people had the money and the time to do it. Anyway there's more of it now than anyone knows. The police know, I said, the figures are so big they don't dare say them.

She was staring at me. It was like we were complete strangers. I must have looked funny, it was the most I'd ever said.

"Don't look like that," she said. "What I fear in you is something you don't know is in you."

What, I asked. I was still angry.

"I don't know. It's lurking somewhere about in this house, this room, this situation, waiting to spring. In a way we're on the same side against it."

That's just talk.

"We all want things we can't have. Being a decent human being is accepting that."

We all take what we can get. And if we haven't had much most of our life we make up for it while the going's good, I said. Of course you wouldn't know about that.

Then she was smiling at me, as if she was much older than me. "You need psychiatric treatment."

The only treatment I need is you to treat me like a friend.

"I am, I am," she said. "Can't you see that?"

There was a big silence, then she broke it.

"Don't you feel this has gone on long enough?"

No, I said.

"Won't you let me go now?"

No.

"You could gag me and tie me up and drive me back to London. I'd not tell a soul."

No.

"But there must be something you want to do with me?"

I just want to be with you. All the time.

"In bed?"

I've told you no.

"But you want to?"

I'd rather not speak about it.

She shut up then.

I don't allow myself to think of what I know is wrong, I said. I don't consider it nice.

"You *are* extraordinary."

Thank you, I said.

"If you let me go, I should want to see you, because you interest me very much."

Like you go to the zoo? I asked.

"To try and understand you."

You'll never do that. (I may as well admit I liked the mystery man side of our talk. I felt it showed her she didn't know everything.)

"I don't think I ever should."

Then suddenly she was kneeling in front of me, with her hands up high, touching the top of her head, being all oriental. She did it three times.

"Will the mysterious great master accept apologies of very humble slave?"

I'll think about it, I said.

"Humble slave very solly for unkind letter."

I had to laugh; she could act anything.

She stayed there kneeling with her hands on the floor beside her, more serious, giving me the look.

"Will you send the letter, then?"

I made her ask again, but then I gave in. It was nearly the big mistake of my life.

The next day I drove up to London. I told her I was going there, like a fool, and she gave me a list of things to buy. There was a lot. (I knew later to keep me busy.) I had to buy special foreign cheese and go to some place in Soho where they had German sausages she liked, and there were some records, and clothes, and other things. She wanted pictures by some artist, it had to be just this one name. I was really happy that day, not a cloud in the sky. I thought she had forgotten about the four weeks, well not forgotten, but accepted I would want more. Talk about a dream-world.

I didn't get back till tea-time and of course went down straight to see her, but I knew at once something was wrong. She didn't look at all pleased to see me and she didn't even look at all the things I'd bought.

I soon saw what it was, it was four stones she had made loose, to make a tunnel, I suppose. There was dirt on the steps. I got one out easy. All the time she sat on the bed not looking. Behind it was stone, so it was all right. But I saw her game—the sausages and the special pictures and all that. All the soft soap.

You tried to escape, I said.

"Oh, shut up!" she cried. I began looking for the thing she had done it with. Suddenly something flew past me and clattered on the floor. It was an old six-inch nail, I don't know how she'd got hold of it.

That's the last time I leave you alone for so long, I said. I can't trust you any more.

She just turned, she wouldn't speak, and I was dead scared she'd go off on a hunger strike again, so I didn't insist. I left her then. Later I brought her her supper. She didn't talk, so I left her.

The next day she was all right again, though she didn't talk, except a word, about the escape that nearly was; she never mentioned it after again. But I saw she had a bad scratch on her wrist, and she made a face when she tried to hold a pencil to draw.

I didn't post the letter. The police are dead cunning with some things. A chap I knew in Town Hall's brother worked at Scotland

Yard. They only needed a pinch of dust and they would tell you where you came from and everything.

Of course when she asked me I went red; I said it was because I knew she didn't trust me, etcetera. Which she seemed to accept. It may not have been kind to her parents, but from what she said they weren't up to much, and you can't think of everybody. First things first, as they say.

I did the same thing over the money she wanted me to send to the H-bomb movement. I wrote out a cheque and showed it to her, but I didn't send it. She wanted proof (the receipt), but I said I had sent it anonymous. I did it to make her feel better (writing the cheque) but I don't see the point of wasting money on something you don't believe in. I know rich people give sums, but in my opinion they do it to get their names published or to dodge the tax-man.

For every bath, I had to screw in the planks again. I didn't like to leave them up all the time. All went off well. Once it was very late (eleven) so I took her gag off when she went in. It was a very windy night, a proper gale blowing. When we came down she wanted to sit in the sitting-room (I got ticked off for calling it the lounge), hands bound of course, there seemed no harm, so I put the electric fire on (she told me imitation logs were the end, I ought to have real log fires, like I did later). We sat there a bit, she sat on the carpet drying her washed hair and of course I just watched her. She was wearing some slacks I bought her, very attractive she looked all in black except for a little red scarf. She had her hair all day before she washed it in two pigtails, one of the great pleasures for me was seeing how her hair was each day. Before the fire, however, it was loose and spread, which I liked best.

After a time she got up and walked round the room, all restless.

She kept on saying the word "bored." Over and over again. It sounded funny, what with the wind howling outside and all.

Suddenly she stopped in front of me.

"Amuse me. Do something."

Well what, I asked. Photos? But she didn't want photos.

"I don't know. Sing, dance, anything."

I can't sing. Or dance.

"Tell me all the funny stories you know."

I don't know any, I said. It was true, I couldn't think of one.

"But you must do. I thought all men had to know dirty jokes."

I wouldn't tell you one if I knew it.

"Why not?"

They're for men.

"What do you think women talk about? I bet I know more dirty jokes than you do."

I wouldn't be surprised, I said.

"Oh, you're like mercury. You won't be picked up."

She walked away, but suddenly she snatched a cushion off a chair, turned and kicked it straight at me. I of course was surprised; I stood up, and then she did the same with another, and then another that missed and knocked a copper kettle off the side-table.

Easy on, I said.

"Come, thou tortoise!" she cried (a literary quotation, I think it was). Anyway, almost at once she pulled a jug thing off the mantelpiece and threw that at me, I think she called catch, but I didn't and it broke against the wall.

Steady on, I said.

But another jug followed. All the time she was laughing, there was nothing vicious exactly, she just seemed to be mad, like a kid. There was a pretty green plate with a cottage moulded in relief that hung by the window and she had that off the wall and smashed that. I don't know why, I always liked that plate and I didn't like to see her break it, so I shouted, really sharp, stop it!

All she did was to put her thumb to her nose and make a rude sign and put her tongue out. She was just like a street boy.

I said, you ought to know better.

"You ought to know better," she said, making fun of me. Then she said, "Please come round this side and then I can get at those beautiful plates behind you." There were two by the door. "Unless you'd like to smash them yourself."

Stop it, I said again, that's enough.

But suddenly she came behind the sofa, going for the plates. I got between her and the door, she tried to dodge under my arm; however, I caught hers.

Then she suddenly changed.

"Let go," she said, all quiet. Of course I didn't, I thought she might be joking still.

But then suddenly she said, "Let go," in a nasty voice that I did at once. Then she went and sat down by the fire.

After a while she said, "Get a broom. I'll sweep up."

I'll do it tomorrow.

"I *want* to clear up." Very my-lady.

I'll do it.

"It's your fault."

Of course.

"You're the most perfect specimen of petit bourgeois squareness I've ever met."

Am I?

"Yes you *are*. You despise the real bourgeois classes for all their snobbishness and their snobbish voices and ways. You do, don't you? Yet all you put in their place is a horrid little refusal to have nasty thoughts or do nasty things or be nasty in any way. Do you

know that every great thing in the history of art and every beautiful thing in life is actually what you call nasty or has been caused
by feelings that you would call nasty? By passion, by love, by hatred, by truth. Do you know that?"

I don't know what you're talking about, I said.

"Yes you do. Why do you keep on using these stupid words—
nasty, nice, proper, right? Why are you so worried about what's
proper? You're like a little old maid who thinks marriage is dirty
and everything except cups of weak tea in a stuffy old room is
dirty. Why do you take all the life out of life? Why do you kill all
the beauty?"

I never had your advantages. That's why.

"You can change, you're young, you've got money. You can
learn. And what have you done? You've had a little dream, the sort
of dream I suppose little boys have and masturbate about, and you
fall over yourself being nice to me so that you won't have to admit
to yourself that the whole business of my being here is nasty,
nasty, nasty—"

She stopped sudden then. "This is no good," she said. "I might
be talking Greek."

I understand, I said. I'm not educated.

She almost shouted. "You're so stupid. Perverse."

"You have money—as a matter of fact, you aren't stupid,
you could become whatever you liked. Only you've got to
shake off the past. You've got to kill your aunt and the house
you lived in and the people you lived with. You've got to be a
new human being."

She sort of pushed out her face at me, as if it was something
easy I could do, but wouldn't.

Some hope, I said.

"Look what you could do. You could . . . you could collect pictures. I'd tell you what to look for, I'd introduce you to people who would tell you about art-collecting. Think of all the poor artists you could help. Instead of massacring butterflies, like a stupid schoolboy."

Some very clever people collect butterflies, I said.

"Oh, clever . . . what's the use of that? Are they human beings?"

What do you mean? I asked.

"If you have to ask, I can't give you the answer."

Then she said, "I always seem to end up by talking down to you. I hate it. It's you. You always squirm one step lower than I can go."

She went like that at me sometimes. Of course I forgave her, though it hurt at the time. What she was asking for was someone different to me, someone I could never be. For instance, all that night after she said I could collect pictures I thought about it; I dreamed myself collecting pictures, having a big house with famous pictures hanging on the walls, and people coming to see them. Miranda there, too, of course. But I knew all the time it was silly; I'd never collect anything but butterflies. Pictures don't mean anything to me. I wouldn't be doing it because I wanted, so there wouldn't be any point. She could never see that.

She did several more drawings of me which were quite good, but there was something in them I didn't like, she didn't bother so much about a nice likeness as what she called my inner character, so sometimes she made my nose so pointed it would have pricked you and my mouth was all thin and unpleasant, I mean more than it really is, because I know I'm no beauty. I didn't dare think about the four weeks being up, I didn't know what would happen, I just thought there would be arguing and she'd sulk and I'd get her to stay another four weeks—I mean I thought I had some sort of power over her, she would do what I wanted. I lived from day

to day, really. I mean there was no plan. I just waited. I even half
expected the police to come. I had a horrible dream one night
when they came and I had to kill her before they came in the
room. It seemed like a duty and I had only a cushion to kill her
with. I hit and hit and she laughed and then I jumped on her and
smothered her and she lay still, and then when I took the cushion
away she was lying there laughing, she'd only pretended to die. I
woke up in a sweat, that was the first time I ever dreamed of
killing anyone.

She started talking about going several days before the end. She
kept on saying that she would never tell a soul, and of course I had
to say I believed her, but I knew even if she meant it the police or
her parents would screw it out of her in the end. And she kept on
about how we'd be friends and she'd help me choose pictures and
introduce me to people and look after me. She was very nice to me
those days; not that of course she didn't have her reasons.

At last the fatal day (November 10th, the 11th was her release
day) came. The first thing she said when I took her in her coffee
was, could we have a celebration party tonight?

What about guests, I said, joking, not that I was feeling light-
hearted, need I add.

"Just you and me. Because . . . oh, well, we've come through,
haven't we?"

Then she said, "And upstairs, in your dining-room?"

To which I agreed. I had no choice.

She gave me a list of things to buy at the posh grocer's in
Lewes, and then she asked if I'd buy sherry and a bottle of cham-
pagne and of course I said I would. I never saw her get so excited.
I suppose I got excited too. Even then. What she felt, I felt.

To make her laugh I said, evening dress, of course. And she

said, "Oh, I wish I had a nice dress. And I must have some more hot water to wash my hair."

I said, I'll buy you a dress. Just tell me like before the colour and so on and I'll see what there is in Lewes.

Funny, I'd been so careful, and there I was, going red. She gave me a smile, however.

"I knew it was Lewes. There's a ticket on one of the cushions. And I'd like either a black dress, or no, a biscuit, stone—oh, wait . . ." and she went to her paint-box and mixed colours like she did before when she wanted a scarf of a special colour when I was going to London. "This colour, and it must be simple, knee-length, not long, sleeves like this (she drew it), or no sleeves, something like this or like this." I always liked it when she drew. She was so quick, fluttery, you felt she couldn't wait to draw whatever it was.

Naturally my thoughts were far from happy that day. It was just like me not to have a plan. I don't know what I thought would happen. I don't even know if I didn't think I would keep the agreement, even though it was forced out of me and forced promises are no promises, as they say.

I actually went into Brighton and there after looking at a lot I saw just the dress in a small shop; you could tell it was real class, at first they didn't want to sell it without a fitting although it was the right size. Well, going back to where I parked the van I passed another shop, a jeweller's, and I suddenly had the idea that she would like a present, also it might make things easier when it came to the point. There was a sapphire and diamond necklace lying on a bit of black velvet, shape of a heart I remember—I mean they'd arranged the necklace into a heart shape. I went in and it was three hundred pounds and I nearly walked right out again, but then my more generous nature triumphed. After all, I had the money. The woman in the shop put it on and it looked really pretty and expensive. It's only small stones, she said, but all very fine water and these Victorian designs. I remembered Miranda talking one day about how she liked Victorian things, so that did it. There was trouble about the cheque, of course. The woman wouldn't take it at first, but I got her to ring my bank and she changed her tune very quick. If I'd spoken in a la-di-da voice and said I was Lord Muck or something, I bet . . . still, I've got no time for that.

It's funny how one idea leads to another. While I was buying the necklace I saw some rings and that gave me the plan I could ask her to marry me and if she said no then it would mean I had to keep her. It would be a way out. I knew she wouldn't say yes. So I bought a ring. It was quite nice; but not very expensive. Just for show.

When I got home I washed the necklace (I didn't like to think of it touching that other woman's skin) and hid it so that I could get it out at the correct time. Then I made all the preparations she said: there were flowers, and I put the bottles on the side-table, and laid out everything really grand hotel, with all the usual precautions, of course. We arranged I was to go down and fetch her at seven. After I took in the parcels I wasn't to see her, it was like it is before a wedding.

What I decided was I would let her come up ungagged and untied just this once, I would take the risk but watch her like a knife and I would have the chloroform and CTC handy, just in case trouble blew up. Say someone knocked at the door, I could use the pad and have her bound and gagged in the kitchen in a very short time, and then open up.

Well, at seven I had my best suit and shirt and a new tie I bought on and I went down to see her. It was raining, which was all to the good. She made me wait about ten minutes and then she came out. You could have knocked me down with a feather. For a moment I thought it wasn't her, it looked so different. She had a lot of French scent which I gave her on and she was really made up for the first time since she was with me; she had the dress on and it really suited her, it was a creamy colour, very simple but elegant, leaving her arms and her neck bare. It wasn't a girl's dress at all, she looked a real woman. Her hair was done up high unlike before, very elegant. Empire, she called it. She looked just like one of those model girls you see in magazines; it really amazed me what she could look like when she wanted. I remember her eyes were different too, she'd drawn black lines round them so she looked sophisticated. Sophisticated, that's exactly the word. Of course, she made me feel all clumsy and awkward. I had the same feeling I did when I had watched an imago emerge, and then to have to kill it. I mean, the beauty confuses you, you don't know what you want to do any more, what you should do.

"Well?" she said. She turned round, showing off.

Very nice, I said.

"Is that all?" She gave me a look under her eyebrows. She looked a real sensation.

Beautiful, I said. I didn't know what to say, I wanted to look at her all the time and I couldn't. I felt sort of frightened, too.

I mean, we seemed further apart than ever. And I knew more and more I couldn't let her go.

Well, I said, shall we go up?

"No cords, no gag?"

It's too late for that, I said. That's all over.

"I think what you're doing today, and tomorrow, is going to be one of the best things that ever happened to you."

One of the saddest, I couldn't help saying.

"No, it's not. It's the beginning of a new life. And a new you." And she reached out her hand and took mine and led me up the steps.

It was pouring and she took one breath only before she went into the kitchen and through the dining-room into the lounge.

"It's nice," she said.

I thought you said that word meant nothing, I said.

"Some things are nice. Can I have a glass of sherry?" I poured us one out each. Well, we stood there, she made me laugh, she kept on pretending that the room was full of people, waving at them, and telling me about them, and them about my new life, and then she put a record on the gramophone, it was soft music, and she looked beautiful. She was so changed, her eyes seemed alive, and what with the French scent she had that filled the room and the sherry and the heat from the fire, real logs, I managed to forget what I had to do later. I even said some silly jokes. Anyway she laughed.

Well, she had a second glass and then we went through to the other room where I'd slipped my present in her place, which she saw at once.

"For me?"

Look and see, I said. She took off the paper and there was this dark blue leather case and she pressed the button and she just didn't say anything. She just stared at them.

"Are they real?" She was awed, really awed.

Of course. They're only little stones, but they're high quality.

"They're fantastic," she said. Then she held out the box to me. "I can't take them. I understand, I think I understand why you've given them to me, and I appreciate it very much, but . . . I can't take them."

I want you to, I said.

"But . . . Ferdinand, if a young man gives a girl a present like this, it can only mean one thing."

What, I asked.

"Other people have nasty minds."

I want you to have them. Please.

"I'll wear them for now. I'll pretend they're mine."

They are yours, I said.

She came round the table with the case.

"Put them on," she said. "If you give a girl jewellery, you must put it on yourself."

She stood there and watched me, right up close to me, then she turned as I picked up the stones and put them round her neck. I had a job fastening them, my hands were trembling, it was the first time I had touched her skin except her hand. She smelt so nice I could have stood like that all the evening. It was like being in one of those adverts come to life. At last she turned and there she was looking at me.

"Are they nice?" I nodded, I couldn't speak. I wanted to say something nice, a compliment.

"Would you like me to kiss you on the cheek?"

I didn't say, but she put her hand on my shoulder and lifted up a bit and kissed my cheek. It must have seemed hot, I was red enough by that time to have started a bonfire.

Well, we had cold chicken and things; I opened the champagne and it was very nice, I was surprised. I wished I'd bought another bottle, it seemed easy to drink, not very intoxicating. Though we laughed a lot, she was really witty, talking with other people that weren't there again and so on.

After supper we made coffee together in the kitchen (I kept a sharp eye open, of course) and took it through to the lounge and she put on jazz records I'd bought her. We actually sat on the sofa together.

Then we played charades; she acted things, syllables of words, and I had to guess what they were. I wasn't any good at it, either acting or guessing. I remember one word she did was "butterfly." She kept on doing it again and again and I couldn't guess. I said aeroplane and all the birds I could think of and in the end she collapsed in a chair and said I was hopeless. Then it was dancing. She tried to teach me to jive and samba, but it meant touching her, I got so confused and I never got the time right. She must have thought I was really slow.

The next thing was she had to go away a minute. I didn't like it, but I knew I couldn't expect her to go downstairs. I had to let her go up and I stood on the stairs where I could see if she did any monkey business with the light (the planks weren't up, I slipped there). The window was high, I knew she couldn't get out without my hearing, and it was quite a drop. Anyhow she came right out, seeing me on the stairs.

"Can't you trust me?" She was a bit sharp.

I said, yes, it's not that.

We went back into the lounge.

"What is it, then?"

If you escaped now, you could still say I imprisoned you. But if I take you home, I can say I released you. I know it's silly, I said. Of course I was acting it a bit. It was a very difficult situation.

Well, she looked at me, and then she said, "Let's have a talk. Come and sit here beside me."

I went and sat.

"What are you going to do when I've gone?"

I don't think about it, I said.

"Will you want to go on seeing me?"

Of course I will.

"You're definitely going to come and live in London? We'll

make you into someone really modern. Someone really interesting to meet."

You'd be ashamed of me with all your friends.

It was all unreal. I knew she was pretending just like I was. I had a headache. It was all going wrong.

"I've got lots of friends. Do you know why? Because I'm never ashamed of them. All sorts of people. You aren't the strangest by a long way. There's one who's very immoral. But he's a beautiful painter so we forgive him. And he's not ashamed. You've got to be the same. Not be ashamed. I'll help you. It's easy if you try."

It seemed the moment. Anyway, I couldn't stand it any longer.

Please marry me, I said. I had the ring in my pocket all ready.

There was a silence.

Everything I've got is yours, I said.

"Marriage means love," she said.

I don't expect anything, I said. I don't expect you to do anything that you don't want. You can do what you like, study art, etcetera. I won't ask anything, anything of you, except to be my wife in name and live in the same house with me.

She sat staring at the carpet.

You can have your own bedroom and lock it every night, I said.

"But that's horrible. It's inhuman! We'll never understand each other. We don't have the same sort of heart."

I've got a heart, for all that, I said.

"I just think of things as beautiful or not. Can't you understand? I don't think of good or bad. Just of beautiful or ugly. I think a lot of nice things are ugly and a lot of nasty things are beautiful."

You're playing with words, I said. All she did was stare at me, then she smiled and got up and stood by the fire, really beautiful. But all withdrawn. Superior.

I suppose you're in love with that Piers Broughton, I said. I wanted to give her a jolt. She was really surprised, too.

"How do you know about him?"

I told her it was in the papers. It said you and him were unofficially engaged, I said.

I saw right off they weren't. She just laughed. "He's the last person I'd marry. I'd rather marry you."

Then why can't it be me?

"Because I can't marry a man to whom I don't feel I belong in all ways. My mind must be his, my heart must be his, my body must be his. Just as I must feel he belongs to me."

I belong to you.

"But you don't! Belonging's two things. One who gives and one who accepts what's given. You don't belong to me because I can't accept you. I can't give you anything back."

I don't want much.

"I know you don't. Only the things that I have to give anyway. The way I look and speak and move. But I'm other things. I have other things to give. And I can't give them to you, because I don't love you."

I said, that changes everything then, doesn't it. I stood up, my head was throbbing. She knew what I meant at once, I could see it in her face, but she pretended not to understand.

"What do you mean?"

You know what I mean, I said.

"I'll marry you. I'll marry you as soon as you like."

Ha ha, I said.

"Isn't that what you wanted me to say?"

I suppose you think I don't know you don't need witnesses and all, I said.

"Well?"

I don't trust you half an inch, I said.

The way she was looking at me really made me sick. As if I wasn't human hardly. Not a sneer. Just as if I was something out of outer space. Fascinating almost.

You think I don't see through all the soft as soap stuff, I said.

She just said, "Ferdinand." Like she was appealing. Another of her tricks.

Don't you Ferdinand me, I said.

"You promised. You can't break your promise."

I can do what I like.

"But I don't know what you want of me. How *can* I prove I'm your friend if you never give me a chance of doing so?"

Shut up, I said.

Then suddenly she acted, I knew it was coming, I was ready for it, what I wasn't ready for was the sound of a car outside. Just as it came up to the house, she reached with her foot like to warm it, but all of a sudden she kicked a burning log out of the heath on to the carpet, at the same moment screamed and ran for the window, then seeing they were padlocked, for the door. But I got her first. I didn't get the chloroform which was in a drawer, speed was the thing. She turned and scratched and clawed at me, still screaming, but I wasn't in the mood to be gentle, I beat down her arms and got my hand over her mouth. She tore at it and bit and kicked, but I was in a panic by then. I got her round the shoulders and pulled her where the drawer was with the plastic box. She saw what it was, she tried to twist away, her head side to side, but I got the pad out and let her have it. All the time listening, of course. And watching the log, it was smouldering badly, the room was full of smoke. Well, soon as she was under good and proper, I let her go and went and put the fire out. I poured the water from a vase over it. I had to act really fast, I decided to get her down while I had time, which I did, laid her on her bed, then upstairs again to make sure the fire was really out and no one about.

I opened the front door very casual, there was no one there, so it was O.K.

Well, then I went down again.

She was still out, on the bed. She looked a sight, the dress all off one shoulder. I don't know what it was, it got me excited, it gave me ideas, seeing her lying there right out. It was like I'd showed who was really the master. The dress was right off her shoulder, I could see the top of one stocking. I don't know what reminded me of it, I remembered an American film I saw once (or was it a magazine) about a man who took a drunk girl home and undressed her and put her to bed, nothing nasty, he just did that and no more and she woke up in his pyjamas.

So I did that. I took off her dress and her stockings and left on certain articles, just the brassière and the other so as not to go the whole hog. She looked a real picture lying there with only what Aunt Annie called strips of nothing on. (She said it was why more women got cancer.) Like she was wearing a bikini.

It was my chance I had been waiting for. I got the old camera and took some photos, I would have taken more, only she started to move a bit, so I had to pack up and get out quick.

I started the developing and printing right away. They came out very nice. Not artistic, but interesting.

I never slept that night, I got in such a state. There were times I thought I would go down and give her the pad again and take other photos, it was as bad as that. I am not really that sort and I was only like it that night because of all that happened and the strain I was under. Also the champagne had a bad effect on me. And everything she said. It was what they call a culmination of circumstances.

Things were never the same again, in spite of all that happened. Somehow it proved we could never come together, she could never understand me, I suppose she would say I never could have understood her, or would have, anyhow.

About what I did, undressing her, when I thought after, I saw it wasn't so bad; not many would have kept control of themselves, just taken photos, it was almost a point in my favour.

I considered what to do, I decided a letter was best. This is what I wrote:

> I am sorry for last night, I dare say you think now you cannot ever forgive me.
> I did say I would not ever use force unless obliged. I think you will admit you did oblige me by what you did.
> Please understand that I did only the necessary. I took your dress off as I thought you might be ill again.
> I showed every respect I could under the circumstances. Please give me the credit for not going as far as some might in the same.
> I will not say any more. Except I must have you here a bit longer.
>
> Yours sincerely, etc.

I didn't put any beginning. I couldn't decide what to call her: Dear Miranda seemed familiar.

Well, I went down and took in her breakfast. It was just like I thought. She was sitting in her chair, staring at me. I said good morning, she didn't reply. I said something—do you want krispies or corn flakes?—she just stared. So I just left her breakfast with the letter on the tray and waited outside and when I went back nothing was touched, the letter was unopened, and she was still

sitting there staring at me. I knew it was no good talking, she had
it in for me good and proper.

She kept it up several days. So far as I know all she had was some
water. At least once a day, when I took in the food she always refused, I tried to argue with her. I took in the letter again and she
read it this time, at least it was torn up, so she touched it. I tried
everything: I spoke gentle, I pretended I was angry, bitter, I
begged her, but it was all no use. Mostly she just sat with her back
to me as if she didn't hear me. I got special things like continental
chocolate, caviare, the best food money could buy (in Lewes) but
it was never touched.

I was beginning to get really worried. But then one morning
when I went in she was standing by her bed with her back to me;
however, she turned as soon as I came in and said good morning.
But in a funny tone. Full of spite.

Good morning, I said. It's nice to hear your voice again.

"Is it? It won't be. You'll wish you never heard it."

That remains to be seen, I answered.

"I'm going to kill you. I realize you'd let me starve to death.
Just the thing you would do."

I suppose I never brought you any food these last days?

She couldn't answer that one, she just stared at me in the old
style.

"You're not keeping *me* prisoner any more. You're keeping
death prisoner."

Have some breakfast anyhow, I said.

Well, from that time on she ate normally, but it wasn't like before. She hardly spoke, if she did it was always sharp and sarcastic,
she was so bad-tempered there was no staying with her. If I was
ever there more than a minute when it wasn't necessary she used to

spit at me to get out. One day soon after, I brought in a plate of perfectly nice baked beans on toast and she just picked it up and hurled
it straight at me. I felt like giving her a good clip over the earhole.
About this time I was fed up with the whole thing, there didn't seem
any point in it, I tried everything, but she would keep on holding
that evening against me. It was like we had reached a dead end.

Then one day she actually asked for something. I got in the habit
of leaving at once after supper before she could shout at me, but
this time she said, stop a minute.

"I want a bath."

It's not convenient tonight, I said. I wasn't ready for that.

"Tomorrow?"

Don't see why not. With parole.

"I'll give my parole." She said it in a nasty hard voice. I knew
what her parole was worth.

"And I want to walk in the cellar." She pushed forward her
hands, and I tied them up. It was the first time I touched her for
days. Well, as usual I went and sat on the steps to the outer door
and she walked up and down in the funny way she had. It was very
windy, you could hear it down there, just the sound of her feet and
the wind above. She didn't speak for quite a time, I don't know
why but I knew she wanted to.

"Are you enjoying life?" she suddenly came out with.

Not much, I answered. Cautious.

She walked to and fro four or five times more. Then she started
to hum music.

That's a nice tune, I said.

"Do you like it?"

Yes, I said.

"Then I don't any more."

Two or three more times she went up and down.

"Talk to me."

What about?

"Butterflies."

What about butterflies?

"Why you collect them. Where you find them. Go on. Just talk."

Well, it seemed odd, but I talked, every time I stopped she said, go on, talk. I must have talked half an hour there, until she stopped and said, that's enough. She went back inside and I took off the cord and she went straight and sat on her bed with her back to me. I asked her if she wanted any tea, she didn't answer, all of a sudden I realized she was crying. It really did things to me when she cried, I couldn't bear to see her so unhappy. I went up close and said, tell me what you want, I'll buy you anything. But she turned round on me, she was crying all right, but her eyes were blazing, she stood up and walked towards me saying get out, get out, get out. It was terrible. She looked really mad.

The next day she was very quiet. Not a word. I got the planks up and everything ready and sure enough she showed she was all ready when she had had her walk (all in silence that time). So I gagged and corded her and took her upstairs and she had her bath and then she came out and put her hands out at once to be tied again and for the gag.

I always went out of the kitchen first with my hand on her just in case, but there was a step there, I fell over it once myself, perhaps that was it, when she fell it seemed natural, and natural that the brushes and bottles and things she carried in a towel (her hands were done in front, so she always carried things up against her front) should all fall out with a noise on the path. She got up all innocent, bending and rubbing her knees and like a proper fool I knelt down to pick the stuff up. Of course I kept a hand on her dressing-gown, but I took my eyes off her which was fatal.

The next thing I knew was I got a terrible blow on the side of the head. Luckily it missed my head, my shoulder or rather my coat-collar took the force. Anyway I fell sideways, half to try and escape the next attack. I was off balance and couldn't reach at her arms, though I still held on to her dressing-gown. I could see her with something in her hands, I suddenly knew it was the old odd-jobs axe; I used it in the garden only that morning where a branch came away off one of the old apple trees with the wind the night before. I knew like in a flash I had slipped at last. Left it out on the sill of the kitchen window and she must have spotted it. Just one mistake, and you lose everything.

For a moment she had me at her mercy, it was a miracle she didn't do me in. She struck down again and I only half got my arm up and I felt a terrible gashing blow in the temple, it made my head ring and the blood seemed to gush out at once. I don't know how I did it, instinct I suppose, but I kicked out sideways and twisted and she fell sideways, nearly on me, I heard the axe hit the stone.

I got my hand on it and tore it away and threw it on the grass and then I got her hands before she could tear the gag off, that was her game. Well we had another fight, only a few seconds, she must have decided it was no good, she'd had her chance and missed it, she suddenly stopped fighting and I got her in her door and down. I was rough, I was feeling very bad, the blood pouring down my face. I pushed her in, and she gave me a very queer look before I slammed the door and got the bolts home. I didn't care about her cords and the gag. Teach her a lesson, I thought.

Well upstairs I went and washed it, I thought I was going to faint when I saw my face, there was blood everywhere. However I was very lucky, the axe wasn't all that sharp and it glanced off my head, it looked a horrible jagged wound but it wasn't deep. I sat a long time with a cloth pressed on it. I never thought I could stand blood like I did, I really surprised myself that evening.

Of course I was bitter about it. If I hadn't felt a bit faint I don't know what I wouldn't have done. It was just about the straw that broke the camel's back, as the saying is, and certain ideas did come into my mind. I don't know what I mightn't have done if she'd kept on as before. Still, that's neither here nor there now.

The next morning I went down, I still had a headache, I was ready to get really nasty if she was, but you could have knocked me down with the feather, the first thing she did was to stand up and ask me how my head was. I knew by the way she asked that she was trying to be different. Kind.

I'm lucky not to be dead, I said.

She looked all pale, serious too. She held out her hands, she had got the gag off, but she must have slept with the cords (she was still in her dressing-gown). I undid them.

"Let me look at it."

I backed away, she had me very jumpy.

"I've nothing in my hands. Did you wash it?"

Yes.

"Disinfectant?"

It's all right.

Well she went and got a small bottle of Dettol she had, she diluted some with cotton wool and came back.

What's the game now, I said.

"I want to dab this on. Sit down. Sit down." The way she said it you knew she meant well. Funny, sometimes you knew she couldn't be lying.

She took the plaster and lint off, very gentle, I felt her wince when she saw it, it wasn't very pretty, but she washed it very softly and put the lint on again.

Thanks very much, I said.

"I'm sorry I did . . . what I did. And I should like to thank you for not retaliating. You had every right to."

It's not easy when you've been like you've been.

"I don't want to talk about anything. Just to say I'm sorry."

I accept your apologies.

"Thank you."

It was all formal, she turned away to have her breakfast, and I waited outside. When I knocked on the door to see if I could clear away, she was dressed and the bed properly made, I asked if she wanted anything but she didn't. She said I was to get TCP ointment for myself, and she handed me the tray with just the ghost of a smile. It doesn't seem much, but it marked a big change. It almost seemed to make the head worth it. I was really happy that morning. Like the sun was coming out again.

After that for two or three days we were neither one thing nor the other. She didn't say much, but she wasn't bitter or cutting at all. Then one day after breakfast she asked me to sit down as I used to in the beginning so she could draw me. It was just to give herself an excuse to talk.

"I want you to help me," she said.

Carry on, I answered.

"I have a friend, a girl, who's got a young man in love with her."

Go on, I said. She stopped. To watch me walk into it, I suppose.

"He's so much in love with her that he's kidnapped her. He's keeping her prisoner."

What a coincidence.

"Isn't it? Well, she wants to be free again and she doesn't want to hurt him. And she just doesn't know what to do. What would you advise?"

Patience, I said.

"What must happen before the young man will release her?"

Anything might happen.

"All right. Don't let's play games. Tell me what I must do to be set free."

I couldn't answer, I thought if I said live with me for ever we'd only be back where we started.

"Marriage is no good. You can't trust me."

Not yet.

"If I went to bed with you?"

She'd stopped drawing. I wouldn't answer.

"Well?"

I didn't think you were that sort, I said.

"I'm just trying to find your price." Just like it was a new washing-machine she was inquiring the pros and cons of.

You know what I want, I said.

"But that's just what I don't!"

You know all right.

"Oh, God. Look. Just answer yes or no. Do you want to go to bed with me?"

Not like we are now.

"What are we like now?"

I thought you were supposed to be the clever one.

She took a deep breath. I liked having her on a bit. "You feel I'm only looking for a way to escape? Whatever I did would be just for that? Is that it?"

I said yes.

"If you felt I was doing it for some other reason. Because I liked you. Just for fun. You would like it then?"

I can buy what you're talking about in London any time I want,
I said.

That shut her up a bit. She started drawing again.

After a bit she said, "You haven't got me here because you find
me sexually attractive."

I find you very attractive, I said. The most.

"You're just like a Chinese box," she said. Then she went on
drawing and we didn't say any more. I tried to, but she said it
spoilt the pose.

I know what some would think, they would think my behaviour
peculiar. I know most men would only have thought of taking an
unfair advantage and there were plenty of opportunities. I could
have used the pad. Done what I liked, but I am not that sort, definitely not that sort at all. She was like some caterpillar that takes
three months to feed up trying to do it in a few days. I knew nothing good would come of it, she was always in such a hurry. People today always want to get things, they no sooner think of it they
want to get it in their hands, but I am different, old-fashioned, I
enjoy thinking about the future and letting things develop all in
good time. Easy does it, as Uncle Dick used to say when he was
into a big one.

What she never understood was that with me it was having.
Having her was enough. Nothing needed doing. I just wanted to
have her, and safe at last.

Two or three days passed. She never said much, but then one day
after lunch she said, "I'm a prisoner for life, aren't I."

I could tell she was just talking, so I said nothing.

"Hadn't we better start being friends again?"

O.K. with me, I said.

"I'd like a bath tonight."

O.K.

"Then could we sit upstairs? It's this room. I get mad for a change."

I said I'd see.

Actually, I lit the fire and got everything ready. Made sure there was nothing she could pick up and have a bash at me with. It's no good pretending I had my old trust in her.

Well, she went up to her bath and it was all like as usual. When she came out I did her hands, no gag, and I followed her downstairs. I noticed she had a lot of her French scent on, she'd done her hair up the way she did it before, and she was wearing a purple and white housecoat I bought her. She wanted some of the sherry we never finished (there was still half a bottle there) and I poured it out and she stood by the log fire looking down into it, holding out her bare feet turn by turn to warm them. We stood there drinking; we didn't say anything but she gave me one or two funny looks, like she knew something I didn't and that made me nervous.

Well she had another glass, and drank it off in a minute and then wanted another.

"Sit down," she said, so I sat down on the sofa where she pointed. For a moment she watched me sitting there. Then she stood in front of me, very funny, looking down at me, moving from foot to foot. Then she came, twist, bang she sat on my knees. It took me right by surprise. Somehow she got her arms right round my head and the next thing was she was kissing me at the mouth. Then laying her head on my shoulder.

"Don't be so stiff," she said.

I was like stunned. It was the last thing.

"Put your arm round me," she said. "There. Isn't that nice?

Am I heavy?" And she leant her head again on my shoulder, while
I had my hand on her waist. She was all warm and perfumed and
I have to say that her housecoat was open very low and fell apart
to above the knees, but she didn't seem to care, she just stretched
her legs along the sofa.

What's up? I said.

"You're so unrelaxed. Just relax. There's nothing to worry
about." Well, I tried, she lay still, but I knew there was something
wrong in the situation.

"Why don't you kiss me?"

I knew something was really on then. I didn't know what to do,
I kissed the top of her head.

"Not like that."

I don't want to, I said.

She sat up still on my knees and looked at me.

"You don't want to?"

I looked away, it was difficult with her tied hands round my
neck, I didn't know what to say to stop her.

"Why not?"

She was laughing at me.

I might go too far, I said.

"So might I."

I knew she was laughing, making fun of me again.

I know what I am, I said.

"What are you?"

Not the sort you like.

"Don't you know there are times when every man is attractive? Eh?" She sort of gave my head a bit of a jerk, like I was
being stupid.

I didn't, I said.

"Well, then."

It's what it could lead to.

"I don't care what it leads to. You *are* slow." And then all of a sudden she was kissing me again, I even felt her tongue.

"Isn't that nice?"

Of course I had to say, yes it was. I didn't know what her real game was, it made me nervous, quite apart from me being very nervous anyhow about kissing and all the other business.

"Come on, then. Try."

Well, she pulled my head round. I had to do it and her mouth was very nice. Very soft.

I know I was weak. I should have told her straight out not to be disgusting. I was very weak. It was like I was drawn on against my will.

She laid her head again so I couldn't see her face.

"Am I the first girl you've ever kissed?"

Don't be daft.

"Just relax. Don't be nervous, don't be ashamed."

Then she turned and was kissing me again, her eyes shut. Of course she'd had three glasses of sherry. What happened then was most embarrassing, I began to feel very worked up and I always understood (from something I heard in the army) that a gentleman always controls himself to the right moment and so I just didn't know what to do. I thought she would be offended and so I tried to sit upright more when she took her mouth away.

"What's wrong. Am I hurting you?"

Yes, I said.

She moved off my knees then, she unhooked her arms from my head, but she still sat very close.

"Won't you undo my hands?"

I got up, I was shamed, I had to go to the window and pretend to do something to the curtain, all the time she watched me over the back of the sofa, kneeling on it.

"Ferdinand. What's wrong?"

Nothing's wrong, I said.

"There's nothing to be frightened of."

I'm not frightened.

"Come back then. Turn out the light. Let's just have the firelight."

I did what she said, I turned out the lights, but I stayed by the window.

"Come on." Very coaxing, she was.

I said, it's not right. You're only pretending.

"Am I?"

You know you are.

"Why don't you come and see?"

I didn't move, all the time I knew it was a bad mistake. The next thing was she went and stood by the fire. I didn't feel excited any more, I felt all cold inside. It was the surprise.

"Come and sit here."

I'm all right here, I said.

Well, suddenly she came to me, she took my hand in her two and pulled me to the fire, I let her. When we were there she held out her hands, she had such a look, so I untied them. At once she came close and kissed me again, for which she had to stand on tiptoe almost.

Then she did something really shocking.

I could hardly believe my eyes, she stood back a step and unfastened her housecoat and she had nothing on beneath. She was stark. I didn't give no more than a quick look, she just stood there, smiling and waiting, you could feel it, for me to make a move. She put up her arms and began to undo her hair. It was deliberate provoking, standing there naked in the shadows and firelight. I couldn't believe it, rather I had to believe it, but I couldn't believe it was what it seemed.

It was terrible, it made me feel sick and trembling, I wished I was on the other side of the world. It was worse than with the prostitute; I didn't respect her, but with Miranda I knew I couldn't stand the shame.

We stood there, she was just in front of me shaking her hair loose and I felt more and more ashamed. The next thing was she came up and began to take off my coat, then it was my tie, and she undid my shirt buttons one after the other. I was like putty in her hands. Then she started pulling my shirt out.

I kept thinking, stop it, stop it, it's wrong, but I was too weak. The next thing was I was naked and she was against me and holding me but I was all tense, it was like a different me and a different she. I know I wasn't normal then, not doing the expected, she did some things which I won't say except that I would never have thought it of her. She lay beside me on the sofa and everything, but I was all twisted inside.

She made me look a proper fool. I knew what she was thinking, she was thinking this was why I was always so respectful. I wanted to do it, I wanted to show her I could do it so I could prove I was really respectful. I wanted her to see I could do it, then I would tell her I wasn't going to, it was below me, and below her, it was disgusting.

Well, we lay for some time still and I felt she was despising me, I was a freak.

In the end she got up off the sofa and kneeled beside me and stroked my head.

"It happens to lots of men, it doesn't matter." You'd think she had all the experience in the world to have heard her.

She went back by the fire and put her housecoat on and sat

there watching me. I got my clothes on. I told her I knew I could never do it. I made up a long story so that she would pity me, it was all lies, I don't know if she believed it; about how I could feel love but could never do it. How that was why I had to keep her.

"But doesn't it please you at all to touch me? You seemed to like kissing me."

I said, it was when it got past the kissing.

"I shouldn't have given you such a shock."

It's not your fault, I said. I'm not like other people. Nobody understands.

"I understand."

I dream about it, I said. It can't ever be real.

"Like Tantalus." She explained who he was.

She was quiet a long time. I felt like giving her the pad. Getting her downstairs and out of it. I wanted to be right alone.

"What kind of doctor told you you could never do it?"

Just a doctor. (It was the lies I told her. I never saw any doctor, of course.)

"A psychiatrist?"

In the army, I said. A psychiatrist.

"What sort of dreams did you have about me?"

All sorts.

"No sexy ones?"

She would go on like that. Never leave it alone.

I'd be holding you, I said. That's all. We would be sleeping side by side with the wind and the rain outside or something.

"Would you like to try that now?"

It wouldn't do any good.

"I'll do it if you want to."

I don't want to, I said.

I wish you never started, I said.

She was silent, it seemed ages.

"Why do you think I did it? Just to escape?"

Not love, I said.

"Shall I tell you?" She stood up. "You must realize that I've sacrificed all my principles tonight. Oh, yes, to escape. I was thinking of that. But I *do* want to help you. You must believe that. To try to show you that sex—sex is just an activity, like anything else. It's not dirty, it's just two people playing with each other's bodies. Like dancing. Like a game." She seemed to think I ought to say something, but I let her talk. "I'm doing something for you I've never done for any man. And—well, I think you owe me something."

I saw her game, of course. She was very artful at wrapping up what she meant in a lot of words. Making you feel you really did owe her something, just like she never started it all in the first place.

"Please say something."

What, I said.

"That you do at least understand what I've just said."

I understand.

"Is that all?"

I don't feel like talking, I said.

"You could have told me. You could have stopped me at the very beginning."

I tried, I said.

She knelt in front of the fire.

"It's fantastic. We're further apart than ever."

I said, you hated me before. Now I suppose you despise me as well.

"I pity you. I pity you for what you are and I pity you for not seeing what I am."

I can see what you are, I said. Don't you think I can't.

I sounded sharp, I'd had enough. She looked round quick, then bent down, her hands covering her face. I think she was pretending to cry a bit. Well in the end she said in a very quiet voice, "Please take me down."

So down we went. She turned when she was inside and I was going to go, having removed her cords.

"We've been naked in front of each other," she said. "We *can't* be further apart."

I was like mad when I got out. I can't explain. I didn't sleep the whole night. It kept on coming back, me standing and lying there with no clothes on, the way I acted and what she must think. I could just see her laughing at me down there. Every time I thought about it, it was like my whole body went red. I didn't want the night to end. I wanted it to stay dark for ever.

I walked about upstairs for hours. In the end I got the van out and drove down to the sea, real fast, I didn't care what happened.

I could have done anything. I could have killed her. All I did later was because of that night.

It was almost like she was stupid, plain stupid. Of course she wasn't really, it was just that she didn't see how to love me in the right way. There were a lot of ways she could have pleased me.

She was like all women, she had a one-track mind.

I never respected her again. It left me angry for days.

Because I could do it.

The photographs (the day I gave her the pad), I used to look at them sometimes. I could take my time with them. They didn't talk back at me.

That was what she never knew.

                              *   *   *

Well, I went down the next morning, and it was like it never happened. She didn't say a word about it, nor did I. I got her breakfast, she said she didn't want anything in Lewes, she went out in
the cellar to walk a bit, and then I locked her back in and went off.
Actually I had a sleep.

   That evening it was different.

   "I want to talk to you."

   Yes, I said.

   "I've tried everything. There's only one thing left for me to
try. I'm going to fast again. I shan't eat until you let me go."

   Thanks for the warning, I said.

   "Unless . . ."

   Oh, so there's an unless, I said.

   "Unless we come to an agreement."

   She seemed to wait. I haven't heard it yet, I said.

   "I'm prepared to accept that you won't let me go at once. But
I'm not prepared to stay any longer down here. I want to be a prisoner upstairs. I want daylight and some fresh air."

   Just like that, I said.

   "Just like that."

   As from this evening, I suppose, I said.

   "Very soon."

   I suppose I get a carpenter in, and the decorators and all.

   She sighed then, she began to get the message.

   "Don't be like this. Please don't be like this." She gave me a
funny look. "All this sarcasm. I didn't mean to hurt you."

   It was no good, she had killed all the romance, she had made
herself like any other woman, I didn't respect her any more, there
was nothing left to respect. I knew her lark, no sooner she was up
out of the room she was as good as gone.

Still, what I thought was I didn't want the no-eating business again, so it was best to play for time.

How soon, I said.

"You could keep me in one of the bedrooms. It could be all barred and boarded up. I could sleep there. Then perhaps you'd tie me up and gag me and let me sit sometimes near an open window. That's all I ask."

That's all, I said. What are people going to think with boarded-up windows all over the place?

"I'd rather starve to death than stay down here. Keep me in chains upstairs. Anything. But let me have some fresh air and daylight."

I'll think about it, I said.

"No. Now."

You're forgetting who's the boss.

"Now."

I can't say now. It needs thinking.

"Very well. Tomorrow morning. Either you tell me I can come up or I don't touch any food. And that will be murder." Really fierce and nasty she looked. I just turned and went.

I thought it all out that night. I knew I had to have time, I had to pretend I would do it. Go through the motions, as they say.

The other thing I thought was something I could do when it came to the point.

The next morning I went down, I said I'd thought things over, I saw her point, I'd looked into the matter, etcetera—one room could be converted, but it would take me a week. I thought she would start sulking but she took it O.K.

"But if this *is* another put-off, I will fast. You know that?"

I'd do it tomorrow, I said. But it needs a lot of wood and bars special. It may take a day or two to get them.

She gave me a good old tight look, but I just took her bucket.

After that, we got on all right, except that I was pretending all the time. We didn't say much, but she wasn't sharp. One night she wanted a bath and she wanted to see the room and what I'd done. Well, I knew she would; I had got some wood and made it look as if I was seriously doing things to the window (it was a back bedroom). She said she wanted one of those old windsor chairs in it (quite like old times, her asking for something) which I got the next day and actually took down and showed her. She wouldn't have it down there, it had to go back up. She said she didn't want anything she had (in the way of furniture) downstairs upstairs. It was dead easy. After she saw the room and the screw-holes she really seemed to think I was going to be soft enough to let her come up.

The idea was I would go down and bring her up and we would have supper upstairs and then she would have her first night upstairs and in the morning she would see daylight.

She got quite gay sometimes. I had to laugh. Well, I say I laugh, but I was nervous, too, when the day came.

The first thing she said when I went down at six was she had my cold, the one I got at the hairdresser in Lewes.

She was all bright and bossy, laughing up her sleeve at me, of course. Only the joke was going to be on her.

"These are my things for tonight. You can bring up the rest tomorrow. Is it ready?" She already asked that at lunch, and I said yes.

I said, it's ready.

"Come on then. Must I be tied?"

There's just one thing, I said. One condition.

"Condition?" Her face dropped. She knew at once.

I've been thinking, I said.

"Yes?" Really burning, her eyes were.

I'd like to take some photographs.

"Of me? But you've taken a lot already."

Not the sort I mean.

"I don't understand." But I could see she did.

I want to take pictures of you like you were the other evening, I said.

She sat on the end of her bed.

"Go on."

And you've got to look as if you enjoyed posing, I said. You got to pose the way I tell you.

Well she just sat there, not saying a word. I thought at least she would get angry. She just sat there wiping her nose.

"If I do it?"

I'll keep my side of the bargain, I said. I got to protect myself. I want some photos of you what you would be ashamed to let anyone else see.

"You mean I'm to pose for obscene photographs so that if I escape I shan't dare tell the police about you."

That's the idea, I said. Not obscene. Just photos you wouldn't want to be published. Art-photographs.

"No."

I'm only asking what you did without asking the other day.

"No, no, no."

I know your game, I said.

"What I did then was wrong. I did it, I did it out of despair that there is nothing between us except meanness and suspicion and hate. This is different. It's vile."

I don't see the difference.

She got up and went up to the end wall.

You did it once, I said. You can do it again.

"God, God, it's like a lunatic asylum." She looked all round the room like I wasn't there, like there was someone else listening or she was going to bust down the walls.

Either you do it or you don't go out at all. No walking out there. No baths. No nothing.

I said, you took me in for a bit. You've just got one idea. Get away from me. Make a fool of me and get the police on to me.

You're no better than a common street-woman, I said. I used to respect you because I thought you were above what you done. Not like the rest. But you're just the same. You do any disgusting thing to get what you want.

"Stop it, stop it," she cried.

I could get a lot more expert than you in London. Any time. And do what I liked.

"You disgusting filthy mean-minded bastard."

Go on, I said. That's just your language.

"You're breaking every decent human law, every decent human relationship, every decent thing that's ever happened between your sex and mine."

Hark at the pot calling the kettle black, I said. You took your clothes off, you asked for it. Now you got it.

"Get out! Get out!"

It was a real scream.

Yes or no, I said.

She turned and picked up an ink-bottle on her table and hurled it at me.

So that was that. I went out and bolted up. I didn't take her any

supper, I let her stew in her own juice. I had the chicken I bought
in case and had some of the champagne and poured the rest down
the sink.

I felt happy, I can't explain, I saw I was weak before, now I was
paying her back for all the things she said and thought about me.
I walked about upstairs, I went and looked at her room, it made me
really laugh to think of her down there, she was the one who was
going to stay below in all senses and even if it wasn't what she de-
served in the beginning she had made it so that she did now. I had
real reasons to teach her what was what.

Well, I got to sleep in the end, I looked at the previous photos and
some books and I got some ideas. There was one of the books
called *Shoes* with very interesting pictures of girls, mainly their
legs, wearing different sorts of shoes, some just shoes and belts,
they were really unusual pictures, artistic.

However, when I went down in the morning, I knocked and
waited as usual before going in, but when I did I was very
surprised she was still in bed, she'd been asleep with her clothes
on just under the top blanket and for a moment she didn't
seem to know where she was and who I was, I just stood there
waiting for her to fly at me, but she just sat up on the edge
of the bed and rested her arms on her knees and her head on
her hands, like it was all a nightmare and she couldn't bear to
wake up.

She coughed. It sounded a bit chesty. She looked a real mess.

So I decided not to say anything then, and went and got her
breakfast. She drank the coffee when I brought it and ate the cereal, the no eating was off, and then she just went back to the same
position, her head on her hands. I knew her game, it was to try and

get my pity. She looked properly beaten but I consider it was all a pose to make me fall on my knees and beg for forgiveness or something daft.

Do you want some Coldrex, I asked. I knew she had the cold all right.

Well, she nodded, her head still in her hands, so I went and got them and when I came back she hadn't changed her position. You could see it was a big act. Like a sulk. So I thought, well, let her sulk away. I can wait. I asked if she wanted anything, she shook her head, so I left her.

That lunch-time she was in bed when I went down. She just looked over the bedclothes at me, she said she wanted just some soup and tea, which I brought, and left. It was more or less the same at supper. She wanted aspirins. She hardly ate anything. But that was the game she played once before. We didn't speak twenty words together all that day.

The next day it was the same, she was in bed when I went in. She was awake though, because she was lying watching me.

Well, I asked. She didn't answer, she just lay there.

I said, if you think you take me in with all this lying in bed lark you're mistaken.

That made her open her mouth.

"You're not a human being. You're just a dirty little masturbating worm."

I acted like I hadn't heard, I just went and got her breakfast. When I went to bring her her coffee, she said "Don't come near me!" Real poison in her voice.

Supposing I just left you here, I said, teasing. What'd you do then?

"If only I had the strength to kill you, I'd kill you. Like a scorpion. I will when I'm better. I'd never go to the police. Prison's too good for you. I'd come and kill you."

I knew she was angry because her game wasn't working. I had the cold, I knew it wasn't much.

You talk too much, I said. You forget who's boss. I could just forget you. Nobody'd know.

She just shut her eyes at that.

I left then, I went into Lewes and got the food. At lunch she seemed to be asleep when I said it was ready, but she made a sort of movement, so I left.

At supper she was still in bed but sitting up and reading her Shakespeare I bought.

I asked her if she was better. Sarcastic, of course.

Well, she just went on reading, wouldn't answer, I nearly snatched the book away to teach her then, but I kept control. Half an hour later, after I had my own supper, I went back and she hadn't eaten and when I commented on that she hadn't, she said, "I feel sick. I think I've got the flu."

However, she was stupid enough to say next, "What would you do if I needed a doctor?"

Wait and see, I answered.

"It hurts so when I cough."

It's only a cold, I said.

"It's *not* a cold." She really shouted at me.

Of course it's a cold, I said. And stop acting. I know your game.

"I am *not* acting."

Oh, no. You never acted in your life, I said. Of course not.

"Oh, God you're not a man, if only you were a man."

Say that again, I said. I had had some more champagne with my supper, there was a shop I found in Lewes with half-bottles, so I was not in the mood for her silliness.

"I said you are not a man."

All right, I said. Get out of bed. Go on, get up. From now on I give the orders.

I had had enough, most men would have had it long before. I went and pulled the bedclothes off her and got hold of her arm to pull her up and she started to fight, scratching at my face.

I said, all right, I'm going to teach you a lesson.

I had the cords in my pocket and after a bit of a struggle I got them on her and then the gag, it was her own fault if they were tight, I got her on a short rope tied to the bed and then I went and fetched the camera and flash equipment. She struggled of course, she shook her head, she looked daggers with her eyes, as they say, she even tried to go all soft, but I kept at her. I got her garments off and at first she wouldn't do as I said but in the end she lay and stood like I ordered (I refused to take if she did not co-operate). So I got my pictures. I took her till I had no more bulbs left.

It was not my fault. How was I to know she was iller than she looked. She just looked like she had a cold.

I got the pictures developed and printed that night. The best ones were with her face cut off. She didn't look much anyhow with the gag, of course. The best were when she stood in her high heels, from the back. The tied hands to the bed made what they call an interesting motif. I can say I was quite pleased with what I got.

The next day she was up when I went in, in her housecoat, like she was waiting for me. What she did was very surprising, she took a step forward and went down on her knees at my feet. Like she was drunk. Her face was very flushed, I did see; she looked at me and she was crying and she had got herself up into a state.

"I'm terribly ill. I've got pneumonia. Or pleurisy. You've got to get a doctor."

I said, get up and go back to bed. Then I went to get her coffee.

When I came back I said, you know you're not ill, if it was pneumonia you couldn't stand up even.

"I can't breathe at nights. I've got a pain here, I have to lie on my left side. Please take my temperature. Look at it."

Well I did and it was a 102 but I knew there were ways you could fake temperatures.

"The air's stifling here."

There's plenty of air, I said. It was her fault for having used that game before.

Anyway I got the chemist in Lewes to give me something he said was very good for congestion and special anti-flu pills and in-haler, all of which she took when offered. She tried to eat some-thing at supper, but she couldn't manage it, she was sick, she did look off-colour then, and I can say that for the first time I had rea-son to believe there might be something in it all. Her face was red, bits of her hair stuck on it with perspiration, but that could have been deliberate.

I cleaned up the sick and gave her her medicines and was going to leave when she asked me to sit on the bed, so she wouldn't have to speak loud.

"Do you think I could speak to you if I wasn't terribly ill? After what you've done."

You asked for what I did, I said.

"You must see I'm really ill."

It's the flu, I said. There's a lot in Lewes.

"It's not the flu. I've got pneumonia. Something terrible. I can't breathe."

You'll be all right, I said. Those yellow pills will do the trick. The chemist said they're the best.

"Not fetching a doctor is murder. You're going to kill me."

I tell you you're all right. It's fever, I said. As soon as she mentioned doctor, I was suspicious.

"Would you mind wiping my face with my flannel?"

It was funny, I did what she said and for the first time for days I felt a bit sorry for her. It was a woman's job, really. I mean it was a time when women need other women. She said thanks.

I'll go now then, I said.

"Don't go. I'll die." She actually tried to catch hold of my arm.

Don't be so daft, I told her.

"You must listen, you must listen," and suddenly she was crying again; I could see her eyes filling with tears and she sort of banged her head from side to side on the pillow. I felt sorry for her by then, as I say, so I sat on the bed and gave her a handkerchief and told her I would never not get a doctor if she was really ill. I even said I still loved her and I was sorry and some other things. But the tears just kept on coming, she hardly seemed to listen. Not even when I told her she looked much better than the day before, which was not strictly true.

In the end she grew calm, she lay there with her eyes shut for a while and then when I moved she said, "Will you do something for me?"

What, I asked.

"Will you stay down here with me and let the door be open for air?"

Well, I agreed, and we turned out the lights in her room, with only the light from outside and the fan, and I sat by her for quite a time. She began to breathe in a funny quick way like she'd just run upstairs, as she said she was stifled, and she spoke several times—once she said, please don't, and another I think she said my name but it was all blurred—well, I felt she was asleep and after I said her name and she didn't answer, I went out and locked up and then set the alarm for early the next morning. I thought she went off to sleep so easy, I wasn't to tell. I thought it was for the best, and I thought the pills might do the trick and she would be better the next morning, with the worst past. I even felt it was a good thing, her being ill, because if she hadn't there would have been a lot of trouble of the old kind.

What I am trying to say is that it all came unexpected. I know what I did next day was a mistake, but up to that day I thought I was acting for the best and within my rights.

2

It's the seventh night.

I keep on thinking the same things. If only they knew. If only *they* knew.

Share the outrage.

So now I'm trying to tell it to this pad he bought me this morning. His kindness.

Calmly.

Deep down I get more and more frightened. It's only surface calm.

No nastiness, no sex thing. But his eyes are mad. Grey with a grey lost light in them. To begin with I watched him all the time. I thought it must be sex, if I turned my back I did it where he couldn't spring at me, and I listened. I had to know exactly where he was in the room.

Power. It's become so *real*.

I know the H-bomb is wrong. But being so weak seems wrong now too.

I wish I knew judo. Could make him cry for mercy.

This crypt-room is so stuffy, the walls squeeze in, I'm listening for him as I write, the thoughts I have are like bad drawings. Must be torn up at once.

Try try try to escape.

It's all I think of.

A strange thing. He fascinates me. I feel the deepest contempt and loathing for him, I can't stand this room, everybody will be wild with worry. I can sense their wild worry.

How can he love me? How can you love someone you don't know?

He wants desperately to please me. But that's what madmen must be like. They aren't deliberately mad, they must be as shocked in a way as everyone else when they finally do something terrible.

It's only this last day or two I could speak about him so.

All the way down here in the van it was nightmare. Wanting to be sick and afraid of choking under the gag. And then being sick. Thinking I was going to be pulled into some thicket and raped and murdered. I was sure that was it when the van stopped, I think that was why I was sick. Not just the beastly chloroform. (I kept on remembering Penny Lester's grisly dormitory stories about how her mother survived being raped by the Japanese, I kept on saying, don't resist, don't resist. And then someone else at Ladymont once said that it takes two men to rape you. Women who let themselves be raped by one man want to be raped.) I know now that wouldn't be his way. He'd use chloroform again, or something. But that first night it was, don't resist, don't resist.

I was grateful to be alive. I am a terrible coward, I don't want to die, I love life so passionately, I never knew how much I wanted to live before. If I get out of this, I shall never be the same.

I don't care what he does. So long as I live.

It's all the vile unspeakable things he *could* do.

I've looked everywhere for a weapon, but there's nothing of any use, even if I had the strength and skill. I prop a chair against the iron door every night, so at least I shall know if he tries to get in without my hearing.

Hateful primitive wash-stand and place.

The great blank door. No keyhole. Nothing.

The silence. I've got a little more used to it now. But it is *terrible*. Never the least sound. It makes me feel I'm always waiting.

Alive. Alive in the way that death is alive.

The collection of books on art. Nearly fifty pounds' worth, I've added them up. That first night it suddenly dawned on me that they were there for *me*. That I wasn't a haphazard victim after all.

Then there were the drawers full of clothes—shirts, skirts, dresses, coloured stockings, an extraordinary selection of week-end-in-Paris underwear, night-dresses. I could see they were about my size. They're too large, but he says he's seen me wear the colours.

Everything in my life seemed fine. There was G.P. But even that was strange. Exciting. Exciting.

Then this.

I slept a little with the light on, on top of the bed. I would have loved a drink, but I thought it might be drugged. I still half expect the food to be doped.

Seven days ago. It seems like seven weeks.

He looked so innocent and worried when he stopped me. He said he'd run over a dog. I thought it might be Misty. Exactly the sort of man you would *not* suspect. The most unwolflike.

Like falling off the edge of the world. There suddenly being an edge.

Every night I do something I haven't done for years. I lie and pray. I don't kneel, I know God despises kneelers. I lie and ask him to comfort M and D and Minny, and Caroline who must feel so guilty and everyone else, even the ones it would do good to suffer for me (or for anyone else). Like Piers and Antoinette. I ask him to help this misery who has me under his power. I ask him to help me. Not to let me be raped or abused and murdered. I ask him for light.

Literally. Daylight.

I can't stand the absolute darkness. He's bought me night-lights. I go to sleep with one glowing beside me now. Before that I left the light on.

Waking up is the worst thing. I wake up and for a moment I think I'm at home or at Caroline's. Then it hits me.

I don't know if I believe in God. I prayed to him furiously in the van when I thought I was going to die (that's a proof *against*, I can hear G.P. saying). But praying makes things easier.

It's all bits and pieces. I can't concentrate. I've thought so many things, and now I can't think of one.

But it makes me feel calmer. The illusion, anyway. Like working out how much money one's spent. And how much is left.

October 15th

He has never had any parents, he's been brought up by an aunt. I can see her. A thin woman with a white face and a nasty tight mouth and mean grey eyes and dowdy beige tea-cosy hats and a thing about dirt and dust. Dirt and dust being everything outside her foul little back-street world.

I told him he was looking for the mother he'd never had, but of course he wouldn't listen.

He doesn't believe in God. That makes me want to believe.

I talked about me. About D and M, in a bright little matter-of-fact voice. He knew about M. I suppose the whole town knows.

My theory is that I have to unmartyr him.

The time in prison. Endless time.

The first morning. He knocked on the door and waited ten minutes (as he always does). It wasn't a nice ten minutes, all the consoling thoughts I'd scraped together during the night ran away and I was left alone. I stood there and said, if he does, don't resist, don't resist. I was going to say, do what you like, but don't kill me. Don't kill me, you can do it again. As if I was washable. Hard-wearing.

It was all different. When he came in he just stood there looking gawky and then at once, seeing him without a hat on, I knew who he was. I suppose I memorize people's features without thinking. I knew he was the clerk from the Town Hall Annexe. The fabulous pools win. His photo in the paper. We all said we'd seen him about.

He tried to deny it, but he went red. He blushes at everything. Simple as sneezing to put him on the defensive. His face has a

sort of natural "hurt" set. Sheepish. No, giraffish. Like a lanky
gawky giraffe. I kept on popping questions, he wouldn't answer,
all he could do was look as if I had no right to ask. As if *this* wasn't
at all what he'd bargained for.

He's never had anything to do with girls. With girls like me,
anyway.

A lilywhite boy.

He's six feet. Eight or nine inches more than me. Skinny, so he
looks taller than he is. Gangly. Hands too big, a nasty fleshy white
and pink. Not a man's hands. Adam's apple too big, wrists too big,
chin much too big, underlip bitten in, edges of nostrils red. Ade-
noids. He's got one of those funny inbetween voices, uneducated
trying to be educated. It keeps on letting him down. His whole
face is too long. Dull black hair. It waves and recedes, it's coarse.
Stiff. Always in place. He always wears a sports coat and flannels
and a pinned tie. Even cuff-links.

He's what people call a "nice young man."

Absolutely sexless (he looks).

He has a way of standing with his hands by his side or behind
his back, as if he doesn't know what on earth to do with them. Respectfully waiting for me to give my orders.

Fish-eyes. They watch. That's all. No expression.

He makes me feel capricious. Like a dissatisfied rich customer
(he's a male assistant in a draper's).

It's his line. The mock-humble. Ever-so-sorry.

I sit and eat my meals and read a book and he watches me. If I
tell him to go, he goes.

He's been secretly watching me for nearly two years. He
loves me desperately, he was very lonely, he knew I would always be "above" him. It was awful, he spoke so awkwardly, he
always has to say things in a roundabout way, he always has to

justify himself at the same time. I sat and listened. I couldn't look at him.

It was his heart. Sicked up all over the hideous tangerine carpet. We just sat there when he had finished. When he got up to go I tried to tell him that I understood, that I wouldn't say anything if he would take me home, but he backed away out. I tried to look very understanding, very sympathetic, but it seemed to frighten him.

The next morning I tried again, I found out what his name was (vile coincidence!), I was very reasonable, I looked up at him and appealed, but once again it just frightened him.

At lunch I told him I could see he was ashamed of what he was doing, and that it wasn't too late. You hit his conscience and it gives, but it doesn't hurt him at all. I am ashamed, he says; I know I ought, he says. I told him he didn't look a wicked person. He said, this is the first wicked thing I've ever done.

It probably is. But he's been saving up.

Sometimes I think he's being very clever. He's trying to enlist my sympathy by pretending he's in the grip of some third thing.

That night I tried not being decent, being sharp and bitchy instead. He just looked more hurt than ever. He's very clever at looking hurt.

Putting the tentacles of his being hurt around me.

His not being my "class."

I know what I am to him. A butterfly he has always wanted to catch. I remember (the very first time I met him) G.P. saying that collectors were the worst animals of all. He meant art collectors, of course. I didn't really understand, I thought he was just trying to shock Caroline—and me. But of course, he is right. They're anti-life, anti-art, anti-everything.

I write in this terrible nightlike silence as if I feel normal. But

I'm not. I'm so sick, so frightened, so alone. The solitude is un-
bearable. Every time the door opens I want to rush at it and out.
But I know now I must save up my escape attempts. Outwit him.
Plan ahead.

    Survive.

October 16th

It's afternoon. I should be in life class. Does the world go on? Does the sun still shine? Last night, I thought—I am dead. This is death. This is hell. There wouldn't be other people in hell. Or just one, like him. The devil wouldn't be devilish and rather attractive, but like him.

I drew him this morning. I wanted to get his face, to illustrate this. But it wasn't any good, and he wanted it. Said he would pay TWO HUNDRED guineas for it. He is mad.

It is me. I am his madness.

For years he's been looking for something to put his madness into. And he found me.

I can't write in a vacuum like this. To no one. When I draw I always think of someone like G.P. at my shoulder.

All parents should be like ours, then sisters really become sisters. They *have* to be to each other what Minny and I are.

Dear Minny.

I have been here over a week now, and I miss you very much, and I miss the fresh air and the fresh faces of all those people I so hated on the Tube and the fresh things that happened every hour of every day if only I could have seen them—their freshness, I mean. The thing I miss most is fresh light. I can't live without light. Artificial light, all the lines lie, it almost makes you long for darkness.

I haven't told you how I tried to escape. I thought about it all night, I couldn't sleep, it was so stuffy, and my tummy's all wrong (he tries his best to cook, but it's hopeless). I pretended something was wrong with the bed, and then I just turned and ran. But I couldn't get the door shut to lock him in and he caught me in the other cellar. I could see daylight through a keyhole.

He thinks of everything. He padlocks the door open. It was worth it. One keyholeful of light in seven days. He foresaw I would try and get out and lock him in.

Then I treated him for three days with a view of my back and my sulky face. I fasted. I slept. When I was sure he wouldn't come in I got up and danced about a bit, and read the art books and drank water. But I didn't touch his food.

And I brought him to terms. His condition was six weeks. A week ago six hours would have been too much. I cried. Brought him down to four weeks. I'm not less horrified at being with him. I've grown to know every inch of this foul little crypt, it's beginning to grow on me like those coats of stones on the worms in rivers. But the four weeks seem less important.

I don't seem to have any energy, any will, I'm constipated in all ways.

Minny, going upstairs with him yesterday. First, the outside air, being in a space bigger than ten by ten by twenty (I've measured it out), being under the stars, and breathing in wonderful wonderful, even though it was damp and misty, wonderful air.

I thought I might be able to run. But he gripped my arm and I was gagged and bound. It was so dark. So lonely. No lights. Just darkness. I didn't even know which way to run.

The house is an old cottage. I think it may be timbered outside, indoors there are a lot of beams, the floors all sag, and the ceilings are very low. A lovely old house really, done up in *the* most excruciating women's magazine "good taste." Ghastliest colour-clashes, mix-up of furniture styles, bits of suburban fuss, phoney antiques, awful brass ornaments. And the pictures! You wouldn't believe me if I described the awfulness of the pictures. He told me some firm did all the furniture choosing and decorating. They must have got rid of all the junk they could find in their store-rooms.

The bath was delicious. I knew he might burst in (no lock on the door, couldn't even shut it, there was a screwed-in bit of wood). But somehow I knew he wouldn't. And it was so lovely to see a bathful of hot water and a proper place that I almost didn't care. I made him wait hours. Just outside. He didn't seem to mind. He was "good."

Nothing makes him mind.

But I've seen a way to get a message out. I could put a message in a little bottle down the place. I could put a bright ribbon round it. Perhaps someone would see it somewhere some day. I'll do it next time.

I listened for traffic, but there was none. I heard an owl. And an aeroplane.

If only people knew what they flew over.

We're all in aeroplanes.

The bathroom window was boarded up. Great screws. I looked everywhere for a weapon. Under the bath, behind the pipes. But there's nothing. Even if I found one I don't know how I'd use it. I watch him and he watches me. We never give each other a chance. He doesn't look very strong, but he's much stronger than me. It would have to be by surprise.

Everything's locked and double-locked. There's even a burglar-alarm on my cell door.

He's thought of everything. I thought of putting a note in laundry. But he doesn't send any. When I asked him about sheets, he said, I buy them new, tell me when you want some more.

Down-the-place is the only chance.

Minny, I'm not writing to you, I'm talking to myself.

When I came out, wearing the least horrid of the shirts he'd bought for me, he stood up (he's been sitting all the time by the door). I felt like the girl-at-the-ball-coming-down-the-grand-staircase. I knocked him over. I suppose it was seeing me in "his" shirt. And with my hair down.

Or perhaps it was just shock at seeing me without the gag. Anyway I smiled and I wheedled and he let me be without the gag and he let me look round. He kept very close to me. I knew that if I made the slightest false step he would leap at me.

Upstairs, bedrooms, lovely rooms in themselves, but all fusty, unlived-in. A strange dead air about everything. Downstairs what he (he would) called "the lounge" is a beautiful room, much bigger than the other rooms, peculiarly square, you don't expect it, with one huge crossbeam supported on three uprights in the middle of the room, and other crossbeams and nooks and delicious angles an architect wouldn't think of once in a thousand years. All massacred, of course, by the furniture. China wild duck on a lovely old fireplace. I couldn't stand it, I got him to retie my hands in front and then I unhooked the monsters and smashed them on the hearth.

That hurt him almost as much as when I slapped his face for not letting me escape.

He makes me change, he makes me want to dance round him, bewilder him, dazzle him, dumbfound him. He's so slow, so unimaginative, so lifeless. Like zinc white. I see it's a sort of tyranny he has over me. He forces me to be changeable, to act. To show off. The hateful tyranny of weak people. G.P. said it once.

The ordinary man is the curse of civilization.

But he's so ordinary that he's extraordinary.

He takes photographs. He wants to take a "portrait" of me.

Then there were his butterflies, which I suppose were rather beautiful. Yes, rather beautifully arranged, with their poor little wings stretched out all at the same angle. And I felt for them, poor dead butterflies, my fellow-victims. The ones he was proudest of were what he called aberrations!

Downstairs he let me watch him make tea (in the outer cellar), and something ridiculous he said made me laugh—or want to laugh. Terrible.

I suddenly realized that I was going mad too, that he was wickedly wickedly cunning. Of course he doesn't mind what I say about him. That I break his miserable china duck. Because suddenly he has me (it's mad, he *kidnapped* me) laughing at him and pouring out his tea, as if I'm his best girl-friend.

I swore at him. I was my mother's daughter. A bitch.

There it is, Minny. I wish you were here and we could talk in the dark. If I could just talk to someone for a few minutes. Someone I love. I make it sound brighter so much brighter than it is.

I'm going to cry again.

It's *so* unfair.

October 17th

I hate the way I have changed.

I accept too much. To begin with I thought I must force myself to be matter-of-fact, not let his abnormality take control of the situation. But he might have planned it. He's getting me to behave exactly as *he* wants.

This isn't just a fantastic situation; it's a fantastic variation of a fantastic situation. I mean, now he's got me at his mercy, he's not going to do what anyone would expect. So he makes me falsely grateful. I'm so lonely. He must realize that. He can make me depend on him.

I'm on edge, I'm nowhere near as calm as I seem (when I read what I've written).

It's just that there's so much time to get through. Endless endless endless time.

What I write isn't natural. It's like two people trying to keep up a conversation.

It's the very opposite of drawing. You draw a line and you know at once whether it's a good or a bad line. But you write a line and it seems true and then you read it again later.

Yesterday evening he wanted to take a photograph of me. I let him take several. I think, he may be careless, someone may see me lying around. But I think he lives quite alone. He must do. He must have spent all last night developing and printing them (as if he'd go to the chemist's! I don't think). Flashlit me's on glossy paper. I didn't like the flashlight. It hurt my eyes.

Nothing has happened today, except that we have come to a sort of agreement about exercise. No daylight yet. But I can go in the outer cellar. I felt sulky so I was sulky. I asked him to go away after lunch and I asked him to go away after supper, and he went away both times. He does everything he's told.

He's bought me a record-player and records and all the things on the huge shopping-list I gave him. He wants to buy things for me. I could ask for anything. Except my freedom.

He's given me an expensive Swiss watch. I say I will use it *while I am here* and give it back when I go. I said I couldn't stand the orangeady carpet any more and he's bought me some Indian and Turkish rugs. Three Indian mats and a beautiful deep purple, rose-orange and sepia white-fringed Turkish carpet (he said it was the only one "they" had, so no credit to his taste).

It makes this cell more liveable in. The floor's very soft and springy. I've broken all the ugly ashtrays and pots. Ugly ornaments don't deserve to exist.

I'm so superior to him. I know this sounds wickedly conceited. But I *am*. And so it's Ladymont and Boadicaea and *noblesse oblige* all over again. I feel I've got to show him how decent human beings live and behave.

He is ugliness. But you can't smash human ugliness.

Three nights ago was so strange. I was so excited at leaving this crypt. I felt so nearly in complete control. It suddenly seemed all rather a grand adventure, something I'd one day soon be telling everyone about. A sort of chess-game with death I'd rather unexpectedly won. A feeling that I *had* run a terrible risk and now everything was going to be all right. That he was going to let me go, even.

Mad.

I have to give him a name. I'm going to call him Caliban.

Piero. I've spent the whole day with Piero, I've read all about him, I've stared at all the pictures in the book, I've lived them. How can I ever become a good painter when I know so little

geometry and mathematics? I'm going to make Caliban buy me
books. I shall become a geometrician. Shattering doubts about
modern art. I thought of Piero standing in front of a Jackson
Pollock, no, even a Picasso or a Matisse. His eyes. I can just see
his eyes.

The things Piero says in a hand. In a fold in a sleeve. I know
all this, we've been told it and told it and I've said it. But today I
really felt it. I felt our whole age was a hoax, a sham. The way
people talk and talk about tachism and cubism and this ism and
that ism and all the long words they use—great smeary clots of
words and phrases. All to hide the fact that either you can paint or
you can't.

I want to paint like Berthe Morisot, I don't mean with her
colours or forms or anything physical, but with her simplicity and
light. I don't want to be clever or great or "significant" or given
all that clumsy masculine analysis. I want to paint sunlight on children's faces, or flowers in a hedge or a street after April rain.

The essences. Not the things themselves.

Swimmings of light on the smallest things.

Or am I being sentimental?

Depressed.

I'm so far from everything. From normality. From light. From
what I want to be.

October 18th

G.P.—You paint with your whole being. First you learn that. The rest is luck.

Good solution: I must not be fey.

This morning I drew a whole series of quick sketches of bowls of fruit. Since Caliban wants to give, I don't care how much paper I waste. I "hung" them and asked him to choose which one was best. Of course he picked all those that looked most like the wretched bowl of fruit. I started to try to explain to him. I was boasting about one of the sketches (the one *I* liked best). He annoyed me, it didn't mean anything to him, and he made it clear in his miserable I'll-take-your-word-for-it way that he didn't really care. To him I was just a child amusing herself.

Blind, blind, other world.

My fault. I was showing off. How could he see the magic and importance of art (not my art, of *art*) when I was so vain?

We had an argument after lunch. He always asks me if he may stay. Sometimes I feel so lonely, so sick of my own thoughts, that I let him. I *want* him to stay. That's what prison does. And there's escape, escape, escape.

The argument was about nuclear disarmament. I had doubts, the other day. But not now.

DIALOGUE BETWEEN MIRANDA AND CALIBAN.

M. *(I was sitting on my bed, smoking. Caliban on his usual chair by the iron door, the fan was going outside)* What do you think about the H-bomb?

C. Nothing much.

M. You must think something.

C. Hope it doesn't drop on you. Or on me.

M. I realize you've never lived with people who take things seriously, and discuss seriously. *(He put on his hurt face.)* Now let's try again. What do you think about the H-bomb?

C. If I said anything serious, you wouldn't take it serious. *(I stared at him till he had to go on.)* It's obvious. You can't do anything. It's here to stay.

M. You don't care what happens to the world?

C. What'd it matter if I did?

M. Oh, God.

C. We don't have any say in things.

M. Look, if there are enough of us who believe the bomb is wicked and that a decent nation could never think of having it, whatever the circumstances, then the government would have to do something. Wouldn't it?

C. Some hope, if you ask me.

M. How do you think Christianity started? Or anything else? With a little group of people who didn't give up hope.

C. What would happen if the Russians come, then? *(Clever point, he thinks.)*

M. If it's a choice between dropping bombs on them, or having them here as our conquerors—then the second, every time.

C. *(check and mate)* That's pacifism.

M. Of course it is, you great lump. Do you know I've walked all the way from Aldermaston to London? Do you know I've given up hours and hours of my time to distribute leaflets and address envelopes and argue with miserable people like you who don't believe anything? Who really deserve the bomb on them?

C. That doesn't prove anything.

M. It's despair at the lack of *(I'm cheating, I didn't say all these things—but I'm going to write what I want to say as well as what I did)* feeling, of love, of reason in the world. It's despair that anyone can even contemplate the idea of dropping a bomb or ordering that it should be dropped. It's despair that so few of us care. It's despair that there's so much brutality and callousness in the world. It's despair that perfectly normal young men can be made vicious and evil because they've won a lot of money. And then do what you've done to me.

C. I thought you'd get on to that.

M. Well, you're part of it. Everything free and decent in life is being locked away in filthy little cellars by beastly people who don't care.

C. I know your lot. You think the whole blooming world's all arranged so as everything ought to be your way.

M. Don't be so wet.

C. I was a private in the army. You can't tell me. My lot just do what they're told *(he was really quite worked up—for him)* and better look out if they don't.

M. You haven't caught up with yourself. You're rich now. You've got *nothing* to be hurt about.

C. Money doesn't make all that difference.

M. Nobody can order you about any more.

C. You don't understand me at all.

M. Oh, yes I do. I know you're not a teddy. But deep down you feel like one. You hate being an underdog, you hate not being able to express yourself properly. They go and smash things, you sit and sulk. You say, I won't help the world. I won't do the smallest good thing for humanity. I'll just think of myself and humanity can go and stew for all I care. *(It's like continually slapping someone across the face—almost a wince.)* What use do you think money is unless it's used? Do you understand what I'm talking about?

C. Yes.

M. Well?

C. Oh . . . you're right. As always.

M. Are you being sarcastic again?

C. You're like my Aunt Annie. She's always going on about the way people behave nowadays. Not caring and all that.

M. You seem to think it's right to be wrong.

C. Do you want your tea?

M. *(superhuman effort)* Look, for the sake of argument, we'll say that however much good you tried to do in society, in fact you'd never do any good. That's ridiculous, but never mind. There's still yourself. I don't think the Campaign for Nuclear Disarmament has much chance of actually affecting the government. It's one of the first things you have to face up to. But we do it to keep our self-respect to show to ourselves, each one to himself or herself, that we care. And to let other people, all the lazy, sulky, hopeless ones like you, know that someone cares. We're trying to shame you into thinking about it, about acting. *(Silence—then I shouted.)* Say something!

C. I know it's evil.

M. Do something, then! *(He gawked at me as if I'd told him to swim the Atlantic.)* Look. A friend of mine went on a march to an American air-station in Essex. You know? They were stopped outside the gate, of course, and after a time the sergeant on guard came out and spoke to them and they began an argument and it got very heated because this sergeant thought that the Americans were like knights of old rescuing a damsel in distress. That the H-bombers were absolutely

necessary—and so on. Gradually as they were arguing they
began to realize that they rather liked the American. Because
he felt very strongly, and honestly, about his views. It wasn't
only my friend. They all agreed about it afterwards. The
only thing that really matters is feeling and living what you
believe—so long as it's something more than belief in your
own comfort. My friend said he was nearer to that American
sergeant than to all the grinning idiots who watched them
march past on the way. It's like football. Two sides may each
want to beat the other, they may even hate each other as
sides, but if someone came and told them football is stupid
and not worth playing or caring about, then they'd feel together. It's *feeling* that matters. Can't you see?

C. I thought we were talking about the H-bomb.

M. Go away. You exhaust me. You're like a sea of cotton wool.

C. *(he stood up at once)* I do like to hear you talk. I do think
about what you say.

M. No, you don't. You put what I say in your mind and wrap it
up and it disappears for ever.

C. If I wanted to send a cheque to the . . . this lot . . . what's the
address?

M. To buy my approval?

C. What's wrong with that?

M. We need money. But we need feeling even more. And I
don't think you've got any feeling to give away. You can't
win that by filling in a football coupon.

C. *(there was an awkward silence)* See you later, then.

*(Exit Caliban. I hit my pillow so hard that it has looked re-
proachful ever since.)*

                    *   *   *

(This evening—as I knew I would and could—I coaxed and bullied him, and he wrote out a cheque for a hundred pounds, which he's promised to send off tomorrow. I know this is right. A year ago I would have stuck to the strict moral point. Like Major Barbara. But the essential is that we have money. Not where the money comes from, or why it is sent.)

October 19th

I have been out.

I was copying all the afternoon (Piero) and I was in the sort of mood where normally I *have* to go out to the cinema or to a coffee-bar, anywhere. But out.

I made him take me by giving myself to him like a slave. Bind me, I said, but take me.

He bound and gagged me, held my arm, and we walked round the garden. Quite a big one. It was very dark, I could just make out the path and some trees. And it *is* very lonely. Right out in the country somewhere.

Then suddenly in the darkness I knew something was wrong with him. I couldn't see him, but I was suddenly frightened, I just knew he wanted to kiss me or something worse. He tried to say something about being very happy; his voice very strained. Choked. And then, that I didn't think he had any deep feelings, but he had. It's so terrible not being able to speak. My tongue's my defence with him, normally. My tongue and my look. There was a little silence, but I knew he was pent up.

All the time I was breathing in beautiful outdoor air. That was good, so good I can't describe it. So living, so full of plant smells and country smells and the thousand mysterious wet smells of the night.

Then a car passed. So there is a road which is used in front of the house. As soon as we heard the engine his grip tightened. I prayed the car would stop, but its lights just swept past behind the house.

Luckily I'd thought it out before. If I ever try to escape, and fail, he'll never let me out again. So I must not jump at the first chance. And I knew, out there, that he would have killed me rather than let me get away. If I'd tried to run for it. (I couldn't have, anyway, he held my arm like a vice.)

But it was terrible. Knowing other people were so near. And knew nothing.

He asked me if I wanted to go round again. But I shook my head. I was too frightened.

Back down here I told him that I had to get the sex business cleared up.

I told him that if he suddenly wanted to rape me, I wouldn't resist, I would let him do what he liked, but that I would never speak to him again. I said I knew he would be ashamed of himself, too. Miserable creature, he looked ashamed enough as it was. It was "only a moment's weakness." I made him shake hands, but I bet he breathed a sigh of relief when he got outside again.

No one would believe this situation. He keeps me *absolutely* prisoner. But in everything else I am mistress. I realize that he encourages it, it's a means of keeping me from being as discontented as I should be.

The same thing happened when I was lameducking Donald last spring. I began to feel he was mine, that I knew all about him. And I hated it when he went off to Italy like that, without telling me. Not because I was seriously in love with him, but because he was vaguely mine and didn't get permission from me.

The isolation he keeps me in. No newspapers. No radio. No TV. I miss the news terribly. I never did. But now I feel the world has ceased to exist.

I ask him every day to get me a newspaper, but it's one of those things where he sticks his heels in. No reason. It's funny, I know it's no good asking. I might just as well ask him to drive me to the nearest station.

I shall go on asking him, all the same.

He swears blind that he sent the CND cheque, but I don't know. I shall ask to see the receipt.

Incident. Today at lunch I wanted the Worcester sauce. He hardly ever forgets to bring anything I might want. But no Worcester sauce. So he gets up, goes out, undoes the padlock holding the door open, locks the door, gets the sauce in the outer cellar, unlocks the door, re-padlocks it, comes back. And then looks surprised when I laugh.

He never gives the locking-unlocking routine a miss. Even if I do get out into the outer cellar unbound, what can I do? I can't lock him in, I can't get out. The only chance I might have is when he comes in with the tray. Sometimes he doesn't padlock the door back first. So *if* I could get past him then, I could bolt him in. But he won't come past the door unless I'm well away from it. Usually I go and take the tray.

The other day I wouldn't. I just leant against the wall by the door. He said, please go away. I just stared at him. He held out the tray. I ignored it. He stood there undecided. Then he bent very cautiously, watching my every move, and put the tray down in the doorway. Then went back into the outer cellar.

I was hungry. He won.

No good. I can't sleep.

It's seemed a funny day. Even for here.

He took a lot more photos of me this morning. He really enjoys it. He likes me to smile at the camera, so twice I pulled shocking faces. He was not amused. Then I put my hair up with one hand and pretended I was a model.

You ought to be a model, he said. Quite serious. He didn't realize I was guying the whole idea.

I know why he likes the photographing business. He thinks it makes me think he's artistic. And of course he hasn't a clue. I mean he gets me in focus, and that's all. No imagination.

It's weird. Uncanny. But there is a sort of relationship between us. I make fun of him, I attack him all the time, but he senses when I'm "soft." When he can dig back and not make me angry. So we slip into teasing states that are almost friendly. It's partly because I'm so lonely, it's partly deliberate (I want to make him relax, both for his own good and so that one day he may make a mistake), so it's part weakness, and part cunning, and part charity. But there's a mysterious fourth part I can't define. It can't be friendship, I loathe him.

Perhaps it's just knowledge. Just knowing a lot about him. And knowing someone automatically makes you feel close to him. Even when you wish he was on another planet.

The first days, I couldn't do anything if he was in the room. I pretended to read, but I couldn't concentrate. But now I sometimes forget he's here. He sits by the door and I read in my chair, and we're like two people who've been married years.

It is not that I have forgotten what other people are like. But other people seem to have lost reality. The only real person in my world is Caliban.

It can't be understood. It just *is*.

October 20th

It's eleven o'clock in the morning.

I've just tried to escape.

What I did was to wait for him to unbolt the door, which opens outwards. Then to push it back as violently as possible. It's only metal-lined on this side, it's made of wood, but it's very heavy. I thought I might hit him with it and knock him out, if I did it at just the right moment.

So as soon as it began to move back, I gave it the biggest push I could manage. It knocked him back and I rushed out, but of course it depended on his being stunned. And he wasn't at all. He must have taken the force of it on his shoulder, it doesn't swing very smoothly.

At any rate he caught my jumper. For a second there was that other side of him I sense, the violence, hatred, absolute determination not to let me go. So I said, all right, and pulled myself away and went back.

He said, you might have hurt me, that door's very heavy.

I said, every second you keep me here, you hurt me.

I thought pacifists didn't believe in hurting people, he said.

I just shrugged and lit a cigarette. I was trembling.

He did all the usual morning routine in silence. Once he rubbed his shoulder in rather an obvious way. And that was that.

Now I'm going to look properly for loose stones. The tunnel idea. Of course I've looked before, but not really closely, literally stone by stone, from top to bottom of each wall.

It's evening. He's just gone away. He brought me my food. But he's been very silent. Disapproving. I laughed out loud when he went away with the supper-things. He behaves exactly as if *I* ought to be ashamed.

He won't be caught by the door trick again. There aren't any loose stones. All solidly concreted in. I suppose he thought of that as well as of everything else.

I've spent most of today thinking. About me. What will happen to me? I've never felt the mystery of the future so much as here. What will happen? What will happen?

It's not only now, in this situation. When I get away. What shall I do? I want to marry, I want to have children, I want to prove to myself that all marriages needn't be like D and M's. I know exactly the sort of person I want to marry, someone with a mind like G.P.'s, only much nearer my own age, and with the looks I like. And without his one horrid weakness. But then I want to use my feelings about life. I don't want to use my skill vainly, for its own sake. But I want to *make* beauty. And marriage and being a mother terrifies me for that reason. Getting sucked down into the house and the house things and the baby-world and the child-world and the cooking-world and the shopping-world. I have a feeling a lazy-cow me would welcome it, would forget what I once wanted to do, and I would just become a Great Female Cabbage. Or I would have to do miserable work like illustrating, or even commercial stuff, to keep the home going. Or turn into a bitchy ginny misery like M (no, I couldn't be like her). Or worst of all be like Caroline, running along pathetically after modern art and modern ideas and never catching up with them because she's someone quite different at heart and yet can never see it.

I think and think down here. I understand things I haven't really thought about before.

Two things. M. I've never really thought of M objectively before, as another person. She's always been my mother I've hated or been ashamed of. Yet of all the lame ducks I've met or heard of, she's the lamest. I've *never* given her enough sympathy. I haven't given her this last year (since I left home) one half of the consideration I've given the beastly creature upstairs just this last week. I feel that I could overwhelm her with love now. Because I haven't felt so sorry for her for years. I've always excused my-self—I've said, I'm kind and tolerant with everyone else, she's the one person I can't be like that with, and there has to be an exception to the general rule. So it doesn't matter. But of course that's wrong. She's the last person that should be an exception to the general rule.

Minny and I have so often despised D for putting up with her. We ought to go down on our knees to him.

The other thing I think about is G.P.

When I first met him I told everyone how marvellous he was. Then a reaction set in, I thought I was getting a silly schoolgirl hero-pash on him, and the other thing began to happen. It was all too emotional.

Because he's changed me more than anything or anybody. More than London, more than the Slade.

It's not just that he's seen so much more life. Had so much more artistic experience. And is known. But he says exactly what he thinks, and he always makes *me* think. That's the big thing. He makes me question myself. How many times have I disagreed with him? And then a week later with someone else I find I'm arguing as he would argue. Judging people by his standards.

He's chipped off all (well, some of, anyway) my silliness, my stupid fussy frilly ideas about life and art, and modern art. My fey-ness. I've never been the same since he told me how he hated fey women. I even learnt the word from him.

List of the ways in which he has altered me. Either directly. Or confirmed alterations in progress.

1. If you are a real artist, you give your whole being to your art. Anything short of that, then you are not an artist. Not what G.P. calls a "maker."

2. You don't gush. You don't have little set-pieces or set-ideas you gush out to impress people with.

3. You *have* to be Left politically because the Socialists are the only people who care, for all their mistakes. They *feel*, they want to better the world.

4. You must *make*, always. You *must* act, if you believe something. Talking about acting is like boasting about pictures you're going to paint. The most *terrible* bad form.

5. If you feel something deeply, you're not ashamed to show your feeling.

6. You accept that you are English. You don't pretend that you'd rather be French or Italian or something else. (Piers always talking about his American grandmother.)

7. But you don't compromise with your background. You cut off all the old you that gets in the way of the maker you. If you're suburban (as I realize D and M are—their laughing at suburbia is just a blind), you throw away (cauterize) the suburbs. If you're working class, you cauterize the working class in you. And the same, whatever class you are, because class is primitive and silly.

(It's not only me. Look at that time Louise's boy-friend—the miner's son from Wales—met him, and how they argued and snarled at each other, and we were all against G.P. for being so contemptuous about working-class people and working-class life. Calling them animals, not human beings. And David Evans, all white and stammering, don't you tell me my father's a bloody animal I've got to kick out of the way, and G.P. saying I've never hurt an animal in my life, you can always make out a case for hurting human beings, but human animals deserve every sympathy. And then David Evans coming up to me last month and actually *admitting* it had changed him, that evening.)

8. You hate the political business of nationality. You hate everything, in politics and art and everything else, that is not genuine and deep and necessary. You don't have any time for silly trivial things. You live seriously. You don't go to silly films, even if you want to; you don't read cheap newspapers; you don't listen to trash on the wireless and the telly; you don't waste time talking about nothing. You *use* your life.

I must have always wanted to believe in those things; I did believe in them in a vague sort of way, before I met him. But he's *made* me believe them; it's the thought of *him* that makes me feel guilty when I break the rules.

If he's made me believe them, that means he's made a large part of the new me.

If I had a fairy godmother—please, make G.P. twenty years younger. And please, make him physically attractive to me.

How he would despise that!

It's odd (and I feel a little guilty) but I have been feeling happier today than at any time since I came here. A feeling—all will turn out for the best. Partly because I did something this morning. I tried to escape. Then, Caliban has accepted it. I mean if he was going to attack me, he'd surely do it at some time when he had a reason to be angry. As he was this morning. He has tremendous self-control, in some ways.

I know I also feel happy because I've been not here for most of the day. I've been mainly thinking about G.P. In his world, not this one here. I remembered so much. I would have liked to write it all down. I gorged myself on memories. This world makes that world seem so real, so living, so beautiful. Even the sordid parts of it.

And partly, too, it's been a sort of indulging in wicked vanity about myself. Remembering things G.P. has said to me, and other people. Knowing I am rather a special person. Knowing I am intelligent, knowing that I am beginning to understand life much better than most people of my age. Even knowing that I shall never be so stupid as to be vain about it, but be grateful, be terribly glad (especially after this) to be alive, to be who I am—Miranda, and unique.

I shall never let anyone see this. Even if it is the truth, it must *sound* vain.

Just as I never let other girls see that I know I am pretty; nobody knows how I've fallen over myself not to take that unfair advantage. Wandering male eyes, even the nicest, I've snubbed.

Minny: one day when I'd been gushing about her dress when she was going out to a dance. She said, shut up. You're so pretty you don't even have to try.

G.P. saying, you've every kind of face.

Wicked.

October 21st

I'm making him cook better. Absolute ban on frozen food. I must have fruit, green vegetables. I have steak. Salmon. I ordered him to get caviare yesterday. It irritates me that I can't think of enough rare foods I haven't had and have wanted to have.

Pig.

Caviare is wonderful.

I've had another bath. He daren't refuse, I think he thinks "ladies" fall down dead if they don't have a bath when they want one.

I've put a message down the place. In a little plastic bottle with a yard of red ribbon round it. I hope it will become un-rolled and someone may see it. Somewhere. Sometime. They ought to find the house easily enough. He was silly to tell me about the date over the door. I had to end by saying THIS IS NOT A HOAX. Terribly difficult not to make it sound like a silly joke. And I said anyone ringing up D and telling him would get £25. I'm going to launch a bottle on the sea (hmm) every time I have a bath.

He's taken down all the brass gewgaws on the landing and stairs. And the horrible viridian-orange-magenta paintings of Majorcan fishing-villages. The poor place sighs with relief.

I like being upstairs. It's nearer freedom. Everything's locked. All the windows in the front of the house have indoor shutters. The others are padlocked. (Two cars passed tonight, but it must be a very unimportant road.)

I've also started to educate him. Tonight in the lounge (my hands tied, of course) we went through a book of paintings. No mind of his own. I don't think he listens half the time. He's thinking about sitting near me and straining to be near without touching. I don't know if it's sex, or fear that I'm up to some trick.

If he does think about the pictures, he accepts everything I say. If I said Michelangelo's *David* was a frying-pan he'd say— "I see."

Such people. I must have stood next to them in the Tube, passed them in the street, of course I've overheard them and I knew they existed. But never really believed they exist. So totally blind. It never seemed possible.

Dialogue. He was sitting still looking at the book with an Art-Is-Wonderful air about him (for my benefit, not because he believes it, of course).

> M. Do you know what's really odd about this house? There aren't any books. Except what you've bought for me.
> C. Some upstairs.
> M. About butterflies.
> C. Others.
> M. A few measly detective novels. Don't you ever read proper books—real books? *(Silence.)* Books about important things by people who really feel about life. Not just paperbacks to kill time on a train journey. You know, books?
> C. Light novels are more my line. *(He's like one of those boxers. You wish he'd lie down and be knocked out.)*
> M. You can jolly well read *The Catcher in the Rye.* I've almost finished it. Do you know I've read it twice and I'm five years younger than you are?
> C. I'll read it.
> M. It's not a punishment.
> C. I looked at it before I brought it down.

M. And you didn't like it.

C. I'll try it.

M. You make me sick.

Silence then. I felt unreal, as if it *was* a play and I couldn't remember who I was in it.

And I asked him earlier today why he collected butterflies.

C. You get a nicer class of people.

M. You can't collect them just because of that.

C. It was a teacher I had. When I was a kid. He showed me how. He collected. Didn't know much. Still set the old way. *(Something to do with the angle of the wings. The modern way is to have them at right angles.)* And my uncle. He was interested in nature. He always helped.

M. He sounds nice.

C. People interested in nature always are nice. You take what we call the Bug Section. That's the Entomological Section of the Natural History Society back home. They treat you for what you are. Don't look down their noses at you. None of that.

M. They're not always nice. *(But he didn't get it.)*

C. You get the snob ones. But they're mostly like I say. A nicer class of people than what you . . . what I meet . . . met in the ordinary way.

M. Didn't your friends despise you? Didn't they think it was sissy?

C. I didn't have any friends. They were just people I worked with. (After a bit he said, they had their silly jokes.)

M. Such as?

C. Just silly jokes.

I didn't go on. I have an irresistible desire sometimes to get to the bottom of him, to drag things he won't talk about out of him. But it's bad. It sounds as if I care about him and his miserable, wet, unwithit life.

When you use words. The gaps. The way Caliban sits, a certain bowed-and-upright posture—why? Embarrassment? To spring at me if I run for it? I can draw it. I can draw his face and his expressions, but words are all so used, they've been used about so many other things and people. I write "he smiled." What does that mean? No more than a kindergarten poster painting of a turnip with a moon-mouth smile. Yet if I draw the smile . . .

Words are so crude, so terribly primitive compared to drawing, painting, sculpture. "I sat on my bed and he sat by the door and we talked and I tried to persuade him to use his money to educate himself and he said he would but I didn't feel convinced." Like a messy daub.

Like trying to draw with a broken lead.

All this is my own thinking.

I need to see G.P. He'd tell me the names of ten books where it's all said much better.

How I hate ignorance! Caliban's ignorance, my ignorance, the world's ignorance! Oh, I could learn and learn and learn and learn. I could cry, I want to learn so much.

Gagged and bound.

I'll put this to bed where it lives under the mattress. Then I'll pray to God for learning.

October 22nd

A fortnight today. I have marked the days on the side of the
screen, like Robinson Crusoe.

I feel depressed. Sleepless. I must, must, must escape.

I'm getting so pale. I feel ill, weak, all the time.

This terrible silence.

He's so without mercy. So incomprehensible. What does he
want? What is to happen?

He must see I'm getting ill.

I told him this evening that I must have some daylight. I made
him look at me and see how pale I am.

Tomorrow, tomorrow. He never says no outright.

Today I've been thinking he could keep me here forever. It
wouldn't be very long, because I'd die. It's absurd, it's diabolical—
but there is no way of escape. I've been trying to find loose stones
again. I could dig a tunnel round the door. I could dig a tunnel right
out. But it would have to be at least twenty feet long. All the earth.
Being trapped inside it. I could never do it. I'd rather die. So it must
be a tunnel round the door. But to do that I must have time. I must
be sure he is away for at least six hours. Three for the tunnel, two to
break through the outer door. I feel it is my best chance, I mustn't
waste it, spoil it through lack of preparation.

I can't sleep.

I must do something.

I'm going to write about the first time I met G.P.

Caroline said, oh, this is Miranda. My niece. And went on
telling him odiously about me (one Saturday morning shopping in

the Village) and I didn't know where to look, although I'd been wanting to meet him. She'd talked about him before.

At once I liked the way he treated her, coolly, not trying to hide he was bored. Not giving way before her, like everyone else. She talked about him all the way home. I knew she was shocked by him, although she wouldn't admit it. The two broken marriages and then the obvious fact that he didn't think much of her. So that I wanted to defend him from the beginning.

Then meeting him walking on the Heath. Having wanted to meet him again, and being ashamed again.

The way he walked. Very self-contained, not loosely. Such a nice old pilot-coat. He said hardly anything, I knew he really didn't want to be with us (with Caroline) but he'd caught us up; he can't have spotted from behind who we were, he was obviously going the same way. And perhaps (I'm being vain) it was something that happened when Caroline was going on in her silly woman-of-advanced-ideas way—just a look between us. I knew he was irritated and he knew I was ashamed. So he went round Kenwood with us and Caroline showed off.

Until she said in front of the Rembrandt, don't you think he got the teeniest bit bored halfway through—I mean I never feel I feel what I ought to feel. You know? And she gave him her stupid listen-to-me laugh.

I was looking at him and his face suddenly went minutely stiff, as if he'd been caught off guard. It wasn't done for me to see, it was the minutest change in the set of his mouth. He just gave her one look. Almost amused. But his voice wasn't. It was icy cold.

I must go now. Goodbye. The goodbye was for me. It wrote me off. Or it said—so you can put up with this? I mean (looking back on it) he seemed to be teaching *me* a lesson. I had to choose. Caroline's way, or his.

And he was gone, we didn't even answer, and Caroline was looking after him, and shrugging and looking at me and saying, well, really.

I watched him go out, his hands in his pockets. I was red. Caroline was furious, trying to slide out of it. ("He's always like that, he does it deliberately.") Sneering at his painting all the way home ("second-rate Paul Nash"—ridiculously unfair). And me feeling so angry with her, and sorry for her at the same time. I couldn't speak. I couldn't be sorry for her, but I couldn't tell her he was right.

Between them Caroline and M have every quality I hate in other women. I had a sort of despair for days afterwards, thinking how much of their rotten, pretentious blood I must have in me. Of course, there are times when I like Caroline. Her briskness. Her enthusiasm. Her kindness. And even all the pretentiousness that's so horrid next to the real thing—well, it's better than nothing. I used to think the world of her when she came to stay. I used to love staying with her. She backed me up when there was the great family war about my future. All that till I lived with her and saw through her. Grew up. (I'm being a Hard Young Woman.)

Then a week later I ran into the lift at the Tube and he was the only other person there. I said hallo, too brightly. Went red again. He just nodded as if he didn't want to speak, and then at the bottom (it was vanity, I couldn't bear to be lumped with Caroline) I said, I'm sorry my aunt said that at Kenwood.

He said, she always irritates me. I knew he didn't want to talk about it. As we went towards the platform, I said, she's frightened of seeming behind the times.

Aren't you?—and he gave me one of his dry little smiles. I thought, he doesn't like me playing at "us" against "her."

We were passing a film poster and he said, that's a good film. Have you seen it? Do.

When we came out on the platform, he said, come round one day. But leave your bloody aunt at home. And he smiled. A little infectious mischievous smile. Not his age, at all. Then he walked off. So by-himself. So indifferent.

So I did go round. One Saturday morning. He was surprised. I had to sit in silence for twenty minutes with him and the weird Indian music. He got straight back on to the divan and lay with his eyes shut, as if I shouldn't have come and I felt I ought never to have come (especially without telling C), and I felt as well that it really was a bit much, a pose. I couldn't relax. At the end he asked me about myself, curtly, as if it was all rather a bore. And I stupidly tried to impress him. Do the one thing I shouldn't. Show off. I kept on thinking, he didn't really mean me to come round.

Suddenly he cut me short and took me round the room and made me look at things.

His studio. The most beautiful room. I always feel happy there. Everything in harmony. Everything expressing only him (it's not deliberate, he hates "interior decoration" and gimmicks and *Vogue*). But it's all him. Toinette, with her silly female *House and Garden* ideas of austere good taste, calling it "cluttered." I could have bitten her head off. The feeling that someone lives all his life in it, works in it, thinks in it, *is* it.

And we thawed out. I stopped trying to be clever.

He showed me how he gets his "haze" effect. Tonksing gouache. With all his little home-made tools.

Some friends of his came in, Barber and Frances Cruikshank. He said, this is Miranda Grey I can't stand her aunt, all in one breath, and they laughed, they were old friends. I wanted to leave. But they were going for a walk, they had come in to make him go with them, and they wanted me to go too. Barber Cruikshank did; he had special seduction eyes for me.

Supposing aunt sees us, G.P. said. Barber's got the foulest reputation in Cornwall.

I said, she's my aunt. Not my duenna.

So we all went to the Vale of Health pub and then on to Kenwood. Frances told me about their life in Cornwall and I felt for the first time in my life that I was among people of an older generation that I understood, real people. And at the same time I couldn't help seeing Barber was a bit of a sham. All those funny malicious stories. While G.P. was the one who led us into all the serious things. I don't mean that he wasn't gay, too. Only he has this strange twist of plunging straight into what matters. Once when he was away getting drinks, Barber asked me how long I'd known G.P. Then he said, I wish to God I'd met someone like G.P. when I was a student. And quiet little Frances said, we think he's the most wonderful person. He's one of the few. She didn't say which few, but I knew what she meant.

At Kenwood G.P. made us split. He took me straight to the Rembrandt and talked about it, without lowering his voice, and I had the smallness to be embarrassed because some other people there stared at us. I thought, we must look like father and daughter. He told me all about the background to the picture, what Rembrandt probably felt like at that time, what he was trying to say, how he said it. As if I knew nothing about art. As if he was trying to get rid of a whole cloud of false ideas I probably had about it.

We went out to wait for the others. He said, that picture moves me very much. And he looked at me, as if he thought I might laugh. One of those flashes of shyness he has.

I said, it moves me now, too.

But he grinned. It can't possibly. Not for years yet.

How do you know?

He said, I suppose there are people who are purely moved by

great art. I never met a painter who was. I'm not. All I think of
when I see that picture is that it has the supreme mastery I have
spent all my life trying to attain. And shall not. Ever. You're
young. You can understand. But you can't feel that yet.

I said, I think I do.

He said, then that's bad. You should be blind to failure. At your
age. Then he said, don't try to be our age. I shall despise you if
you do.

He said, you're like a kid trying to see over a six-foot wall.

That was the first time. He hated me for attracting him. The
Professor Higgins side of him.

Later, when the Cruikshanks came out, he said, as they walked
towards us, Barber's a womanizer. Refuse to meet him if he asks.

I gave him a surprised look. He said, smiling at them, not you,
I can't stand the pain for Frances.

Back in Hampstead I left them and went on home. All the way
back there I'd realized that G.P. was making sure Barber Cruikshank and I shouldn't be left alone. They (Barber) asked me to
come to see them if I was ever in Cornwall.

G.P. said, see you one day. As if he didn't care whether he did
or not.

I told Caroline I'd met him by chance. He had said he was
sorry (lie). If she'd rather I didn't see him, I wouldn't. But I found
him very stimulating to be with, full of ideas, I *needed* to meet such
people. It was too bad of me, I knew she would do the decent
thing if I put it like that. I was my own mistress—and so on.

And then she said, darling, you know I'm the last person to
be a prude, but his reputation . . . there *must* be fire, there's so
much smoke.

I said, I'd heard about it. I could look after myself.

It's her own fault. She shouldn't insist on being called Caroline and treated like a girl in so many ways. I can't respect her as an aunt. As a giver of advice.

Everything's changing. I keep on thinking of him: of things he said and I said, and how we neither of us really understood what the other meant. No, he understood, I think. He counts possibilities so much faster than I can. I'm growing up so quickly down here. Like a mushroom. Or is it that I've lost my sense of balance? Perhaps it's all a dream. I jab myself with the pencil. But perhaps that's a dream, too.

If he came to the door now I should run into his arms. I should want him to hold my hand for weeks. I mean I believe I *could* love him in the other way, his way, now.

The curse is with me. I'm a bitch to C. No mercy. It's the lack of privacy on top of everything else. I made him let me walk in the cellar this morning. I think I could hear a tractor working. And sparrows. So daylight, sparrows. An aeroplane. I was crying.

My emotions are all topsy-turvy, like frightened monkeys in a cage. I felt I was going mad last night, so I wrote and wrote and wrote myself into the other world. To escape in spirit, if not in fact. To prove it still exists.

I've been making sketches for a painting I shall do when I'm free. A view of a garden through a door. It sounds silly in words. But I see it as something very special, all black, umber, dark, dark grey, mysterious angular forms in shadow leading to the distant soft honey-whitish square of the light-filled door. A sort of horizontal shaft.

I sent him away after supper and I've been finishing *Emma*. I *am* Emma Woodhouse. I feel for her, of her and in her. I have a different sort of snobbism, but I understand her snobbism. Her priggishness. I admire it. I know she does wrong things, she tries to organize other people's lives, she can't see Mr. Knightley is a man in a million. She's temporarily silly, yet all the time one knows she's basically intelligent, alive. Creative, determined to set the highest standards. A real human being. Her faults are my faults: her virtues I must *make* my virtues.

And all day I've been thinking—I shall write some more about G.P. tonight.

There was the time I took some of my work round for him to look at. I took the things I thought *he* would like (not just the clever-clever things, like the perspective of Ladymont). He didn't say a thing as he looked through them. Even when he was looking at the ones (like the *Carmen at Ivinghoe*) that I think are my best (or did then). And at the end he said, they're not much good. In my opinion. But a bit better than I expected. It was as if he had turned and hit me with his fist, I couldn't hide it. He went on, it's quite useless if I think of your feelings in any way at all. I can see you're a draughtsman, you've a fairish sense of colour and what-not, sensitive. All that. But you wouldn't be at the Slade if you hadn't.

I wanted him to stop but he would go on. You've obviously seen quite a lot of good painting. Tried not to plagiarize too flagrantly. But this thing of your sister—Kokoschka, a mile off. He must have seen my cheeks were red because he said, is all this rather disillusioning? It's meant to be.

It nearly killed me. I know he was right; it *would* have been ridiculous if he hadn't said exactly what he thought. If he'd just kind-uncled me. But it hurt. It hurt like a series of slaps across the face. I'd made up my mind that he would like some of my work. What made it worse was his coldness. He seemed so absolutely serious and clinical. Not the faintest line of humour or tenderness, even of sarcasm, on his face. Suddenly much, much older than me.

He said, one has to learn that painting well—in the academic and technical sense—comes right at the bottom of the list. I mean, you've got that ability. So have thousands. But the thing I look for isn't here. It just isn't here.

Then he said, I know this hurts. As a matter of fact, I nearly asked you not to bring this round. But then I thought . . . there's a sort of eagerness about you. You'd survive.

You knew they wouldn't be any good, I said.

I expected just about this. Shall we forget you brought them? But I knew he was challenging me.

I said, tell me in detail what is wrong with this. And I gave him one of the street scenes.

He said, it's quite graphic, well composed, I can't tell you details. But it's not living art. It's not a limb of your body. I don't expect you to understand this at your age. It can't be taught you. You either have it one day, or you don't. They're teaching you to express personality at the Slade—personality in general. But however good you get at translating personality into line or paint it's no go if your personality isn't worth translating. It's all luck. Pure hazard.

He spoke in fits and starts. And there was a silence. I said, shall I tear them up? and he said, now you're being hysterical.

I said, I've got so much to learn.

He got up and said, I think you've got something in you. I don't know. Women very rarely have. I mean most women just want to be good at something, they've got good-at minds, and they mean deftness and a flair and good taste and what-not. They can't ever understand that if your desire is to go to the furthest limits of yourself then the actual form your art takes doesn't seem important to you. Whether you use words or paint or sounds. What you will.

I said, go on.

He said, it's rather like your voice. You put up with your voice and speak with it because you haven't any choice. But it's what you say that counts. It's what distinguishes all great art from the other kind. The technically accomplished buggers are two a penny in any period. Especially in this great age of universal education. He was sitting on his divan, talking at my back. I had to stare out of the window. I thought I was going to cry.

He said, critics spiel away about superb technical accomplishment. Absolutely meaningless, that sort of jargon. Art's cruel. You can get away with murder with words. But a picture is like a window straight through to your inmost heart. And all you've done here is build a lot of little windows on to a heart full of other fashionable artists' paintings. He came and stood beside me and picked out one of the new abstracts I'd done at home. You're saying something here about Nicholson or Pasmore. Not about yourself. You're using a camera. Just as *trompe-l'oeil* is mischannelled photography, so is painting in someone else's style. You're photographing here. That's all.

I'll never learn, I said.

It's to unlearn, he said. You've nearly finished the learning. The rest is luck. No, a little more than luck. Courage. Patience.

We talked for hours. He talked and I listened.

It was like wind and sunlight. It blew all the cobwebs away. Shone on everything. Now I write down what he said, it seems so obvious. But it's something in the way he says things. He is the *only* person I know who always seems to mean what he says when he talks about art. If one day you found he didn't, it would be like a blasphemy.

And there is the fact that he *is* a good painter, and I know he will be quite famous one day, and this influences me more than it should. Not only what he is, what he will be.

I remember later he said (Professor Higgins again). You don't really stand a dog's chance anyhow. You're too pretty. The art of love's your line: not the love of art.

I'm going to the Heath to drown myself, I said.

I shouldn't marry. Have a tragic love *affaire*. Have your ovaries cut out. Something. And he gave me one of his really wicked looks out of the corners of his eyes. It wasn't just that. It was frightened in a funny little-boy way, too. As if he'd said something he knew he shouldn't have, to see how I would react. And suddenly he seemed much younger than me.

He so often seems young in a way I can't explain.

He so often seems young in a way I can't explain. Perhaps it's that he's made me look at myself and see that what I believe is old and stuffy. People who teach you cram old ideas, old views, old ways, into you. Like covering plants with layer after layer of old earth; it's no wonder the poor things so rarely come up fresh and green.

But G.P. has. I didn't recognize it as fresh-green-shootiness for a long time. But now I do.

Another bad day. I made sure it was bad for Caliban, too. Sometimes he irritates me so much that I could scream at him. It's not so much the way he looks, though that's bad enough. He's always so respectable, his trousers always have creases, his shirts are always clean. I really think he'd be happier if he wore starched collars. So utterly not with it. And he stands. He's the most tremendous stander-around I've ever met. Always with that I'm-sorry expression on his face, which I begin to realize is *actually* contentment. The sheer joy of having me under his power, of being able to spend all and every day staring at me. He doesn't care what I say or how I feel—my feelings are meaningless to him—it's the fact that he's got me.

I could scream abuse at him all day long; he wouldn't mind at all. It's me he wants, my look, my outside; not my emotions or my mind or my soul or even my body. Not anything *human*.

He's a collector. That's the great dead thing in him.

What irritates me most about him is his way of speaking. Cliché after cliché after cliché, and all so old-fashioned, as if he's spent all his life with people over fifty. At lunch-time today he said, I called in with regard to those records they've placed on order. I said, Why don't you just say, "I asked about those records you ordered?"

He said, I know my English isn't correct, but I try to make it correct. I didn't argue. That sums him up. He's got to be correct, he's got to do whatever was "right" and "nice" before either of us was born.

I know it's pathetic, I know he's a victim of a miserable Nonconformist suburban world and a miserable social class, the horrid timid copycatting genteel in-between class. I used to think D and M's class the worst. All golf and gin and bridge and cars and the right accent and the right money and having been to the right school and hating the arts (the theatre being a pantomime at Christmas and *Hay Fever* by the Town Rep—Picasso and Bartók dirty words unless you wanted to get a laugh). Well, that is foul. But Caliban's England is fouler.

It makes me sick, the blindness, deadness, out-of-dateness, stodginess and, yes, sheer jealous malice of the great bulk of England.

G.P. talks about the Paris rat. Not being able to face England any more. I can understand that so well. The feeling that England stifles and smothers and crushes like a steamroller over everything fresh and green and original. And that's what causes tragic failures like Matthew Smith and Augustus John—they've done the Paris rat and they live ever after in the shadow of Gauguin and Matisse or whoever it may be—just as G.P. says he once lived under the shadow of Braque and suddenly woke up one morning to realize that all he had done for five years was a lie, because it was based on Braque's eyes and sensibilities and not his own.

Photography.

It's all because there's so little hope in England that you have to turn to Paris, or somewhere abroad. But you have to force yourself to accept the truth—that Paris is always an escape *downwards* (G.P.'s words)—not saying anything against Paris, but you have to face up to England and the apathy of the environment (these are all G.P.'s words and ideas) and the great deadweight of the Calibanity of England.

And the real saints are people like Moore and Sutherland who fight to be English artists in England. Like Constable and Palmer and Blake.

Another thing I said to Caliban the other day—we were listening to jazz—I said, don't you dig this? And he said, in the garden. I said he was so square he was hardly credible. Oh, that, he said.

Like rain, endless dreary rain. Colour-killing.

I've forgotten to write down the bad dream I had last night. I always seem to get them at dawn, it's something to do with the stuffiness of this room after I've been locked in it for a night. (The relief—when he comes and the door is open, and the fan on. I've asked him to let me go straight out and breathe the cellar air, but he always makes me wait till I've had breakfast. As I think he might not let me have my half-hour in midmorning if he let me go out earlier, I don't insist.)

The dream was this. I'd done a painting. I can't really remember what it was like but I was very pleased with it. It was at home. I went out and while I was out I knew something was wrong. I had to get home. When I rushed up to my room M was there sitting at the pembroke table (Minny was standing by the wall—looking frightened, I think G.P. was there, too, and other people, for some peculiar reason) and the picture was in shreds—great long strips of canvas. And M was stabbing at the table top with her secateurs and I could see she was white with rage. And I felt the same. The most wild rage and hatred.

I woke up then. I have never felt such rage for M—even that day when she was drunk and hit me in front of that hateful boy Peter Catesby. I can remember standing there with her slap on my cheek and feeling ashamed, outraged, shocked, everything . . . but sorry for her. I went and sat by her bed and held her hand and let her cry and forgave her and defended her with Daddy and Minny. But this dream seemed so real, so terribly natural.

I've accepted that she tried to stop me from becoming an artist. Parents always misunderstand their children (no, I won't misunderstand mine), I knew I was supposed to be the son and surgeon poor D never was able to be. Carmen will be that now. I mean I have forgiven them their fighting against my ambition for their ambitions. I won, so I must forgive.

But that hatred in that dream. It was so real.

I don't know how to exorcise it. I could tell it to G.P. But there's only the slithery scratch of my pencil on this pad.

Nobody who has not lived in a dungeon could understand how *absolute* the silence down here is. No noise unless I make it. So I feel near death. Buried. No outside noises to help me be living at all. Often I put on a record. Not to hear music, but to hear *something*.

I have a strange illusion quite often. I think I've become deaf. I have to make a little noise to prove I'm not. I clear my throat to show myself that everything's quite normal. It's like the little Japanese girl they found in the ruins of Hiroshima. Everything dead; and she was singing to her doll.

October 25th

I must must must escape.

I spent hours and hours today thinking about it. Wild ideas. He's so cunning, it's incredible. Foolproof.

It must seem I never try to escape. But I can't try every day, that's the trouble. I have to space out the attempts. And each day here is like a week outside.

Violence is no good. It must be cunning.

Face-to-face, I can't be violent. The idea makes me feel weak at the knees. I remember wandering with Donald somewhere in the East End after we'd been to the Whitechapel and we saw a group of teddies standing round two middle-aged Indians. We crossed the street, I felt sick. The teddies were shouting, chivvying and bullying them off the pavement on to the road. Donald said, what can one do, and we both pretended to shrug it off, to hurry away. But it was beastly, their violence and our fear of violence. If he came to me now and knelt and handed me the poker, I couldn't hit him.

It's no good. I've been trying to sleep for the last half-hour, and I can't. Writing here is a sort of drug. It's the only thing I look forward to. This afternoon I read what I wrote about G.P. the day before yesterday. And it seemed vivid. I know it seems vivid because my imagination fills in all the bits another person wouldn't understand. I mean, it's vanity. But it seems a sort of magic, to be able to call my past back. And I just can't live in this present. I would go mad if I did.

I've been thinking today of the time I took Piers and Antoinette to meet him. The black side of him. No, I was stupid.

They'd come up to Hampstead to have coffee and we were to go
to the Everyman, but the queue was too long. So I let them bully
me into taking them round.

It was vanity on my part. I'd talked too much about him. So
that they began to hint that I couldn't be so very friendly if I was
afraid to take them round to meet him. And I fell for it.

I could see he wasn't pleased at the door, but he asked us up.
And oh, it was terrible. *Terrible.* Piers was at his slickest and
cheapest and Antoinette was almost parodying herself, she was so
sex-kittenish. I tried to excuse everyone to everyone else. G.P. was
in such a weird mood. I knew he could withdraw, but he went out
of his way to be rude. He could have seen Piers was only trying to
cover up his feeling of insecurity.

They tried to get him to discuss his own work, but he
wouldn't. He started to be outrageous. Four-letter words. All
sorts of bitter cynical things about the Slade and various
artists—things I know he doesn't believe. He certainly managed
to shock me and Piers, but of course Antoinette just went one
better. Simpered and trembled her eyelashes, and said something
fouler still. So he changed tack. Cut us short every time we tried
to speak (me too).

And then I did something even more stupid than the having
gone there in the first place. There was a pause, and he obviously
thought we would go. But I idiotically thought I could see Antoinette and Piers looking rather amused and I was sure it was because they felt I didn't know him as well as I'd said. So I had to try
to prove to them that I could manage him.

I said, could we have a record, G.P.?

For a moment he looked as if he would say no, but then he said,
why not? Let's hear someone saying something. For a change. He
didn't give us any choice, he just went and put a record on.

He lay on the divan with his eyes closed, as usual, and Piers and Antoinette obviously thought it *was* a pose.

Such a thin strange quavering noise, and such a tense awkward atmosphere had built up; I mean it was the music on top of everything else. Piers started to smirk and Antoinette had a fit of—she can't giggle, she's too slinky, her equivalent—and I smiled. I admit it. Piers cleaned out his ear with his little finger and then leant on his elbow with his forehead on outstretched fingers—and shook his head every time the instrument (I didn't know what it was then) vibrated. Antoinette half-choked. It was awful. I knew he would hear.

He did. He saw Piers cleaning his ears again. And Piers saw himself being seen and put on a clever sort of don't-mind-us smile. G.P. jumped up and turned off the player. He said, you don't like it? Piers said, have I got to like it?

I said, Piers, that wasn't funny.

Piers said, I wasn't making a noise, was I? Have we got to like it?

G.P. said, get out.

Antoinette said, I'm afraid I always think of Beecham. You know. Two skeletons copulating on a tin roof?

G.P. said (frightening, his face, he can look devilish), first, I'm delighted that you should admire Beecham. A pompous little duckarsed bandmaster who stood against everything creative in the art of his time. Second, if you can't tell that from a harpsichord, Christ help you. Third (to Piers) I think you're the smuggest young layabout I've met for years and you (me)—are *these* your friends?

I stood there, I couldn't say anything, he made me furious, they made me furious and anyhow I was ten times more embarrassed than furious.

Piers shrugged, Antoinette looked bewildered, but vaguely

amused, the bitch, and I was red. It makes me red again to think of
it (and of what happened later—how could he?).

Take it easy, said Piers. It's only a record. I suppose he was
angry, he must have known it was a stupid thing to say.

You think that's only a record, G.P. said. Is that it? It's just a
record? Are you like this stupid little bitch's aunt—do you think
Rembrandt got the teeniest bit bored when he painted? Do you think
Bach made funny faces and giggled when he wrote that? Do you?

Piers looked deflated, almost frightened. Well, DO YOU?
shouted G.P.

He was terrible. Both ways. He was terrible, because he had
started it all, he had determined to behave in that way. And won-
derfully terrible, because passion is something you never see. I've
grown up among people who've always tried to hide passion. He
was raw. Naked. Trembling with rage.

Piers said, we're not as old as you are. It was pathetic, feeble.
Showed him up for what he really is.

Christ, said G.P. Art students. ART students.

I can't write what he said next. Even Antoinette looked shocked.

We just turned and went. The studio door slammed behind us
when we were on the stairs. I hissed a damn-you at Piers at the
bottom and pushed them out. Darling, he'll murder you, said Antoinette. I shut the door and waited. After a moment I heard the
music again. I went up the stairs and very slowly opened the door.
Perhaps he heard, I don't know, but he didn't look up and I sat on
a stool near the door until it was finished.

He said, what do you want, Miranda?

I said, to say I'm sorry. And to hear you say you're sorry.

He went and stared out of the window.

I said, I know I was stupid, I may be little, but I'm not a bitch.

He said, you try (I think he didn't mean, you try to be a bitch).

I said, you could have told us to go away. We would have understood.

There was a silence. He turned to look at me across the studio. I said, I'm very sorry.

He said, go home. We can't go to bed together. When I stood up, he said, I'm glad you came back. It was decent of you. Then he said, you would.

I went down the stairs and he came out behind me. I don't want to go to bed with you, I'm speaking about the situation. Not us. Understand?

I said, of course I understand.

And I went on down. Being female. Wanting to make him feel I was hurt.

As I opened the bottom door he said, I've been hitting it. He must have seen I didn't understand, because he added, drinking.

He said, I'll telephone you.

He did, he took me to a concert, to hear the Russians play Shostakovich. And he was *sweet*. That's just what he was. Even though he never apologized.

October 26th

I don't trust him. He's bought this house. If he lets me go he'll have to trust me. Or he'll have to sell it and disappear before I can (could) get to the police. Either way it would be unlike him.

It's too depressing, I *have* to believe he'll keep his word.

He spends pounds and pounds on me. It must be nearly two hundred already. Any book, any record, any clothes. He has all my sizes. I sketch what I want, I mix up the colours as a guide. He even buys all my underwear. I can't put on the black and peach creations he bought before, so I told him to go and get something sensible at Marks and Spencer. He said, can I buy a lot together? Of course it must be agony for him to go shopping for me (what does he do at the chemist's?), so I suppose he prefers to get it all over in one go. But what can they think of him? One dozen pants and three slips and vests and bras. I asked him what they said when he gave the order and he went red. I think they think I'm a bit peculiar, he said. It was the first time I've really laughed since I came here.

Every time he buys me something I think it is proof that he's not going to kill me or do anything else unpleasant.

I shouldn't, but I like it when he comes in at lunch-time from wherever he goes. There are always parcels. It's like having a perpetual Christmas Day and not even having to thank Santa Claus. Sometimes he brings things I haven't asked for. He always brings flowers, and that is nice. Chocolates, but he eats more of them than I do. And he keeps on asking me what I'd like him to buy.

I know he's the Devil showing me the world that can be mine. So I don't sell myself to him. I cost him a lot in little things, but I know he wants me to ask for something big. He's dying to make me grateful. But he shan't.

An awful thought that came to me today: they will have suspected G.P. Caroline is bound to give the police his name. Poor man. He will be sarcastic and they won't like it.

I've been trying to draw him today. Strange. It is hopeless. Nothing like him.

I know he is short, only an inch or two more than me. (I've always dreamed tall men. Silly.)

He is going bald and he has a nose like a Jew's, though he isn't (not that I'd mind if he was). And the face is too broad. Battered, worn; battered and worn and pitted into a bit of a mask, so that I never quite believe whatever expression it's got on. I glimpse things I think must come from behind; but I'm never very sure. He puts on a special dry face for me sometimes. I see it go on. It doesn't seem dishonest, though, it seems just G.P. Life is a bit of a joke, it's silly to take it seriously. Be serious about art, but joke a little about everything else. Not the day when the H-bombs drop, but the "day of the great fry-up." "When the great fry-up takes place." Sick, sick. It's his way of being healthy.

Short and broad and broad-faced with a hook-nose; even a bit Turkish. Not really English-looking at all.

I have this silly notion about English good looks. Advertisement men.

Ladymont men.

October 27th

The tunnel round the door is my best bet. I feel I *must* try it soon. I think I've worked out a way of getting him away. I've been looking very carefully at the door this afternoon. It's wood faced with iron on this side. Terribly solid. I could never break it down or lever it open. He's made sure there's nothing to break and lever with, in any case.

I've begun to collect some "tools." A tumbler I can break. That will be something sharp. A fork and two teaspoons. They're aluminium, but they might be useful. What I need most is something strong and sharp to pick out the cement between the stones with. Once I can make a hole through them it shouldn't be too difficult to get round into the outer cellar.

This makes me feel practical. Businesslike. But I haven't done anything.

I feel more hopeful. I don't know why. But I do.

October 28th

G.P. as an artist. Caroline's "second-rate Paul Nash"—horrid, but there is something in it. Nothing like what he would call "photography." But not absolutely individual. I think it's just that he arrived at the same conclusions. And either he sees that (that his landscapes have a Nashy quality) or he doesn't. Either way, it's a criticism of him. That he neither sees it nor says it.

I'm being objective about him. His faults.

His hatred of abstract painting—even of people like Jackson Pollock and Nicholson. Why? I'm more than half convinced intellectually by him, but I still *feel* some of the paintings he says are bad are beautiful. I mean, he's too jealous. He condemns too much.

I don't mind this. I'm trying to be honest about him, and about myself. He hates people who don't "think things through"—and he does it. Too much. But he has (except over women) principles. He makes most people with so-called principles look like empty tin-cans.

(I remember he once said about a Mondrian—"it isn't whether you like it, but whether you ought to like it"—I mean, he dislikes abstract art on principle. He ignores what he *feels*.)

I've been leaving the worst to last. Women.

It must have been about the fourth or fifth time I went round to see him.

There was the Nielsen woman. I suppose (now) they'd been to bed together. I was so naïve. But they didn't seem to mind my coming. They needn't have answered the bell. And she was rather nice to me in her glittery at-home sort of way. Must be forty—what could he see in her? Then a long time after that, it was May, and I'd been the night before, but he was out (or in bed with someone?) and that evening he was in and alone, and we talked some time (he was telling me about John Minton) and then he put on an Indian record and we were quiet. But he didn't shut his eyes that time, he was looking at me and I was embarrassed. When the *raga* ended there was a silence. I said, shall I turn it? but he said, no. He was in the shadow, I couldn't see him very well.

Suddenly he said, Would you like to come to bed?

I said, no I wouldn't. He caught me by surprise and I sounded foolish. Frightened.

He said, his eyes still on me, ten years ago I would have married you. You would have been my second disastrous marriage.

It wasn't really a surprise. It had been waiting for weeks.

He came and stood by me. You're sure?

I said, I haven't come here for that. At all.

It seemed so unlike him. So crude. I think now, I know now, he was being kind. Deliberately obvious and crude. Just as he sometimes lets me beat him at chess.

He went to make Turkish coffee and he said through the door, you're misleading. I went and stood in the kitchen door, while he watched the vriki. He looked back at me. I could swear you want it sometimes.

How old are you? I said.

I could be your father. Is that what you mean?

I hate promiscuity, I said. I didn't mean that.

He had his back turned to me. I felt angry with him, he seemed so irresponsible. I said, anyhow, you don't attract me that way in the least.

He said, with his back still turned, what do you mean by promiscuity?

I said, going to bed for pleasure. Sex and nothing else. Without love.

He said, I'm very promiscuous then. I never go to bed with the people I love. I did once.

I said, you warned me against Barber Cruikshank.

I'm warning you against myself now, he said. He stood watching the vriki. You know the Ashmolean Uccello? *The Hunt?* No? The design hits you the moment you see it. Apart from all the other technical things. You know it's faultless. The professors with Middle-European names spend their lives working out what the great inner secret is, that thing you feel at the first glance. Now, I see you have the great inner secret, too. God knows what it is. I'm not a Middle-European professor, I don't really care *how* it is. But you have it. You're like Sheraton joinery. You won't fall apart.

He spoke it all in a very matter-of-fact voice. Too.

It's hazard, of course, he said. The genes.

He lifted the vriki off the gas-ring at the last possible moment. The only thing is, he said, there's that scarlet point in your eye. What is it? Passion? Stop?

He stood staring at me, the dry look.

It's not bed, I said.

But for someone?

For no one.

I sat on the divan and he on his high stool by the bench.

I've shocked you, he said.

I was warned.

By aunt?

Yes.

He turned and very slowly, very carefully, poured the coffee into the cups.

He said, all my life I've had to have women. They've mostly brought me unhappiness. The most has been brought by the relationships that were supposed to be pure and noble. There—he pointed at a photo of his two sons—that's the fine fruit of a noble relationship.

I went and got my coffee and leant against the bench, away from him.

Robert's only four years younger than you are now, he said. Don't drink it yet. Let the grounds settle.

He didn't seem at ease. As if he had to talk. Be on the defensive. Disillusion me and get my sympathy at the same time.

He said, lust is simple. You reach an understanding at once. You both want to get into bed or one of you doesn't. But love. The women I've loved have always told me I'm selfish. It's what makes them love me. And then be disgusted with me. Do you know what they always think is selfishness? He was scraping the glue away from a broken Chinese blue-and-white bowl he'd bought in the Portobello Road, and repaired, two fiendishly excited horsemen chasing a timid little fallow-deer. Very short-fingered, sure hands. Not that I will paint in my own way, live in my own way, speak in my own way—they don't mind that. It even excites them. But what they can't stand is that I hate them when *they* don't behave in their own way.

It was as if I was another man.

People like your bloody aunt think I'm a cynic, a wrecker of homes. A rake. I've never seduced a woman in my life. I like bed, I like the female body, I like the way even the shallowest of women become beautiful when their clothes are off and they think they're taking a profound and wicked step. They always do, the first time. Do you know what is almost extinct in your sex?

He looked sideways at me, so I shook my head.

Innocence. The one time you see it is when a woman takes her clothes off and cannot look you in the eyes (as I couldn't then).

Just that first Botticelli moment of the first time of her taking her clothes off. Soon shrivels. The old Eve takes over. The strumpet. Exit Anadyomene.

Who's she? I asked.

He explained. I was thinking, I shouldn't let him talk like this, he's drawing a net round me. I didn't think it, I *felt* it.

He said, I've met dozens of women and girls like you. Some I've known well, some I've seduced against their better nature and my better nature, two I've even married. Some I've hardly known at all, just stood beside them at an exhibition, in the Tube, wherever.

After a while he said, you've read Jung?

No, I said.

He's given your species of the sex a name. Not that it helps. The disease is just as bad.

Tell me the name, I said.

He said, you don't tell diseases their names.

Then there was a strange silence, as if we'd come to a full stop, as if he'd expected me to react in some other way. Be more angry or shocked, perhaps. I was shocked and angry afterwards (in a peculiar way). But I'm glad I didn't run away. It was one of those evenings when one grows up. I suddenly knew I had either to behave like a shocked girl who had still been at school that time the year before; or like an adult.

You're a weird kid, he said at last.

Old-fashioned, I said.

You'd be a bloody bore if you weren't so pretty.

Thank you.

I didn't really expect you to go to bed with me, he said.

I know, I said.

He gave me a long look. Then he changed, he got out the

chess-board and we played chess and he let me beat him. He wouldn't admit it, but I am sure he did. We hardly said anything, we seemed to communicate through the chessmen, there was something very symbolic about my winning. That he wished me to feel. I don't know what it was. I don't know whether it was that he wanted me to see my "virtue" triumphed over his "vice," or something subtler, that sometimes losing is winning.

The next time I went he gave me a drawing he had done. It was of the vriki and the two cups on the bench. Beautifully drawn, absolutely simple, absolutely without fuss or nervousness, absolutely free of that clever art-student look the drawings of simple objects I do have.

Just the two cups and the little copper vriki and his hand. Or a hand. Lying by one of the cups, like a plaster cast. On the back he wrote, *Après,* and the date. And then, *pour "une" princesse lointaine.* The *"une"* was very heavily underlined.

I wanted to go on about Toinette. But I'm too tired. I want to smoke when I write, and it makes the air so stuffy.

October 29th

(Morning.) He's gone into? Lewes.

Toinette.

It was a month after the evening of the record. I ought to have guessed, she had been purring over me for days, giving me arch looks. I thought it was something to do with Piers. And then one evening I rang the bell and then I noticed the lock was up, so I pushed the door open and looked up the stairs, at the same time as Toinette looked down round the door. And we were looking at each other. After a moment she came out on the landing and she was dressing. She didn't say anything, she just gestured me to come up and into the studio and what was worst, I was red, and she was not. She was just amused.

Don't look so shocked, she said. He'll be back in a minute. He's just gone out for . . . but I never heard what it was, because I went.

I've never really analyzed why I was *so* angry and *so* shocked and *so* hurt. Donald, Piers, David, everyone knows she lives in London as she lived in Stockholm—she's told me herself, they've told me. And G.P. had told me what he was like.

It was not just jealousy. It was that someone like G.P. could be so close to someone like her—someone so real and someone so shallow, so phoney, so loose. But why should he have considered me at all? There's not a single reason.

He's twenty-one years older than I am. Nine years younger than D.

For days afterwards it wasn't G.P. I was disgusted with, but myself. At my narrow-mindedness. I forced myself to meet, to listen to Toinette. She didn't crow at all. I think that must have been G.P.'s doing. He ordered her not to.

She went back the next day. She said it was to say she was sorry. And (her words), "It just happened."

I was so jealous. They made me feel older than they were. They were like naughty children. Happy-with-a-secret. Then that I was frigid. I couldn't bear to see G.P. In the end, it must have been a week later, he rang me up again one evening at Caroline's. He didn't sound guilty. I said I was too busy to see him. I wouldn't go round that evening, no. If he had pressed, I would have refused. But he seemed to be about to ring off, and I said I'd go round the next day. I so wanted him to know I was hurt. You can't be hurt over a telephone.

Caroline said, I think you're seeing too much of him.

I said, he's having an *affaire* with that Swedish girl.

We even had a talk about it. I was very fair. I defended him. But in bed I lay and accused him to myself. For hours.

The first thing he said the next day was (no pretending)—has she been a bitch to you?

I said, no. Not at all. Then, as if I didn't care, why should she?

He smiled. I know what you're feeling, he seemed to say. It made me want to slap his face. I couldn't look as if I didn't care, which made it worse.

He said, men are vile.

I said, the vilest thing about them is that they can say that with a smile on their faces.

That is true, he said. And there was silence. I wished I hadn't come, I wished I'd cut him out of my life. I looked at the bedroom door. It was ajar, I could see the end of the bed.

I said, I'm not able to put life in compartments yet. That's all.

Look, Miranda, he said, those twenty long years that lie between you and me. I've more knowledge of life than you, I've lived more and betrayed more and seen more betrayed. At your age one is bursting with ideals. You think that because I can sometimes see what's trivial and what's important in art that I ought to be more virtuous. But I don't want to be virtuous. My charm (if there is any) for you is simply frankness. And experience. Not goodness. I'm not a good man. Perhaps morally I'm younger even than you are. Can you understand that?

He was only saying what I felt. I was stiff and he was supple, and it ought to be the other way round. The fault all mine. But I kept on thinking, he took me to the concert, and he came back here to her. I remembered times when I rang the bell and there had been no answer. I see now it was all sexual jealousy, but then it seemed a betrayal of principles. (I still don't know—it's all muddled in my mind. I can't judge.)

I said, I'd like to hear Ravi Shankar. I couldn't say, I forgive you.

So we listened to that. Then played chess. And he beat me. No reference to Toinette, except at the very end, on the stairs, when he said, it's all over now.

I didn't say anything.

She only did it for fun, he said.

But it was never the same. It was a sort of truce. I saw him a few times more, but never alone, I wrote him two letters when I was in Spain, and he sent a postcard back. I saw him once at the beginning of this month. But I'll write about that another time. And I'll write about the strange talk I had with the Nielsen woman.

Something Toinette said. She said, he talked about his boys and I felt so sorry for him. How they used to ask him not to go to their posh prep school, but to meet them in the town. Ashamed to have him seen. How Robert (at Marlborough) patronizes him now.

He never talked to me about them. Perhaps he secretly thinks I belong to the same world.

A little middle-class boarding-school prig.

*   *   *

(Evening.) I tried to draw G.P. from memory again today.
Hopeless.

C sat reading *The Catcher in the Rye* after supper. Several times
I saw him look to see how many pages more he had to read.

He reads it only to show me how hard he is trying.

I was passing the front door tonight (bath) and I said, well, thank
you for a lovely evening, goodbye now. And I made as if to open the
door. It was locked, of course. It seems stuck, I said. And he didn't
smile, he just stood watching me. I said, It's only a joke. I know, he
said. It's very peculiar—he made me feel a fool. Just by not smiling.

Of course G.P. was always trying to get me into bed. I don't know
why but I see that more clearly now than I ever did at the time. He
shocked me, bullied me, taunted me—never in nasty ways.
Obliquely. He didn't ever force me in any way. Touch me. I mean,
he's respected me in a queer way. I don't think he really knew
himself. He wanted to shock me—to him or away from him, he
didn't know. Left it to chance.

More photos today. Not many. I said it hurt my eyes too much.
And I don't like him always ordering me about. He's terribly ob-
sequious, would I do this, would I oblige by . . . no he doesn't say
"oblige." But it's a wonder he doesn't.

You ought to go in for beauty comps, he said when he was
winding up his film.

Thank you, I said. (The way we talk is mad, I don't see it till I
write it down. He talks as if I'm free to go at any minute, and I'm
the same.)

I bet you'd look smashing in a wotchermercallit, he said.

I looked puzzled. One of those French swimming things, he said.

A bikini? I asked.

I can't allow talk like that, so I stared coldly at him. Is that what
you mean?

To photograph like, he said, going red.

And the weird thing is, I know he means exactly that. He didn't
mean to be nasty, he wasn't hinting at anything, he was just being
clumsy. As usual. He meant literally what he said. I would be interesting to photograph in a bikini.

I used to think, it must be there. It's very deeply suppressed,
but it must be there.

But I don't any more. I don't think he's suppressing anything.
There's nothing to suppress.

A lovely night-walk. There were great reaches of clear sky, no
moon, sprinkles of warm white stars everywhere, like milky diamonds, and a beautiful wind. From the west. I made him take me
round and round, ten or twelve times. The branches rustling, an
owl hooting in the woods. And the sky all wild, all free, all wind
and air and space and stars.

Wind full of smells and far-away places. Hopes. The sea. I am
sure I could smell the sea. I said (later, of course I was gagged outside), are we near the sea? And he said, ten miles. I said, near
Lewes. He said, I can't say. As if someone else had strictly forbid-
den him to speak. (I often feel that with him—a horrid little cring-
ing good nature dominated by a mean bad one.)

Indoors it couldn't have been more different. We talked about
his family again. I'd been drinking scrumpy. I do it (a little) to see
if I can get him drunk and careless, but so far he won't touch it.
He's not a teetotaller, he says. So it's all part of his warderishness.
Won't be corrupted.

M. Tell me some more about your family.
C. Nothing more to tell. That'd interest *you*.

M. That's not an answer.

C. It's like I said.

M. As I said.

C. I used to be told I was good at English. That was before I knew you.

M. It doesn't matter.

C. I suppose you got the A level and all that.

M. Yes, I did.

C. I got O level in Maths and Biology.

M. *(I was counting stitches—jumper—expensive French wool)* Good, seventeen, eighteen, nineteen . . .

C. I won a prize for hobbies.

M. Clever you. Tell me more about your father.

C. I told you. He was a representative. Stationery and fancy goods.

M. A commercial traveller.

C. They call them representatives now.

M. He got killed in a car-crash before the war. Your mother went off with another man.

C. She was no good. Like me. *(I gave him an icy look. Thank goodness his humour so rarely seeps out.)*

M. So your aunt took you over.

C. Yes.

M. Like Mrs. Joe and Pip.

C. Who?

M. Never mind.

C. She's all right. She kept me out of the orphanage.

M. And your cousin Mabel. You've never said anything about her.

C. She's older than me. Thirty. There's her older brother, he went out to Australia after the war to my Uncle Steve. He's a real Australian. Been out there years. I never seen him.

M. And haven't you any other family?

C. There's relations of Uncle Dick. But they and Aunt Annie never got on.

M. You haven't said what Mabel's like.

C. She's deformed. Spastic. Real sharp. Always wants to know everything you've done.

M. She can't walk?

C. About the house. We had to take her out in a chair.

M. Perhaps I've seen her.

C. You haven't missed much.

M. Aren't you sorry for her?

C. It's like you have to be sorry for her all the time. It's Aunt Annie's fault.

M. Go on.

C. She like makes everything round her deformed too. I can't explain. Like nobody else had any right to be normal. I mean she doesn't complain outright. It's just looks she gives, and you have to be dead careful. Suppose, well, I say not thinking one evening, I nearly missed the bus this morning, I had to run like billy-o, sure as fate Aunt Annie would say, think yourself lucky you can run. Mabel wouldn't say anything. She'd just look.

M. How vile!

C. You had to think very careful about what you said.

M. Carefully.

C. I mean carefully.

M. Why didn't you run away? Live in digs?

C. I used to think about it.

M. Because they were two women on their own. You were being a gent.

C. Being a charley, more like it. *(Pathetic, his attempts at being a cynic.)*

M. And now they're in Australia making your other relations miserable.

C. I suppose so.

M. Do they write letters?

C. Yes. Not Mabel.

M. Would you read one to me one day?

C. What for?

M. I'd be interested.

C. *(great inner struggle)* I got one this morning. I've got it on
me. *(A lot of argy-bargy, but in the end he took the letter from
out of his pocket.)* They're stupid.

M. Never mind. Read it out. All of it.

He sat by the door, and I knitted, knitted, knitted—I can't remember the letter word for word, but it was something like this:
Dear Fred (that's the name she calls me by, he said, she doesn't like
Ferdinand—red with embarrassment). Very pleased to have yours
and as I said in my last it's your money, God has been very kind to
you and you mustn't fly up in the face of his kindness and I wish
you had not taken this step, your Uncle Steve says property's more
trouble than it's worth. I notice you don't answer my question
about the woman to clean. I know what men are and just remember what they say cleanliness is next to godliness. I have no right
and you have been very generous, Fred, Uncle Steve and the boys
and Gertie can't understand why you didn't come here with us,
Gert only said this morning that you ought to be here, your place
is with us, but don't think I am not grateful. I hope the Lord will
forgive me but this has been a great experience and you wouldn't
know Mabel, she is brown in the sun here, it is very nice, but I
don't like the dust. Everything gets dirty and they live in a different way to what we do at home, they speak English more like

Americans (even Uncle Steve) than us. I shan't be sorry to get home to Blackstone Rd, it worries me to think of the damp and the dirt, I hope you did what I said and aired all the rooms and linen like I said and got a good cleaning woman in like I said the same as with you, I hope.

Fred I am worried with all that money you won't lose your head, there are a lot of clever dishonest people (she means women, he said) about these days, I brought you up as well as I could and if you do wrong it's the same as if I did. I shan't show this to Mabel she says you don't like it. I know you are over age (over 21, she means, he said) but I worry about you because of all that happened (she means me being an orphan, he said).

We liked Melbourne, it is a big town. Next week we are going to Brisbane to stay with Bob again and his wife. She wrote a nice letter. They will meet us at the station. Uncle Steve, Gert and the children send their love. So does Mabel and your everloving.

Then she says I needn't worry about money, it's lasting very well. Then she hopes I got a woman who will work, she says the young ones don't clean proper nowadays.

(There was a long silence then.)

M. Do you think it's a nice letter?

C. She always writes like that.

M. It makes me want to be sick.

C. She never had any real education.

M. It's not the *English*. It's her nasty mind.

C. She took me in.

M. She certainly did. She took you in, and she's gone on taking you in. She's made an absolute fool out of you.

C. Thank you very much.

M. Well, she has!

C. Oh, you're right. As per usual.

M. Don't say that! *(I put down my knitting and closed my eyes.)*

C. She never bossed me about half as much as you do.

M. I don't boss you. I try to teach you.

C. You teach me to despise her and think like you, and soon you'll leave me and I'll have no one at all.

M. Now you're pitying yourself.

C. It's the one thing you don't understand. You only got to walk into a room, people like you, and you can talk with anyone, you understand things, but when . . .

M. *Do* shut up. You're ugly enough without starting to whine.

I picked up my knitting and put it away. When I looked round he was standing there with his mouth open, trying to say something. And I knew I'd hurt him, I know he deserves to be hurt, but there it is. I've hurt him. He looked so glum. And I remembered he'd let me go out in the garden. I felt mean.

I went to him and said I was sorry and held out my hand, but he wouldn't take it. It was queer, he really had a sort of dignity, he was really hurt (perhaps that was it) and showing it. So I took his arm and made him sit down again, and I said, I'm going to tell you a fairy story.

Once upon a time (I said, and he stared bitterly bitterly at the floor) there was a very ugly monster who captured a princess and put her in a dungeon in his castle. Every evening he made her sit with him and ordered her to say to him, "You are very handsome, my lord." And every evening she said, "You are very ugly, you monster." And then the monster looked very hurt and sad and stared at the floor. So one evening the princess said, "If you do this thing and that thing you might be handsome," but the monster said, "I can't, I can't." The princess said, "Try, try." But the monster said, "I can't, I can't." Every evening it was the same. He asked her to lie, and she wouldn't. So the princess began to think that he really enjoyed being a monster and very ugly. Then one day she saw he was crying when she'd told him, for the fiftieth time, that he was ugly. So she said, "You can become very handsome if you do just one thing. Will you do it?" Yes, he said, at last, he would try to do it. So she said, then set me free. And he set her free. And suddenly, he wasn't ugly any more, he was a prince who had been bewitched. And he followed the princess out of the castle. And they both lived happily ever afterwards.

I knew it was silly as I was saying it. Fey. He didn't speak, he kept staring down.

I said, now it's your turn to tell a fairy story.

He just said, I love you.

And yes, he had more dignity than I did then and I felt small, mean. Always sneering at him, jabbing him, hating him and showing it. It was funny, we sat in silence facing each other and I had a feeling I've had once or twice before, of the most peculiar closeness to him—*not* love or attraction or sympathy in any way. But linked destiny. Like being shipwrecked on an island—a raft—together. In *every* way not wanting to be together. But together.

I feel the sadness of his life, too, terribly. And of those of his miserable aunt and his cousin and their relatives in Australia. The great dull hopeless weight of it. Like those Henry Moore drawings of the people in the Tubes during the blitz. People who would never see, feel, dance, draw, cry at music, feel the world, the west wind. Never *be* in any real sense.

Just those three words, said and meant. I love you.

They were quite hopeless. He said it as he might have said, I have cancer.

His fairy story.

October 31st

Nothing. I psycho-analyzed him this evening.

He would sit so stiffly beside me.

We were looking at Goya's etchings. Perhaps it was the etchings themselves, but he sat and I thought he wasn't really looking at them. But thinking only of being so close to me.

His inhibition. It's absurd. I talked at him as if he could easily be normal. As if he wasn't a maniac keeping me prisoner here. But a nice young man who wanted a bit of chivvying from a jolly girl-friend.

It's because I never see anyone else. He becomes the norm. I forget to compare.

Another time G.P. It was soon after the icy douche (what he said about my work). I was restless one evening. I went round to his flat. About ten. He had his dressing-gown on.

I was just going to bed, he said.

I wanted to hear some music, I said. I'll go away. But I didn't. He said, it's late.

I said I was depressed. It had been a beastly day and Caroline had been so silly at supper.

He let me go up and made me sit on the divan and he put on some music and turned out the lights and the moon came through the window. It fell on my legs and lap through the skylight, a lovely slow silver moon. Sailing. And he sat in the armchair on the other side of the room, in the shadows.

It was the music.

The *Goldberg Variations.*

There was one towards the end that was very slow, very simple, *very* sad, but so beautiful beyond words or drawing or anything but music, beautiful there in the moonlight. Moon-music, so silvery, so far, so noble.

The two of us in that room. No past, no future. All intense deep that-time-only. A feeling that everything must end, the music, ourselves, the moon, everything. That if you get to the heart of things you find sadness for ever and ever, everywhere; but a beautiful silver sadness, like a Christ face.

Accepting the sadness. Knowing that to pretend it was all gay was treachery. Treachery to everyone sad at that moment, everyone ever sad, treachery to such music, such truth.

In all the fuss and anxiety and the shoddiness and the business of London, making a career, getting pashes, art, learning, grabbing frantically at experience, suddenly this silent silver room full of that music.

Like lying on one's back as we did in Spain when we slept out looking up between the fig-branches into the star-corridors, the great seas and oceans of stars. Knowing what it was to be *in* a universe.

I cried. In silence.

At the end he said, now can I go to bed? Gently, making fun of me a little bit, bringing me back to earth. And I went. I don't think we said anything. I can't remember. He had his little dry smile, he could see I was moved.

His perfect tact.

I would have gone to bed with him that night. If he had asked. If he had come and kissed me.

Not for his sake, but for being alive's.

November 1st

A new month, and new luck. The tunnel idea keeps nagging at me, but the difficulty till now has been something to dig the concrete out with. Then yesterday as I was doing my prison-exercise in the outer cellar I saw a nail. A big old one, down against the wall in the far corner. I dropped my handkerchief so that I could get a closer look. I couldn't pick it up, he watches me so closely. And it's awkward with bound hands. Then today, when I was by the nail (he always sits on the steps up), I said (I did it on purpose) run and get me a cigarette. They're on the chair by the door. Of course he wouldn't. He said, what's the game?

I'll stay here, I won't move.

Why don't you get them yourself?

Because sometimes I like to remember the days when men were nice to me. That's all.

I didn't think it would work. But it did. He suddenly decided that there wasn't anything I could possibly do, nothing I could pick up. (He locks things away in a drawer when I come out here.) So he went through the door. Only a second. But I stooped like lightning and got the nail up and into my skirt pocket—specially put on—and I was standing exactly as he left me when he jumped back. So I got my nail. And made him think he could trust me. Two birds with one stone.

Nothing. But it seems a tremendous victory.

I've started putting my plan into effect. For days I've been telling Caliban that I don't see why D and M and everyone else should be left in the dark about whether I still exist. At least he could tell them I'm alive and all right. Tonight after supper I told him he could buy paper from Woolworth's and use gloves and so on. He tried to wriggle out of it, as usual. But I kept at him. Every objection I squashed. And in the end I felt he really was beginning to think he might do it for me.

I told him he could post the letter in London, to put the police off the track. And that I wanted all sorts of things from London. I've got to get him away from here for at least three or four hours. Because of the burglar alarms. And then I'm going to try my tunnel. What I've been thinking is that as the walls of this cellar (and the outer one) are stones—not stone—then behind the stones these must be earth. All I have to do is to get through the skin of stones and then I shall be in soft earth (I imagine).

Perhaps it's all wild. But I'm in a fever to try it.

The Nielsen woman.

I'd met her twice more at G.P.'s, when there were other people there—one was her husband, a Dane, some kind of importer. He spoke perfect English, so perfect it sounded wrong. Affected.

I met her one day when she was coming out of the hair-dresser's and I'd been in to make an appointment for Caroline. She had on that special queasy-bright look women like her put on for girls of my age. What Minny calls welcome-to-the-tribe-of-women. It means they're going to treat you like a grown-up, but they don't really think you are and anyhow they're jealous of you.

She would take me for coffee. I was silly, I should have lied. It was all rhubarb, about me, about her daughter, about art. She knows people and tried to dazzle me with names. But it's what people feel about art that I respect. Not what or who they know.

I know she can't be a lesbian, but she clings like that to one's words. Things in her eyes she doesn't dare tell you. But wants you to ask her to.

You don't know what's gone on and what still goes on between G.P. and me, she seemed to say. I dare you to ask me.

She talked on and on about Charlotte Street in the late 'thirties and the war. Dylan Thomas. G.P.

He likes you, she said.

I know, I answered.

But it was a shock. Both that she should know (had he told her?) and that she wanted to discuss it. I know she did.

He's always fallen for the really pretty ones, she said.

She wanted *terribly* to discuss it.

Then it was her daughter.

She said, she's sixteen now. I just can't get across to her. Sometimes when I talk to her I feel like an animal in a zoo. She just stands outside and watches me.

I knew she'd said it before. Or read it somewhere. You can always tell.

They're all the same, women like her. It's not the teenagers and daughters who are different. We haven't changed, we're just young. It's the silly new middle-aged people who've got to be young who've changed. This desperate silly trying to stay with us. They can't be with us. We don't want them to be with us. We don't want them to wear our clothes-styles and use our language and have our interests. They imitate us so badly that we can't respect them.

But it made me feel, that meeting with her, that G.P. did love me (want me). That there's a deep bond between us—his loving me in his way, my liking him very much (even loving him, but not sexually) in my way—a feeling that we're groping towards a compromise. A sort of fog of unsolved desire and sadness between us. Something other people (like the N woman) couldn't ever understand.

Two people in a desert, trying to find both themselves and an oasis where they can live together.

I've begun to think more and more like this—it is terribly cruel of fate to have put these twenty years between us. Why couldn't he be my age, or me his? So the age thing is no longer the all-important factor that puts love right out of the question but a sort of cruel wall fate has built between us. I don't think any more, the wall is between us, I think, the wall keeps us apart.

He produced the paper after supper, and dictated an absurd letter that I had to write out.

Then the trouble started. I had prepared a little note, written in my smallest writing, and I slipped it into the envelope when he wasn't looking. It was very small, and in the best spy stories wouldn't have been noticed.

He did.

It upset him. Made him see things in the cold light of reality. But he was genuinely shocked that I should be frightened. He can't imagine himself killing or raping me, and that is something.

I let him have his pet, but in the end I went and tried to be nice to him (because I knew I must get him to send that letter). It *was* a job. I've never known him in such a huff.

Wouldn't he call it a day, and let me go home?

No.

What did he want to do with me then? Take me to bed?

He gave me such a look, as if I was being really disgusting.

Then I had an inspiration. I acted a little charade. His oriental slave. He likes me to play the fool. The stupidest things I do he calls witty. He has even got in the habit of joining in, stumbling after me (not that I'm very dazzling) like a giraffe.

So I got him to let me write another letter. He looked in the envelope again.

Then I talked him into going to London, as my plan requires. I gave him a ridiculous list of things (most of them I don't want, but it'll keep him busy) to buy. I told him it was impossible to trace a letter posted in London. So he finally agreed. He likes me to wheedle, the brute.

One request—no, I don't ask him for things, I order them. I

commanded him to try and buy a George Paston. I gave him a list
of galleries where he might find things by G.P. I even tried to get
him to go to the studio.

But as soon as he heard it was in Hampstead, he smelt a rat. He
wanted to know if I knew this George Paston. I said, no, well, just
by name. But it didn't sound very convincing; and I was afraid he
wouldn't buy any of his pictures anywhere. So I said, he's a casual
friend of mine, he's quite old, but he's a very good painter, and he
badly needs money and I should very much like some of his pictures. We could hang them on the walls. If you bought straight
from him we wouldn't be paying money to the galleries, but I can
see you're frightened to go, I said, so there's an end to it. Of
course he didn't fall for *that*.

He wanted to know if G.P. was one of these paintpot-at-the-
wall chaps. I just gave him a look.

C. I was only joking.

M. Then don't.

After a bit, he said, he would want to know where I came from
and all.

I told him what he could say, and he said he'd think about it.
Which is Calibanese for "no." It was too much to expect; and there
probably won't be anything in any of the galleries.

And I don't worry because I'm not going to be here this time
tomorrow. I'm going to escape.

He'll go off after breakfast. He's going to leave my lunch. So
I shall have four or five hours (unless he cheats and doesn't get all
I've asked, but he's never failed before).

I felt sorry for Caliban this evening. He *will* suffer when I am
gone. There will be nothing left. He'll be alone with all his sex neurosis and his class neurosis and his uselessness and his emptiness.
He's asked for it. I'm not really sorry. But I'm not absolutely unsorry.

November 4th

I couldn't write yesterday. Too fed up.

I was so stupid. I got him away all yesterday. I had hours to escape. But I never really thought of the problems. I saw myself scooping out handfuls of soft loamy earth. The nail was useless, it wouldn't dig the cement properly. I thought it would crumble away. It was terribly hard. I took hours to get one stone out. There wasn't earth behind, but another stone, a bigger one, chalk, and I couldn't even find where its edge was. I got another stone out of the wall, but it didn't help. There was the same huge stone behind. I began to get desperate, I saw the tunnel was no good. I hit violently at the door, I tried to force it with the nail, and managed to hurt my hand. That's all. All I had at the end was a sore hand and broken fingernails.

I'm just not strong enough, without tools. Even with tools.

In the end I put the stones back and powdered (as well as I could) the cement and mixed it with water and talcum powder to camouflage the hole. It's typical of the states I get in here—I suddenly told myself that the digging would have to be done over a number of days, the only stupid thing was to expect to do it all in one.

So I spent a long time trying to hide the place.

But it was no good, little bits fell out, and I'd started in the most obvious place, where he's bound to spot it.

So I gave up. I suddenly decided it was all petty, stupid, useless. Like a bad drawing. Unrescuable.

When he came at last, he saw it at once. He always sniffs round as soon as he enters. Then he started to see how far I had gone. I sat on the bed and watched him. In the end I threw the nail at him.

*   *   *

He's cemented the stones back. He says it's solid chalk behind all the way round.

I wouldn't speak to him all the evening, or look at the things he'd bought, even though I could see one of them was a picture-frame.

I took a sleeping-pill and went to bed straight after supper.

Then, this morning (I woke up early) before he came down, I decided to pass it off as something unimportant. To be normal.

Not to give in.

I unpacked all the things he'd bought. First of all, there was G.P.'s picture. It is a drawing of a girl (young woman), a nude, not like anything else of his I have seen, and I think it must be something he did a long time ago. It is *his*. It has his simplicity of line, hatred of fussiness, of Topolskitis. She's half-turned away, hanging up or taking down a dress from a hook. A pretty face? It's difficult to say. Rather a heavy Maillol body. It's not worth dozens of things he's done since.

But real.

I kissed it when I unwrapped it. I've been looking at some of the lines not as lines, but as things he has touched. All morning. Now.

Not love. Humanity.

Caliban was surprised that I seemed so positively gay when he came in. I thanked him for all he had bought. I said, you can't be a proper prisoner if you don't try to escape and now don't let's talk about it—agreed?

He said that he'd telephoned every gallery I gave him the name of. There was only the one thing.

Thank you very much, I said. May I keep it down here? And when I go, I'll give it to you. (I shan't—he said he'd rather have a drawing of mine, in any case.)

I asked him if he had posted the letter. He said he had, but I saw he was going red. I told him I believed him and that it would

be such a dirty trick not to post the letter that I was sure he must
have posted it.

I feel almost certain he funked it, as he funked the cheque. It
would be just like him. But nothing I say will make him post it. So
I've decided that I will suppose he has posted it.

Midnight. I had to stop. He came down.

We've been playing the records he bought.

Bartók's *Music for Percussion and Celesta.*

The loveliest.

It made me think of Collioure last summer. The day we went,
all four of us with the French students, up through the ilexes to the
tower. The ilexes. An absolutely new colour, amazing chestnut,
rufous, burning, bleeding, where they had cut away the cork. The
cicadas. The wild azure sea through the stems and the heat and the
smell of everything burnt in it. Piers and I and everyone except
Minny got a bit tipsy. Sleeping in the shade, waking up staring
through the leaves at the cobalt blue sky, thinking how impossible
things were to paint, how can some blue pigment ever mean the
living blue light of the sky. I suddenly felt I didn't want to paint,
painting was just showing off, the thing was to experience and experience for ever more.

The beautiful clean sun on the blood-red stems.

And coming back I had a long talk with the nice shy boy, Jean-
Louis. His bad English and my bad French, yet we understood
each other. Terribly timid he was. Frightened of Piers. Jealous of
him. Jealous of his throwing an arm round me, the silly lout Piers
is. And when I discovered he was going to be a priest.

Piers was so crude afterwards. That stupid clumsy frightened-
of-being-soft English male cruelty to the truth. He couldn't see
that of course poor Jean-Louis liked me, of course he was sexually attracted, but there was this other thing, it wasn't really shy-

ness, it was a determination to try to be a priest and to live in the world. A simply colossal effort of coming to terms with oneself. Like destroying all the paintings one's ever done and making a new start. Only he had to do it every day. Every time he saw a girl he liked. And all Piers could say was: I bet he's having dirty dreams about you.

So ghastly, that arrogance, that insensitivity, of boys who've been to public schools. Piers is always going on about how he hated Stowe. As if that solves everything, as if to hate something means it can't have affected you. I always know when he doesn't understand something. He gets cynical, he says something shocking.

When I told G.P. about it much later, he just said, poor frog, he was probably on his knees praying to forget you.

Watching Piers throw stones out to sea—where was it?—somewhere near Valencia. So beautiful, like a young god, all golden-brown, with his dark hair. His swimming-slip. And Minny said (she was lying beside me, oh, it's so clear) she said, wouldn't it be wonderful if Piers was dumb.

And then she said, could you go to bed with him?

I said, no. Then, I don't know.

Piers came up then and wanted to know what she was smiling about.

Nanda's just told me a secret, she said. About you.

Piers made some feeble joke and went off to get the lunch from the car with Peter.

What's the secret, I wanted to know.

Bodies beat minds, she said.

Clever Carmen Grey always knows what to say.

I knew you'd say that, she said. She was doodling in the sand and I was on my tummy watching her. She said, what I mean is he's so terribly good-looking, one could forget he's so stupid. You might think, I could marry him and teach him. Couldn't you? And you know you couldn't. Or you could go to bed with him just for fun and one day you'd suddenly find you were in love with his body and you couldn't live without it and you'd be stuck with his rotten mind for ever and ever.

Then she said, doesn't it terrify you?

Not more than so many other things.

I'm serious. If you married him I'd never speak to you again.

And she was serious. That very quick grey shy look she puts on, like a little lance. I got up and kissed her on the way up and went to meet the boys. And she sat there, still looking down at the sand.

We're both terrible lookers-through. We can't help it. But she's always said, I believe this, I shall act like this. It's got to be someone you at least feel is your equal, who can look through as well as you. And the body thing's always got to be second. And I've always secretly thought, Carmen will be another spinster. It's too complicated for set ideas.

But now I think of G.P. and I compare him to Piers. And Piers has got nothing on his side. Just a golden body throwing stones aimlessly into the sea.

November 5th

I gave him hell tonight.

I started throwing things around upstairs. First cushions and then plates. I've been longing to break them.

But I was beastly, really. Spoilt. He suffered it all. He's so weak. He ought to have slapped me across the face.

He did catch hold of me, to stop me breaking another of his wretched plates. We so rarely touch. I hated it. It was like icy water.

I lectured him. I told him all about himself and what he ought to do in life. But he doesn't listen. He likes me to talk about him. It doesn't matter what I say.

I won't write any more. I'm reading *Sense and Sensibility* and I must find out what happens to Marianne. Marianne is me; Eleanor is me as I ought to be.

What happens if he has a crash? A stroke. Anything.

I die.

I couldn't get out. All I did the day before yesterday was to prove it.

November 6th

It's afternoon. No lunch.

Another escape. So nearly, it seemed at one point. But it never was. He's a devil.

I tried the appendicitis trick. I thought of it weeks ago. I've always thought of it as a sort of last resort. Something I must not bungle through unpreparedness. I didn't write about it here, in case he found this.

I rubbed talc into my face. Then when he knocked on the door this morning I swallowed a whole lot of saved-up salt and water and pressed my tongue and the timing was perfect, he came in and saw me being sick. I put on a tremendous act. Lying on the bed with my hair in a mess and holding my tummy. Still in my pyjamas and dressing-gown. Groaning a little, as if I was being terribly brave. All the time he stood and said, what's wrong, what's wrong? And we had a sort of desperate broken conversation, Caliban trying to get out of taking me to hospital, I insisting that he must. And then suddenly he seemed to give way. He muttered something about it being "the end" and rushed out.

I heard the iron door go (I was still staring at the wall) but no bolts. Then the outer door. And there was silence. It was weird. So sudden, so complete. It had worked. I pulled on some socks and shoes and ran to the iron door. It had sprung back an inch or two—was open. I thought it might be all a trap. So I kept up the act, I opened the door and said his name in a quiet voice and hobbled weakly across the cellar and up the steps. I could see the light, he hadn't locked the outer door, either. It flashed across my mind that it was just what he would do, he wouldn't go to the doctor. He'd run away. Crack up completely. But he'd take the van. So I would hear the engine. But I couldn't. I must have waited several minutes, I should have known but I couldn't bear the suspense. I pulled the door open and rushed out. And he was there. At once. In all the daylight.

Waiting.

I couldn't pretend I was ill. I'd put shoes on. He had something (a hammer?) in his hand, peculiar wide eyes, I'm sure he was going to attack me. We sort of stood poised for a moment, neither of us knowing what to do. Then I turned and ran back. I don't know why, I didn't stop to think. He came after me, but he stopped when he saw me go inside (as I instinctively knew he would—the only safe place from him was down here). I heard him come and the bolts were shot to.

I know it was the right thing to do. It saved my life. If I had screamed or tried to escape he would have battered me to death. There are moments when he is possessed, quite out of his own control.

His trick.

(Midnight.) He brought me supper down here. He didn't say a word. I'd spent the afternoon doing a strip cartoon of him. The Awful Tale of a Harmless Boy. Absurd. But I have to keep the reality and the horror at bay. He starts by being a nice little clerk, ends up as a drooling horror-film monster.

When he was going I showed it to him. He didn't laugh, he simply looked at it carefully.

It's only natural, he said. He meant, that I should make such fun of him.

I am one in a row of specimens. It's when I try to flutter out of line that he hates me. I'm meant to be dead, pinned, always the same, always beautiful. He knows that part of my beauty is being alive, but it's the dead me he wants. He wants me living-but-dead. I felt it terribly strong today. That my being alive and changing and having a separate mind and having moods and all that was becoming a nuisance.

He is solid; immovable, iron-willed. He showed me one day what he called his killing-bottle. I'm imprisoned in it. Fluttering against the glass. Because I can see through it I still think I can escape. I have hope. But it's all an illusion.

A thick round wall of glass.

November 7th

How the days drag. Today. Intolerably long.

My one consolation is G.P.'s drawing. It grows on me. On one. It's the only living, unique, created thing here. It's the first thing I look at when I wake up, the last thing at night. I stand in front of it and stare at it. I know every line. He made a fudge of one of her feet. There's something slightly unbalanced about the whole composition, as if there's a tiny bit missing somewhere. But it lives.

After supper (we're back to normal) Caliban handed me *The Catcher in the Rye* and said, I've read it. I knew at once by his tone that he meant—"and I don't think much of it."

I feel awake, I'll do a dialogue.

M. Well?

C. I don't see much point in it.

M. You realize this is one of the most brilliant studies of adolescence ever written?

C. He sounds a mess to me.

M. Of course he's a mess. But he realizes he's a mess, he tries to express what he feels, he's a human being for all his faults. Don't you even feel sorry for him?

C. I don't like the way he talks.

M. I don't like the way you talk. But I don't treat you as below any serious notice or sympathy.

C. I suppose it's very clever. To write like that and all.

M. I gave you that book to read because I thought you would feel identified with him. You're a Holden Caulfield. He doesn't fit anywhere and you don't.

C. I don't wonder, the way he goes on. He doesn't try to fit.

M. He tries to construct some sort of reality in his life, some
    sort of decency.
C. It's not realistic. Going to a posh school and his parents hav-
    ing money. He wouldn't behave like that. In my opinion.
M. I know what you are. You're the Old Man of the Sea.
C. Who's he?
M. The horrid old man Sinbad had to carry on his back.
    That's what you are. You get on the back of everything
    vital, everything trying to be honest and free, and you bear
    it down.

I won't go on. We argued—no, we don't argue, I say things
and he tries to wriggle out of them.

It's true. He is the Old Man of the Sea. I can't stand stupid people like Caliban, with their great deadweight of pettiness and selfishness and meanness of every kind. And the few have to carry it all.
The doctors and the teachers and the artists—not that they haven't
their traitors, but what hope there is, is with them—with us.

Because I'm one of them.

I'm one of them. I feel it and I've tried to prove it. I felt it during my last year at Ladymont. There were the few of us who
cared, and there were the silly ones, the snobbish ones, the would-
be debutantes and the daddy's darlings and the horsophiles and the
sex-cats. I'll never go back to Ladymont. Because I couldn't stand
that suffocating atmosphere of the "done" thing and the "right"
people and the "nice" behaviour. (Boadicaea writing "in spite of
her weird political views" on my report—how dared she?) I *will*
not be an old girl of such a place.

Why *should* we tolerate their beastly Calibanity? Why should
every vital and creative and good person be martyred by the great
universal stodge around?

In this situation I'm a representative.

A martyr. Imprisoned, unable to grow. At the mercy of this resentment, this hateful millstone envy of the Calibans of this world. Because they all hate us, they hate us for being different, for not being them, for their own not being like us. They persecute us, they crowd us out, they send us to Coventry, they sneer at us, they yawn at us, they blindfold themselves and stuff up their ears. They do anything to avoid having to take notice of us and respect us. They go crawling after the great ones among us when they're dead. They pay thousands and thousands for the Van Goghs and Modiglianis they'd have spat on at the time they were painted. Guffawed at. Made coarse jokes about.

I hate them.

I hate the uneducated and the ignorant. I hate the pompous and the phoney. I hate the jealous and the resentful. I hate the crabbed and the mean and the petty. I hate all ordinary dull little people who aren't ashamed of being dull and little. I hate what G.P. calls the New People, the new-class people with their cars and their money and their tellies and their stupid vulgarities and their stupid crawling imitation of the bourgeoisie.

I love honesty and freedom and giving. I love making, I love doing. I love being to the full, I love everything which is not sitting and watching and copying and dead at heart.

G.P. was laughing at my being Labour one day (early on). I remember he said, you are supporting the party which brought the New People into existence—do you realize that?

I said (I was shocked, because from what he had said about other things, I thought he must be Labour, I knew he had been a Communist once), I'd rather we had the New People than poor people.

He said, the New People are still the poor people. Theirs is the new form of poverty. The others hadn't any money and these haven't any soul.

He suddenly said, have you read *Major Barbara?*

How it proved people had to be saved financially before you could save their souls.

They forgot one thing, he said. They brought in the Welfare State, but they forgot Barbara herself. Affluence, affluence, and not a soul to see.

I know he's wrong somewhere (he was exaggerating). One *must* be on the Left. Every decent person I've ever met has been anti-Tory. But I see what he feels, I mean I feel it myself more and more, this awful deadweight of the fat little New People on everything. Corrupting everything. Vulgarizing everything. Raping the countryside, as D says in his squire moods. Everything mass-produced. Mass-everything.

I know we're supposed to face the herd, control the stampede—it's like a Wild West film. Work for them and tolerate them. I shall never go to the Ivory Tower, that's the most despicable thing, to choose to leave life because it doesn't suit you. But sometimes it is frightening, thinking of the struggle life is if one takes it seriously.

All this is talk. Probably I shall meet someone and fall in love with him and marry him and things will seem to change and I shan't care any more. I shall become a Little Woman. One of the enemy.

But this *is* what I feel these days. That I belong to a sort of band of people who have to stand against all the rest. I don't know who they are—famous men, dead and living, who've fought for the right things and created and painted in the right way, and un-famous people I know who don't lie about things, who try not to be lazy, who try to be human and intelligent. Yes, people like G.P., for all his faults. His Fault.

They're not even good people. They have weak moments. Sex moments and drink moments. Coward and money moments. They have holidays in the Ivory Tower. But a part of them is one with the band.

The Few.

November 9th

I'm vain. I'm not one of them. I *want* to be one of them, and that's not the same thing.

Of course, Caliban is not typical of the New People. He's hopelessly out of date (he will call the record-player, the "gramophone"). And there's his lack of confidence. They're not ashamed of themselves. I remember D saying they think they're all equal to the best as soon as they have a telly and a car. But deep down Caliban's one of them—there's this hatred of the unusual, this wanting everybody to be the same. And the awful misuse of money. Why should people have money if they don't know how to use it?

It sickens me every time I think of all the money Caliban has won; and of all the other people like him who win money.

So selfish, so evil.

G.P. said, that day, the honest poor are the moneyless vulgar rich. Poverty forces them to have good qualities and pride in other things besides money. Then when they have money they don't know what to do with it. They forget all the old virtues, which weren't real virtues anyway. They think the only virtue is to make more money and to spend. They can't imagine that there are people to whom money is nothing. That the most beautiful things are quite independent of money.

I'm not being frank. I still want money. But I know that it's wrong. I believe G.P.—I don't have to believe him when he says it, I can see it's true—he hardly worries about money at all. He has just enough to buy his materials, to live, to have a working holiday every year, to manage. And there're a dozen others—Peter. Bill McDonald. Stefan. They don't live in the world of money. If they have it they spend it. If they don't they go without.

Persons like Caliban have no head for money. They've only got to have a little, like the New People, and they become beastly. All the horrid people who wouldn't give me money when I was collecting. I could tell, I only had to look in their faces. Bourgeois people give because they're embarrassed if you pester them. Intelligent people give or at least they look honestly at you and say no. They're not ashamed not to give. But the New People are too mean to give and too small to admit it. Like the horrid man in Hampstead (he was one of them) who said, I'll give you half a dollar if you can prove it doesn't go into someone's pocket. He thought he was being funny.

I turned my back on him, which was wrong, because my pride was less important than the children. So I put a half-crown in for him later.

But I still hate him.

With Caliban it's as if somebody made him drink a whole bottle of whisky. He can't take it. The only thing that kept him decent before was being poor. Being stuck to one place and one job.

It's like putting a blind man in a fast car and telling him to drive where and how he likes.

A nice thing to end with. The Bach record came today, I've played it twice already. Caliban said it was nice, but he wasn't "musical." However, he sat with the right sort of expression on his face. I'm going to play the parts I like again. I'm going to lie in bed in the darkness and the music and think I'm with G.P. and he's lying over there with his eyes shut and his pitted cheek and his Jew's nose; as if he was on his own tomb. Only there's nothing of death in him.

Even so. This evening Caliban was late coming down.

Where've you been, I snapped at him. He just looked surprised, said nothing. I said, you seem so late.

Ridiculous. I wanted him to come. I often want him to come. I'm as lonely as that.

November 10th

We had an argument this evening about his money. I said he ought to give most of it away. I tried to shame him into giving some away. But he won't trust anything. That's what's really wrong with him. Like my man in Hampstead, he doesn't trust people to collect money and use it for the purpose they say they will. He thinks everyone is corrupt, everyone tries to get money and keep it.

It's no good my saying I know it's used for the right purpose. He says, how do you know? And of course I can't tell him. I can only say I feel sure—it *must* go where it's needed. Then he smiles as if I'm too naïve to have any right on my side.

I accused him (not very bitterly) of not having sent the CND cheque. I challenged him to produce a receipt. He said the gift was anonymous, he hadn't sent his address. It was on the tip of my tongue to say, I shall go and find out when I'm free. But I didn't. Because it would be one more reason for him not to set me free. He was red, I'm sure he was lying, as he lied about the letter to D and M.

It's not so much a lack of generosity—a real miserliness. I mean (forgetting the absurdity of the situation), he is generous to me. He spends hundreds of pounds on me. He'd kill me with kindness. With chocolates and cigarettes and food and flowers. I said I'd like some French perfume the other evening—it was just a whim, really, but this room smells of disinfectant and Airwick. I have enough baths, but I don't feel clean. And I said I wished I could go and sniff the various scents to see which I liked best. He came in this morning with *fourteen* different bottles. He'd ransacked all the chemists' shops. It's mad. Forty pounds' worth. It's like living in the Arabian Nights. Being the favourite in the harem. But the one perfume you really want is freedom.

If I could put a starving child before him and give it food and let him watch it grow well, I know he'd give money. But everything beyond what he pays for and sees himself get is suspicious to him. He doesn't believe in any other world but the one he lives in and sees. He's the one in prison; in his own hateful narrow present world.

November 12th

The last night but one. I daren't think about it, about not escaping. I've kept reminding him, recently. But now I feel I should have sprung it on him more or less suddenly. Today I decided that I would organize a little party tomorrow night. I shall say I feel differently towards him, that I want to be his friend and lameduck him in London.

It won't be altogether a lie, I feel a responsibility towards him that I don't really understand. I so often hate him, I think I ought to forever hate him. Yet I don't always. My pity wins, and I do want to help him. I think of people I could introduce him to. He could go to Caroline's psychiatrist friend. I'd be like Emma and arrange a marriage for him, and with happier results. Some little Harriet Smith, with whom he could be mousy and sane and happy.

I know I have to steel myself against not being freed. I tell myself it's a chance in a hundred that he'll keep his word.

But he must keep his word.

G.P.

I hadn't seen him for two months, more than two months. Being in France and Spain and then at home. (I did try to see him twice, but he was away all September.) There was a postcard in answer to my letters. That was all.

I telephoned him and asked him if I could go round, the first evening I was back with Caroline. He said the next day, there were some people there that evening.

He seemed glad to see me. I was trying to look as if I hadn't tried to look pretty. I had.

And I told him all about France and Spain and the Goyas and Albi and everything else. Piers. And he listened, he wouldn't

really say what he had been doing, but later he showed me some
of the things he'd done in the Hebrides. And I felt ashamed. Because we'd none of us done much, we'd been too busy lying in the
sun (I mean too lazy) and looking at great pictures to do much
drawing or anything.

I said (having gushed for at least an hour) I'm talking too much.
He said, I don't mind.

He was getting the rust off an old iron wheel with some acid.
He'd seen it in a junk-shop in Edinburgh, and brought it all the
way down. It had strange obtuse teeth, he thought it was part of
an old church clock. Very elegant tapered spoke-arms. It was
beautiful.

We didn't say anything for a while, I was leaning beside him
against his bench watching him clean off the rust. Then he said,
I've missed you.

I said, you can't have.

He said, you've disturbed me.

I said (knight to cover his pawn), have you seen Antoinette?

He said, no. I thought I told you I gave her the boot. He looked
sideways. His lizard look. Still shocked? I shook my head.

Forgiven?

I said, there was nothing to forgive.

He said, I kept on thinking about you in the Hebrides. I wanted
to show you things.

I said, I wished you were with us in Spain.

He was busy emery-papering between the teeth. He said, it's
very old, look at this corrosion. Then, in the same tone, in fact I
decided that I want to marry you. I didn't say anything and I
wouldn't look at him.

He said, I asked you to come here when I was alone, because
I've been thinking quite hard about this. I'm twice your age, I

ought to take things like this in my stride—Christ only knows it's not the first time. No, let me finish now. I've decided I've got to stop seeing you. I was going to tell you that when you came in. I can't go on being disturbed by you. I shall be if you keep on coming here. This isn't a roundabout way of asking you to marry me. I'm trying to make it quite impossible. You know what I am, you know I'm old enough to be your father, I'm not reliable at all. Anyhow, you don't love me.

I said, I can't explain it. There isn't a word for it.

Precisely, he answered. He was cleaning his hands with petrol. Very clinical and matter-of-fact. So I have to ask you to leave me to find my peace again.

I stared at his hands. I was shocked.

He said, in some ways you're older than I am. You've never been deeply in love. Perhaps you never will be. He said, love goes on happening to you. To men. You become twenty again, you suffer as twenty suffers. All the dotty irrationalities of twenty. I may seem very reasonable at the moment, but I don't feel it. When you telephoned I nearly peed in my pants with excitement. I'm an old man in love. Stock comedy figure. Very stale. Not even funny.

Why do you think I'll never be deeply in love, I said. He took a terribly long time to clean his hands.

He said, I said perhaps.

I'm only just twenty.

He said, an ash tree a foot high is still an ash tree. But I did say perhaps.

And you're not old. It's nothing to do with our ages.

He gave me a faintly hurt look then, smiled and said, you must leave me some loophole.

We went to make coffee, the wretched little kitchen, and I

thought, anyhow I couldn't face up to living here with him—just the domestic effort. A vile irrelevant wave of bourgeois cowardice.

He said, with his back to me, until you went away I thought it was just the usual thing. At least I tried to think it was. That's why I misbehaved myself with your Swedish friend. To exorcise you. But you came back. In my mind. Again and again, up north. I used to go out of the farmhouse at night, into the garden. Look south. You do understand?

Yes, I said.

It was you, you see. Not just the other thing.

Then he said, it's a sudden look you have. When you're not a kid any more.

What sort of look?

The woman you will be, he said.

A nice woman?

A much more than nice woman.

There's no word to say how he said it. Sadly, almost unwillingly. Tenderly, but a shade bitterly. And honestly. Not teasing, not being dry. But right out of his real self. I'd been looking down all the time we were talking, but he made me look up then, and our eyes met and I know something passed between us. I could feel it. Almost a physical touch. Changing us. His saying something he totally meant, and my feeling it.

He remained staring at me, so that I was embarrassed. And still he stared. I said, please don't stare at me like that.

He came and put his arm round my shoulders then and led me gently towards the door. He said, you are very pretty, at times you're beautiful. You are sensitive, you are eager, you try to be honest, you manage to be both your age and natural and a little priggish and old-fashioned at the same time. You even play chess quite well. You're just the daughter I'd like to have. That's probably why I've wanted you so much these last few months.

He pushed me through the door, face forward, so I couldn't see him.

I can't say such things to you without turning your head. And you mustn't turn your head, in any sense. Now, go.

I felt him press my shoulders an instant. And he kissed the back of my head. Pushed me away. And I went two or three steps down the stairs before I stopped and looked back. He was smiling, but it was a sad smile.

I said, please don't let it be too long.

He just shook his head. I don't know if he meant "no, not too long" or "it's no good hoping it will be anything else but very long." Perhaps he didn't know himself. But he looked sad. He looked sad all through.

Of course I *looked* sad. But I didn't really feel sad. Or it wasn't a sadness that hurt, not an all-through one. I rather enjoyed it. Beastly, but I did. I sang on the way home. The romance, the mystery of it. Living.

I thought I knew I didn't love him. I'd won that game.

And what has happened since?

That first day or two, I kept on thinking he would telephone, that it was all a sort of whim. Then I would think, I shan't see him again for months, perhaps years, and it seemed ridiculous. Unnecessary. Stupid beyond belief. I hated what seemed *his* weakness. I thought, if he's like this, to hell with him.

That didn't last very long. I decided to decide that it was for the best. He was right. It was best to make a clean break. I would concentrate on work. Be practical and efficient and everything that I'm not really by nature.

All that time I kept thinking, do I love him? Then, obviously, there was so much doubt, I couldn't.

And now I have to write down what I feel now. Because I have changed again. I know it. I feel it.

Looks; I know it is idiotically wrong to have preconceived notions about looks. Getting excited when Piers kisses me. Having to stare at him sometimes (not when he would notice, because of his vanity) but feeling his looks intensely. Like a beautiful drawing of something ugly. You forget about the ugliness. I know Piers is morally and psychologically ugly—just plain and dull, phoney.

But even there I've changed.

I think about G.P. holding me and caressing me.

There's a sort of nasty perverted curiosity in me—I mean, all the women he's had and all the things he must know about being in bed.

I can imagine his making love to me and it doesn't disgust me. Very expert and gentle. Fun. All sorts of things, but not *the* thing. If it's to be for life.

Then there's his weakness. The feeling that he would probably betray me. And I've always thought of marriage as a sort of young adventure, two people of the same age setting out together, discovering together, growing together. But I would have nothing to tell him, nothing to show him. All the helping would be on his side.

I've seen so little of the world. I know that G.P. in many ways represents a sort of ideal now. His sense of what counts, his independence, his refusal to do what the others do. His standing apart. It has to be someone with those qualities. And no one else I've met has them as he has. People at the Slade *seem* to have them—but

they're so young. It's easy to be frank and to hell with convention
when you're our age.

Once or twice I've wondered whether it wasn't all a trap. Like
a sacrifice in chess. Supposing I had said on the stairs, do what you
like with me, but don't send me away?

No, I won't believe that of him.

Time-lag. Two years ago I couldn't have dreamed of falling in
love with an older man. I was always the one who argued for equal
ages at Ladymont. I remember being one of the most disgusted
when Susan Grillet married a Beastly Baronet nearly three times
her age. Minny and I used to talk about guarding against being
"father" types (because of M) and marrying father-husbands. I
don't feel that any more. I think I need a man older than myself
because I always seem to see through the boys I meet. And I don't
feel G.P. is a father-husband.

It's no good. I could go on writing arguments for and against
all night.

Emma. The business of being between inexperienced girl and
experienced woman and the awful problem of *the* man. Caliban is
Mr. Elton. Piers is Frank Churchill. But is G.P. Mr. Knightley?

Of course G.P. has lived a life and has views that would make
Mr. Knightley turn in his grave. But Mr. Knightley could never
have been a phoney. Because he was a hater of pretence, selfishness, snobbism.

And they both have the one man's name I really can't stand.
George. Perhaps there's a moral in that.

November 18th

I have eaten nothing for five days. I've drunk some water. He brings me food, but I have touched *not one crumb*.

Tomorrow I am going to start eating again.

About half an hour ago, I stood up and felt faint. Had to sit down again. I haven't felt ill so far. Just tummy pains and a bit weak. But this was something different. A warning.

I'm not going to die for him.

I haven't needed food. I have been so full of hatred for him and his beastliness.

His vile cowardice.

His selfishness.

His Calibanity.

November 19th

For all that time, I didn't want to write. Sometimes I wanted to. Then it seemed weak. Like accepting things. I knew as soon as I wrote it down I'd go off the boil. But now I think it needs writing down. Recording. He did *this* to me.

Outrage.

What little friendship, humanity, good nature there was between us has gone.

From now on we are enemies. Both ways. He said things that showed *he* hates me as well.

He resents my existence. That's exactly it.

He doesn't realize it fully yet, because he's trying to be nice to me at the moment. But he's much nearer than he was. One day soon he's going to wake up and say to himself—I hate her.

Something nasty.

When I came round from the chloroform I was in bed. I had my last underclothes on, but he must have taken everything else off.

I was furious, that first night. Mad with disgust. His beastly gloating hands touching me. Peeling my stockings off. Loathsome.

Then I thought of what he might have done. And hadn't. I decided not to fly at him.

But silence.

To shout at someone suggests that there's still contact.

Since then I've thought two things.

First: he's weird enough to have undressed me without thinking, according to some mad notion of the "proper" thing to do. Perhaps he thought I couldn't lie in bed with my clothes on.

And then that perhaps it was a sort of reminder. Of all the

things he might have done, but hadn't. His chivalry. And I accept that. I have been lucky.

But I even find it frightening that he didn't do anything. What is he?

There is a great rift between us now. It can never be bridged.

He says now he will release me in another four weeks. Just talk. I don't believe him. So I've warned him I'm going to try to kill him. I would now. I wouldn't think twice about it.

I've seen how wrong I was before. How blind.

I prostituted myself to Caliban. I mean, I let him spend all that money on me, and although I told myself it was fair, it wasn't. Because I felt vaguely grateful, I've been nice to him. Even my teasing was nice, even my sneering and spitting at him. Even my breaking things. Because it takes notice of him. And my attitude should have been what it will be from now on—ice.

Freeze him to death.

He is absolutely inferior to me in all ways. His one superiority is his ability to keep me here. That's the only power he has. He can't behave or think or speak or do anything else better than I can—nearly as well as I can—so he's going to be the Old Man of the Sea until I shake him off somehow.

It will have to be by force.

I've been sitting here and thinking about God. I don't think I believe in God any more. It is not only me, I think of all the millions who must have lived like this in the war. The Anne Franks. And back through history. What I feel I *know* now is that God doesn't intervene. He lets us suffer. If you pray for liberty then you may get relief just because you pray, or because things happen anyhow which bring you liberty. But God can't hear. There's nothing human like hearing or seeing or pitying or helping about him. I mean perhaps God has created the world and the fundamental laws of matter and evolution. But he can't care about the individuals. He's planned it so some individuals are happy, some sad, some lucky, some not. Who is sad, who is not, he doesn't know, and he doesn't care. So he doesn't exist, really.

These last few days I've felt Godless. I've felt cleaner, less muddled, less blind. I still believe in a God. But he's so remote, so cold, so mathematical. I see that we have to live as if there is no God. Prayer and worship and singing hymns—all silly and useless.

I'm trying to explain why I'm breaking with my principles (about never committing violence). It is still my principle, but I see you have to break principles sometimes to survive. It's no good trusting vaguely in your luck, in Providence or God's being kind to you. You have to act and fight for yourself.

The sky is absolutely empty. Beautifully pure and empty.

As if the architects and builders would live in all the houses they built! Or could live in them all. It's obvious, it stares you in the face. There *must* be a God and he *can't* know anything about us.

(Same evening.) I've been very mean with him all day. Several times he's tried to speak, but I've shut him up. Did I want him to bring me anything? I said, I want nothing. I am your prisoner. If you give me food I shall eat it to keep alive. Our relations from now on are strictly those of a prisoner and a warder. Now please leave me alone.

Luckily I've plenty to read. He'll go on bringing me cigarettes (if he doesn't I shan't ask him for them) and food. That's all I want of him.

He's not human; he's an empty space disguised as a human.

November 20th

I'm making him wish he never set eyes on me. He brought in some baked beans for lunch. I was reading on the bed. He stood for a moment and then started to go out. I jumped to the table, picked up the plate and hurled it at him. I don't like baked beans, he knows it, I suppose he'd been lazy. I wasn't in a temper, I just pretended. He stood there with the filthy little bits of orange sauce on his so-clean clothes and looking sheepish. I don't want any lunch, I snapped at him. And turned my back.

I ate chocolates all the afternoon. He didn't reappear until supper-time. There was caviare and smoked salmon and cold chicken (he buys them ready-cooked somewhere)—all things he knows I like—and a dozen other things he knows I like, the cunning brute. It's not the buying them that's cunning, it's just that I can't help being grateful (I didn't actually say I was grateful, but I wasn't sharp), it's that he presents them so humbly, with such an air of please-don't-thank-me and I-deserve-it-all. When he was arranging my supper-things on the table, I had an irresistible desire to giggle. Awful. I wanted to collapse on the bed and scream. He was so perfectly himself. And I am so cooped up.

Down here my moods change so rapidly. All determination to do one thing one hour; all for another the next.

It's no use. I'm not a hater by nature. It's as if somewhere in me a certain amount of good-will and kindness is manufactured every day; and it must come out. If I bottle it up, then it bursts out.

I wasn't nice to him, I don't want to be nice to him, I shan't be nice to him. But it was a struggle not to be ordinary to him. (I mean little things like "that was a nice meal.") As it was I said nothing. When he said, "Will that be all" (like a butler), I said,

"Yes, you can go now," and turned my back. He would have got a shock if he could have seen my face. It was smiling, and when he shut the door, I was laughing. I couldn't help it again. Hysteria.

Something I have been doing a lot these last days. Staring at myself in the mirror. Sometimes I don't seem real to myself, it suddenly seems that it isn't my reflection only a foot or two away. I have to look aside. I look all over my face, at my eyes, I try to see what my eyes say. What I am. Why I'm here.

It's because I'm so lonely. I have to look at an intelligent face. Anyone who has been locked away like this would understand. You become very real to yourself in a strange way. As you never were before. So much of you is given to ordinary people, suppressed, in ordinary life. I watch my face and I watch it move as if it is someone else's. I stare myself out.

I sit with myself.

Sometimes it's like a sort of spell, and I have to put my tongue out and wrinkle my nose to break it.

I sit down here in the absolute silence with my reflection, in a sort of state of mystery.

In a trance.

It's the middle of the night. I can't sleep.

I hate myself.

I nearly became a murderess tonight.

I shall never be the same again.

It is difficult to write. My hands are bound. I've got the gag off.

It all began at lunch. I realized that I was having to struggle not to be nice to him. Because I felt I must talk to someone. Even him. At least he is a human being. When he went away after lunch, I wanted to call him back to talk. What I felt was quite different from what I decided I should feel two days ago. So I made a new decision. I could never hit him with anything down here. I've watched him so much with that in mind. And he never turns his back to me. Besides, there's no weapon. So I thought, I've got to get upstairs and find something, some means. I had several ideas.

Otherwise I was afraid I would fall into the old trap of pitying him.

So I was a bit nicer at supper-time and said I needed a bath (which I did). He went away, came back, we went up. And there, it seemed a sign, specially left for me, was a small axe. It was on the kitchen window-sill, which is next to the door. He must have been chopping wood outside and forgotten to hide it. My always being down here.

We passed indoors too quickly for me to do anything then.

But I lay in the bath and thought. I decided it must be done. I had to catch up the axe and hit him with the blunt end, knock him out. I hadn't the least idea where on the head was the best place to hit or how hard it had to be.

Then I asked to go straight back. As we went out through the kitchen door, I dropped my talcum powder and things and stood to one side, towards the window-sill, as if I was looking to see where they'd gone. He did just what I wanted and bent forward to pick them up. I wasn't nervous, I picked the axe up very neatly, I didn't scrape the blade and it was the blunt end. But then . . . it was like waking up out of a bad dream. I had to hit him and I couldn't but I had to.

Then he began to straighten up (all this happened in a flash, really) and I did hit him. But he was turning and I didn't hit straight. Or hard enough. I mean, I lashed out in a panic at the last moment. He fell sideways, but I knew he wasn't knocked out, he still kept hold of me, I suddenly felt I had to kill him or he would kill me. I hit him again, but he had his arm up, at the same time he kicked out and knocked me off my feet.

It was too horrible. Panting, straining, like animals. Then suddenly I knew it was—I don't know, undignified. It sounds absurd, but that was it. Like a statue lying on its side. Like a fat woman trying to get up off the grass.

We got up, he pushed me roughly towards the door, keeping a tight hold of me. But that was all. I had a funny feeling it was the same for him—disgusting.

I thought someone may have heard, even though I couldn't call out. But it was windy. Wet and cold. No one would have been out.

I've been lying on the bed. I soon stopped crying. I've been lying for hours in the dark and thinking.

I am ashamed. I let myself down vilely.

I've come to a series of decisions. Thoughts.

Violence and force are wrong. If I use violence I descend to his level. It means that I have no real belief in the power of reason, and sympathy and humanity. That I lameduck people only because it flatters me, not because I believe they need my sympathy. I've been thinking back to Ladymont, to people I lameducked there. Sally Margison. I lameducked her just to show the Vestal Virgins that I was cleverer than they. That I could get her to do things for me that she wouldn't do for them. Donald and Piers (because I've lameducked him in a sense, too)—but they're both attractive young men. There were probably hundreds of other people who needed lameducking, my sympathy, far more than those two. And anyway, most girls would have jumped at the chance of lameducking them.

I've given up too soon with Caliban. I've got to take up a new attitude with him. The prisoner-warder idea was silly. I won't spit at him any more. I'll be silent when he irritates me. I'll treat him as someone who needs all my sympathy and understanding. I'll go on trying to teach him things about art. Other things.

There's only one way to do things. The right way. Not what they meant by "the Right Way" at Ladymont. But the way you feel is right. My own right way.

I am a moral person. I am not ashamed of being moral. I will not let Caliban make me immoral; even though he deserves all my hatred and bitterness *and* an axe in his head.

(Later.) I've been nice to him. That is, not the cat I've been lately. As soon as he came in I made him let me look at his head, and I dabbed some Dettol on it. He was nervous. I make him jumpy. He doesn't trust me. That is precisely the state I shouldn't have got him into.

It's difficult, though. When I'm being beastly to him, he has such a way of looking sorry for himself that I begin to hate myself. But as soon as I begin to be nice to him, a sort of self-satisfaction seems to creep into his voice and his manner (very discreet, he's been humility itself all day, no reproach about last night, of course) and I begin to want to goad and slap him again.

A tightrope.

But it's cleared the air.

(Night.) I tried to teach him what to look for in abstract art after supper. It's hopeless. He has it fixed in his poor dim noddle that art is fiddling away (he can't understand why I don't "rub out") until you get an exact photographic likeness and that making lovely cool designs (Ben Nicholson) is vaguely immoral. I can see it makes a nice pattern, he said. But he won't concede that "making a nice pattern" is art. With him, it's that certain words have terribly strong undertones. Everything to do with art embarrasses him (and I suppose fascinates him). It's *all* vaguely immoral. He knows great art is great, but "great" means locked away in museums and spoken about when you want to show off. Living art, modern art shocks him. You can't talk about it with him because the word "art" starts off a whole series of shocked, guilty ideas in him.

I wish I knew if there were many people like him. Of course I know the vast majority—especially the New People—don't care a damn about any of the arts. But is it because they are like him? Or because they just couldn't care less? I mean, does it really bore them (so that they don't need it at all in their lives) or does it secretly shock and dismay them, so that they have to pretend to be bored?

November 23rd

I've just finished *Saturday Night and Sunday Morning*. It's shocked me. It's shocked me in itself and it's shocked me because of where I am.

It shocked me in the same way as *Room at the Top* shocked me when I read it last year. I know they're very clever, it must be wonderful to be able to write like Alan Sillitoe. Real, un-phoney. Saying what you mean. If he was a painter it would be wonderful (he'd be like John Bratby, much better) he'd be able to set Nottingham down and it would be wonderful in paint. Because he painted so well, put down what he saw, people would admire him. But it isn't enough to write well (I mean choose the right words and so on) to be a good writer. Because I think *Saturday Night and Sunday Morning* is disgusting. I think Arthur Seaton is disgusting. And I think the most dis-gusting thing of all is that Alan Sillitoe doesn't show that he's disgusted by his young man. I think they think young men like that are really rather fine.

I hated the way Arthur Seaton just doesn't care about anything outside his own little life. He's mean, narrow, selfish, brutal. Be-cause he's cheeky and hates his work and is successful with women, he's supposed to be vital.

The only thing I like about him is the feeling that there is some-thing there that could be used for good if it could be got at.

It's the inwardness of such people. Their not caring what hap-pens anywhere else in the world. In life.

Their being-in-a-box.

Perhaps Alan Sillitoe wanted to attack the society that pro-duces such people. But he doesn't make it clear. I know what he's done, he's fallen in love with what he's painting. He started out to paint it as ugly as it is, but then its ugliness conquered him, and he started trying to cheat. To prettify.

It shocked me too because of Caliban. I see there's something of Arthur Seaton in him, only in him it's turned upside down. I mean, he has that hate of other things and other people outside his own type. He has that selfishness—it's not even an honest selfishness, because he puts the blame on life and then enjoys being selfish with a free conscience. He's obstinate, too.

This has shocked me because I think everyone now except *us* (and we're contaminated) has this selfishness and this brutality, whether it's hidden, mousy, and perverse, or obvious and crude. Religion's as good as dead, there's nothing to hold back the New People, they'll grow stronger and stronger and swamp us.

No, they won't. Because of David. Because of people like Alan Sillitoe (it says on the back he was the son of a labourer). I mean the intelligent New People will always revolt and come across to our side. The New People destroy themselves because they're so stupid. They can never keep the intelligent ones with them. Especially the young ones. We want something better than just money and keeping up with the Joneses.

But it's a battle. It's like being in a city and being besieged. They're all around. And we've got to hold out.

It's a battle between Caliban and myself. He is the New People and I am the Few.

I must fight with my weapons. Not his. Not selfishness and brutality and shame and resentment.

He's worse than the Arthur Seaton kind.

If Arthur Seaton saw a modern statue he didn't like, he'd smash it. But Caliban would drape a tarpaulin round it. I don't know which is worse. But I think Caliban's way is.

I'm getting desperate to escape. I can't get any relief from drawing or playing records or reading. The burning burning need I have (all prisoners must have) is for other people. Caliban is only half a person at the best of times. I want to see dozens and dozens of strange faces. Like being terribly thirsty and gulping down glass after glass of water. Exactly like that. I read once that nobody can stand more than ten years in prison, or more than one year of solitary confinement.

One just can't imagine what prison is like from outside. You think, well, there'd be lots of time to think and read, it wouldn't be too bad. But it is too bad. It's the slowness of time. I'll swear all the clocks in the world have gone centuries slower since I came here.

I shouldn't complain. This is a luxury prison.

And there's his diabolical cunning about the newspapers and radio and so on. I never read the papers very much, or listened to the news. But to be totally cut off. It's so strange. I feel I've lost all my bearings.

I spend hours lying on the bed thinking about how to escape. Endless.

November 25th

(Afternoon.) This morning I had a talk with him. I got him to sit as a model. Then I asked him what he really wanted me to do. Should I become his mistress? But that shocked him. He went red and said he could buy *that* in London.

I told him he was a Chinese box. And he is.

The innermost box is that I should love him; in all ways. With my body, with my mind. Respect him and cherish him. It's so utterly impossible—even if I could overcome the physical thing, how could I ever look in any way but down on him?

Battering his head on a stone wall.

I don't want to die. I feel full of endurance. I shall *always* want to survive. I will survive.

November 26th

The only unusual thing about him—how he loves me. Ordinary New People couldn't love anything as he loves me. That is blindly. Absolutely. Like Dante and Beatrice.

He enjoys being hopelessly in love with me. I expect Dante was the same. Mooning around knowing it was all quite hopeless and getting lots of good creative material from the experience.

Though of course Caliban can't get anything but his own miserable pleasure.

People who don't *make* anything. I hate them.

How frightened of dying I was in those first days. I don't want to die because I keep on thinking of the future. I'm *desperately* curious to know what life will bring to me. What will happen to me, how I'll develop, what I'll be in five years' time, in ten, in thirty. The man I will marry and the places I will live in and get to know. Children. It isn't just a selfish curiosity. This is the worst possible time in history to die. Space-travel, science, the whole world waking up and stretching itself. A new age is beginning. I know it's dangerous. But it's wonderful to be alive in it.

I love, I adore *my* age.

I keep on having thoughts today. One was: uncreative men plus opportunity-to-create equals evil men.

Another one was: killing him was breaking my word to what I believe. Some people would say—you're only a drop, your word-breaking is only a drop, it wouldn't matter. But all the evil in the world's made up of little drops. It's silly talking about the unimportance of the little drops. The little drops and the ocean are the same thing.

*   *   *

I've been daydreaming (not for the first time) about living with
G.P. He deceives me, he leaves me, he is brutal and cynical with
me, I am in despair. In these daydreams there isn't much sex, it's
just our living together. In rather romantic surroundings. Sea-
and-island northern landscapes. White cottages. Sometimes in the
Mediterranean. We are together, very close in spirit. All silly magazine stuff, really, in the details. But there is the closeness of spirit.
That is something real. And the situations I imagine (where he
forsakes me) are real. I mean, it kills me to think of them.

Sometimes I'm not very far from utter despair. No one knows I
am alive any more. I'm given up for dead by now, I'm accepted for
dead. There's that—the real situation. And there are the future
situations I sit on the bed here and think about: my *utter* love for
some man; I know I can't do things like love by halves, I know I
have love pent up in me, I shall throw myself away, lose my heart
and my body and my mind and soul to some cad like G.P. Who'll
betray me. I feel it. Everything is tender and rational at first in my
daydreams of living with him, but I know it wouldn't be in fact. It
would be all passion and violence. Jealousy. Despair. Sour. Something would be killed in me. He would be hurt, too.

If he really loved me he couldn't have sent me away.

If he really loved me he would have sent me away.

November 27th

Midnight.

I'll never escape. It drives me mad. I must must must do something. I feel as if I'm at the earth's heart. I've got the whole weight of the whole earth pressing in on this little box. It grows smaller smaller smaller. I can feel it contracting.

I want to scream sometimes. Till my voice is raw. To death.

I can't write it. There aren't the words.

Utter despair.

I've been like that all day. A kind of endless panic in slow-motion.

What can he have thought when he first got me here?

Something's gone wrong in his plans. I'm not acting like the girl of his dreams I was. I'm his pig in a poke.

Is that why he keeps me? Hoping the dream Miranda will appear?

Perhaps I should be his dream-girl. Put my arms round him and kiss him. Praise him, pat him, stroke him. Kiss him.

I didn't mean that. But it's made me think.

Perhaps I really should kiss him. More than kiss him. Love him. Make Prince Charming step out.

I'm thinking hours between each sentence I write.

I've got to make him feel that finally I've been touched by his chivalry and so on and so on . . .

This is extraordinary.

He would have to act.

I am sure I can do it. At least he's scrupulously clean. He never smells of anything but soap.

I'm going to sleep on it.

November 28th

I've come to a tremendous decision today.

I've imagined being in bed with him.

It's useless just kissing him. I've got to give him such a tremendous shock that he'll have to release me. Because you can't very well imprison someone who's given herself to you.

I shall be in his power. I couldn't ever go to the police. I should only want to hush it up.

It's so obvious. It stares one in the face.

Like a really good sacrifice at chess.

It's like drawing. You can't nibble at a line. The boldness *is* the line.

I thought out all the sex facts. I wish I knew a little more about men, I wish I was absolutely sure, that I didn't have to go on things heard, read, half understood, but I'm going to let him do what Piers wanted to do in Spain—what they call Scotch love. Get me into bed if he wants. Play with me if he wants. But not the final thing. I'm going to tell him it's my time of the month, if he tries to go too far. But I think he'll be so shocked that I shall be able to make him do what I want. I mean, I'm going to do all the seducing. I know it would be a terrible risk with ninety-nine men out of a hundred, but I think he's the hundredth. He'll stop when I tell him.

Even if it came to the point. He didn't stop. I'd take the risk.

There are two things. One's the need to make him let me go. The other's me. Something I wrote on Nov. 7th—"I love being to the full, I love everything which is not sitting and watching." But I'm not being to the full at all. I'm just sitting and watching. Not only here. With G.P.

All this Vestal Virgin talk about "saving yourself up" for the right man. I've always despised it. Yet I've always held back.

I'm mean with my body.

I've got to get this meanness out of the way.

I've got sunk in a sort of despair. Something will happen, I say. But nothing will, unless I make it.

I must act.

Another thing I wrote (one writes things and the implications shriek—it's like suddenly realizing one's deaf), "I must fight with my weapons. Not his. Not selfishness and brutality and shame and resentment."

Therefore with generosity (I give myself) and gentleness (I kiss the beast) and no-shame (I do what I do of my own free will) and forgiveness (he can't help himself).

Even a baby. *His* baby. Anything. For freedom.

The more I think about it the more I feel sure that this is the way. He has some secret. He must want me physically.

Perhaps he's "no good."

Whatever it is, it will come out.

We'll know where we are.

I haven't written much about G.P. these last days. But I think about him a great deal. The first and last thing I look at every day is his picture. I begin to hate that unknown girl who was his model. He must have gone to bed with her. Perhaps she was his first wife. I shall ask him when I get out.

Because the first thing I shall do—the first real positive thing, after I've seen the family, will be to go to see him. To tell him that he has been always in my thoughts. That he is the most important person I have ever met. The most real. That I *am* jealous of every woman who has ever slept with him. I still can't say that I love him. But now I begin to see that it's because I don't know what love is. I'm Emma with her silly little clever-clever theories of love and marriage, and love is something that comes in different clothes, with a different way and different face, and perhaps it takes a long time for you to accept it, to be able to call it love.

Perhaps he would be dry and cold when it came to it. Say I'm too young, he wasn't ever really serious, and—a thousand things. But I'm not afraid. I would risk it.

Perhaps he's in mid-*affaire* with somebody else.

I'd say, I've come back because I'm not sure any more that I'm not in love with you.

I'd say, I've been naked with a man I loathed. I've been at bottom. I'd let him have me.

But I still couldn't bear to see him sneaking off with someone else. Reducing it all to sex. I should wither up and die inside if he did.

I know it's not very emancipated of me.

This is what I feel.

Sex doesn't matter. Love does.

This afternoon I wanted to ask Caliban to post a letter to G.P. from me. Quite mad. Of course he wouldn't. He'd be jealous. But I so need to be walking up the stairs and pushing open the studio door, and seeing him at his bench, looking over his shoulder at me, as if he's not in the least interested to see who it is. Standing there, with his faint, faint smile and eyes that understand things so quickly.

This is useless. I'm thinking of the price before the painting.

Tomorrow. I must act *now*.

I started today really. I've called him Ferdinand (not Caliban) three times, and complimented him on a horrid new tie. I've smiled at him, I've dutifully tried to look as if I like everything about him. He certainly hasn't given any sign of having noticed it. But he won't know what's hit him tomorrow.

*   *   *

I can't sleep. I've got up again and put on G.P.'s clavichord record.
Perhaps he's been listening to it, too, and thinking of me. The In-
vention I like best is the one after the one he loves best—he loves
the fifth, and I the sixth. So we lie side by side in Bach. I always
used to think Bach was a bore. Now he overwhelms me, he is *so*
human, so full of moods and gentleness and wonderful tunes and
things so simple-deep I play them over and over again as once I
used to copy drawings I liked.

I think, perhaps I'll just try putting my arms round him and kissing him. No more. But he'd grow to like that. It would drag on.
It's got to be a shock.

All this business, it's bound up with my bossy attitude to life. I've
always known where I'm going, how I want things to happen. And
they *have* happened as I have wanted, and I have taken it for
granted that they have because *I* know where I'm going. But I
have been lucky in all sorts of things.

I've always tried to happen to life; but it's time I let life happen
to me.

November 30th

Oh, God.

    I've done something terrible.

    I've got to put it down. Look at it.

    It is so amazing. That I did it. That what happened happened.
That he is what he is. That I am what I am. Things left like this.
Worse than ever before.

    I decided to do it this morning. I knew I had to do something extraordinary. To give myself a shock as well as him.

    I arranged to have a bath. I was nice to him all day.

    I dolled myself up after the bath. Oceans of Mitsouko. I stood
in front of the fire, showing my bare feet for his benefit. I was
nervous. I didn't know if I could go through with it. And having
my hands bound. But I had three glasses of sherry quickly.

    I shut my eyes then and went to work.

    I made him sit down and then I sat down on his lap. He was so
stiff, so shocked, that I had to go on. If he'd clutched at me, perhaps I'd have stopped. I let the housecoat fall open, but he just sat
there with me on his lap. As if we had never met before and this
was some silly party game. Two strangers at a party, who didn't
much like each other.

    In a nasty perverted way it was exciting. A woman-in-me
reaching to a man-in-him. I can't explain, it was also the feeling
that he didn't know what to do. That he was sheer virgin. There
was an old lady of Cork who took a young priest for a walk. I
must have been drunk.

    I had to force him to kiss me. He made a sort of feeble pretence
of being afraid that he might lose his head. I don't care if you do,
I said. And I kissed him again. He did kiss me back then, as if he

wanted to press his wretched thin inhibited mouth right through my head. His mouth was sweet. He smelt clean and I shut my eyes. It wasn't so bad.

But then he suddenly went away by the window and he wouldn't come back. He wanted to run away, but he couldn't, so he stood by his desk, half turned, while I knelt half-naked by the fire and let my hair down, just to make it quite obvious. In the end I had to go up to him and bring him back to the fire. I made him undo my hands, he was like someone in a trance, and then I undressed him and I undressed myself.

I said, don't be nervous, I want to do this. Just be natural. But he wouldn't, he wouldn't. I did *everything* I could.

But nothing happened. He wouldn't thaw out. He did hold me tight once. But it wasn't natural. Just a desperate imitation of what he must think the real thing's like. Pathetically unconvincing.

He can't do it.

There's no man in him.

I got up, we were lying on the sofa, and knelt by him and told him not to worry. Mothered him. We put our clothes back on.

And gradually it all came out. The truth about him. And later, his real self.

A psychiatrist has told him he won't ever be able to do it.

He said he used to imagine us lying in bed together. Just lying. Nothing else. I offered to do that. But he didn't want to. Deep down in him, side by side with the beastliness, the sourness, there is a tremendous innocence. It rules him. He must protect it.

He said he loved me, even so.

I said, what you love is your own love. It's not love, it's selfishness. It's not me you think of, but what you feel about me.

I don't know what it is, he said.

And then I made a mistake, I felt it had all been a sacrifice in vain,

I felt I had to make him appreciate what I'd done, that he ought to let me go—so I tried to tell him. And his true self came out.

He got beastly. Wouldn't answer me.

We were further apart than ever. I said I pitied him and he flew at me. It was terrible. It made me cry.

The terrible coldness, the inhumanity of it.

Being his prisoner. Having to stay. Still.

And realizing at last that this is what he is.

Impossible to understand. What is he? What does he want? Why am I here if he can't do it?

As if I'd lit a fire in the darkness to try and warm us. And all I'd done was to see his real face by it.

The last thing I said was—We can't be further apart. We've been naked in front of each other.

But we are.

I feel better now.

I'm glad nothing worse happened. I was mad to take the risk.

It's enough to have survived.

He's been down, I've been out in the cellar, and it is absolutely plain. He's angry with me. He's never been angry like this before. This isn't a pet. It's a deep suppressed anger.

It makes me furious. Nobody could ever understand how much I put into yesterday. The effort of giving, of risking, of understanding. Of pushing back every natural instinct.

It's him. And it's this weird male thing. Now I'm no longer nice. They sulk if you don't give, and hate you when you do. Intelligent men must despise themselves for being like that. Their illogicality.

Sour men and wounded women.

Of course, I've discovered his secret. He hates that.

I've thought and thought about it.

He must always have known he couldn't do anything with me. Yet all his talk about loving me. That must mean something.

This is what I think it is. He can't have any normal pleasure from me. His pleasure is keeping me prisoner. Thinking of all the other men who would envy him if they knew. Having me.

So my being nice to him is ridiculous. I want to be so unpleasant that he gets no pleasure from having me. I'm going to fast again. Have absolutely nothing to do with him.

Strange ideas.

That I've done for the first time in my life something original. Something hardly anyone else can have done. I steeled myself when we were naked. I learnt what "to steel oneself" meant.

The last of the Ladymont me. It's dead.

I remember driving Piers's car somewhere near Carcassonne. They all wanted me to stop. But I wanted to do eighty. And I kept my foot down until I did. The others were frightened. So was I.

But it proved I could do it.

*   *   *

(Late afternoon.) Reading *The Tempest* again all the afternoon. Not the same at all, now what's happened has happened. The pity Shakespeare feels for his Caliban, I feel (beneath the hate and disgust) for my Caliban. Half-creatures.

"Not honour'd with a human shape."

"Caliban my slave, who never yields us kind answer."

"Whom stripes may move, not kindness."

> PROS. . . . and lodged thee
> In mine own cell, till thou didst seek to violate
> The honour of my child.
> CAL. O ho, O ho!—Would't had been done!
> Thou didst prevent me; I had peopled else
> This isle with Calibans. . . .

Prospero's contempt for him. His knowing that being kind is useless.

Stephano and Trinculo are the football pools. Their wine, the money he won.

Act III, scene 2. "I cried to dream again." Poor Caliban. But only because *he* never won the pools.

"I'll be wise hereafter."

"O brave new world."

O sick new world.

He's just gone. I said I would fast unless he let me come upstairs. Fresh air and daylight every day. He hedged. He was beastly. Sarcastic. He actually said I was "forgetting who was boss."

He's changed. He frightens me now.

I've given him until tomorrow morning to make up his mind.

December 2nd

I'm to go upstairs. He's going to convert a room. He said it would take a week. I said, all right, but if it's another put-off . . .

We'll see.

I lay in bed last night and thought of G.P. I thought of being in bed with him. I wanted to be in bed with him. I wanted the marvellous, the fantastic ordinariness of him.

His promiscuity is creative. Vital. Even though it hurts. He creates love and life and excitement around him; he lives, the people he loves remember him.

I've always felt like it sometimes. Promiscuous. Anyone I see, even just some boy in the Tube, some man, I think what would he be like in bed. I look at the mouths and their hands, put on a prim expression and think about them having me in bed.

Even Toinette, getting into bed with anyone. I used to think it was messy. But love is beautiful, any love. Even just sex. The only thing that is ugly is this frozen lifeless utter lack-love between Caliban and me.

This morning I was imagining I'd escaped and that Caliban was in court. I was speaking *for* him. I said his case was tragic, he needed sympathy and psychiatry. Forgiveness.

I wasn't being noble. I despise him too much to hate him.

It's funny. I probably should speak for him.

I knew we shouldn't be able to meet again.

I could never cure him. Because I'm his disease.

December 3rd

I shall go and have an *affaire* with G.P.

I'll marry him if he wants.

I want the adventure, the risk of marrying him.

I'm sick of being young. Inexperienced.

Clever at knowing but not at living.

I want his children in me.

My body doesn't count any more. If he just wants that he can have it. I couldn't ever be a Toinette. A collector of men.

Being cleverer (as I thought) than most men, and cleverer than all the girls I knew. I always thought I knew more, felt more, understood more.

But I don't even know enough to handle Caliban.

All sorts of bits left over from Ladymont days. From the days when I was a nice little middle-class doctor's daughter. They've gone now. When I was at Ladymont I thought I could manipulate a pencil very nicely. And then when I went to London, I began to find I couldn't. I was surrounded by people who were just as skilled as I was. More so. I haven't begun to know how to handle my life—or anyone else's.

I'm the one who needs lameducking.

It's like the day you realize dolls are dolls. I pick up my old self and I see it's silly. A toy I've played with too often. It's a little sad, like an old golliwog at the bottom of the cupboard.

Innocent and used-up and proud and silly.

G.P.

I shall be hurt, lost, battered and buffeted. But it will be like being in a gale of light, after this black hole.

It's simply that. He has the secret of life in him. Something spring-like. Not immoral.

It's as if I'd only seen him at twilight; and now suddenly I see him at dawn. He is the same, but everything is different.

I looked in the mirror today and I could see it in my eyes. They look much older and younger. It sounds impossible in words. But that's exactly it. I am older and younger. I am older because I have learnt, I am younger because a lot of me consisted of things older people had taught me. All the mud of their stale ideas on the shoe of me.

The new shoe of me.

The power of women! I've never felt so full of mysterious power. Men are a joke.

We're so weak physically, so helpless with things. Still, even today. But we're stronger than they are. We can stand their cruelty. They can't stand ours.

I think—I will give myself to G.P. He can have me. And whatever he does to me I shall still have my woman-me he can never touch.

All this is wild talk. But I feel full of urges. New independence.

I don't think about now. Today. I know I'm going to escape. I feel it. I can't explain. Caliban can never win against me.

I think of paintings I shall do.

Last night I thought of one, it was a sort of butter-yellow (farm-butter-yellow) field rising to a white luminous sky and the sun just rising. A strange rose-pink, I knew it exactly, full of hushed stillness, the beginning of things, lark-song without larks.

Two strange contradictory dreams.

The first one was very simple. I was walking in the fields, I don't know who I was with, but it was someone I liked very much, a man. G.P. perhaps. The sun shining on young corn. And suddenly we saw swallows flying low over the corn. I could see their backs gleaming, like dark blue silk. They were very low, twittering all around us, all flying in the same direction, low and happy. And I felt full of happiness. I said, how extraordinary, look at the swallows. It was very simple, the unexpected swallows and the sun and the green corn. I was filled with happiness. The *purest* spring feeling. Then I woke up.

Later I had another dream. I was at the window on the first floor of a large house (Ladymont?) and there was a black horse below. It was angry, but I felt safe because it was below and outside. But suddenly it turned and galloped at the house and to my horror it leapt gigantically up and straight at me with bared teeth. It came crashing through the window. Even then I thought, it will kill itself, I am safe. But it sprawled and flailed round in the small room and I suddenly realized it was going to attack me. There was nowhere to escape. I woke again, I had to put on the light.

It was violence. It was all I hate and all I fear.

December 4th

I shan't go on keeping a diary when I leave here. It's not healthy.
It keeps me sane down here, gives me somebody to talk to. But it's
vain. You write what you want to hear.

It's funny. You don't do that when you draw yourself. No
temptation to cheat.

It's sick, sick, all this thinking about me. Morbid.

I long to paint and paint *other* things. Fields, southern houses,
landscapes, vast wide-open things in vast wide-open light.

It's what I've been doing today. Moods of light recalled from
Spain. Ochre walls burnt white in the sunlight. The walls of Avila.
Cordoba courtyards. I don't try to reproduce the place, but the
light of the place.

Fiat lux.

I've been playing the Modern Jazz Quartet's records over and
over again. There's no night in their music, no smoky dives.
Bursts and sparkles and little fizzes of light, starlight, and sometimes high noon, tremendous everywhere light, like chandeliers of
diamonds floating in the sky.

December 5th

G.P.

The Rape of Intelligence. By the moneyed masses, the New People.

Things he says. They shock you, but you remember them. They stick. Hard, meant to last.

I've been doing skyscapes all day. I just draw a line an inch from the bottom. That's the earth. Then I think of nothing but the sky. June sky, December, August, spring-rain, thunder, dawn, dusk. I've done dozens of skies. Pure sky, nothing else. Just the simple line and the skies above.

A strange thought: I would not want this not to have happened. Because if I escape I shall be a completely different and I think better person. Because if I don't escape, if something dreadful happened, I shall still know that the person I was and would have stayed if this hadn't happened was not the person I now want to be.

It's like firing a pot. You have to risk the cracking and the warping.

Caliban's very quiet. A sort of truce.

I'm going to ask to go up tomorrow. I want to see if he's actually doing anything.

Today I asked him to bind me and gag me and let me sit at the foot of the cellar steps with the door out open. In the end he agreed. So I could look up and see the sky. A pale grey sky. I saw birds fly across, pigeons, I think. I heard outside sounds. This is the first proper daylight I've seen for two months. It lived. It made me cry.

December 6th

I've been up for a bath and we've been looking at the room I shall occupy. He has done some things. He's going to see if he can't find an antique windsor chair. I drew it for him.

It's made me feel happy.

I'm restless. I can't write here. I feel half-escaped already.

The thing that made me feel he was more normal was this little bit of dialogue.

> M. *(we were standing in the room)* Why don't you just let me come and live up here as your guest? If I gave you my word of honour?
>
> C. If fifty people came to me, real honest respectable people, and swore blind you wouldn't escape, I wouldn't trust them. I wouldn't trust the whole world.
>
> M. You can't go all through life trusting no one.
>
> C. You don't know what being alone is.
>
> M. What do you think I've been these last two months?
>
> C. I bet a lot of people think about you. Miss you. I might be dead for all anyone I knew ever cared.
>
> M. Your aunt.
>
> C. Her.
>
> *(There was a silence.)*
>
> C. *(he suddenly burst out with it)* You don't know what you are. You're everything. I got nothing if you go.
>
> *(And there was a great silence.)*

December 7th

He's bought the chair. He brought it down. It's nice. I wouldn't have it down here. I don't want anything from down here. A complete change.

Tomorrow I'm going upstairs for good. I asked him afterwards, last night. And he agreed. I haven't got to wait the whole week.

He's gone into Lewes to buy more things for the room. We're going to have a celebration supper.

He's been much nicer, these last two days.

I'm not going to lose my head and try and rush out at the first chance. He'll watch me, I know. I can't imagine what he'll do. The window will be boarded and he'll lock the door. But there'll be ways of seeing daylight. Sooner or later there'll be a chance (if he doesn't let me go of his own accord) to run for it.

But I know it will be only one chance. If he caught me escaping he'd put me straight back down here.

So it must be a really good chance. A sure one.

I tell myself I must prepare for the worst.

But something about him makes me feel that this time he will do what he has said.

I've caught his cold. It doesn't matter.

Oh my God my God I could kill myself.

He's going to kill me with despair.

I'm still down here. He never meant it.

He wants to take photographs. That's his secret. He wants to take my clothes off and . . . oh God I never knew till now what loathing was.

He said unspeakable things to me. I was a street-woman, I asked for what he suggested.

I went mad with rage. I threw a bottle of ink at him.

He said that if I didn't do it he'd stop me having baths or going out in the cellar. I'll be here all the time.

The hate between us. It came seething out.

I've caught his wretched cold. I can't think straight.

I couldn't kill myself, I'm too angry with him.

He's always abused me. From the very beginning. That story about the dog. He uses my heart. Then turns and tramples on it.

He hates me, he wants to defile me and break me and destroy me. He wants me to hate myself so much that I destroy myself.

The final meanness. He's not bringing me any supper. I'm to fast, on top of everything else. Perhaps he's going to leave me to starve. He's capable of it.

I've got over the shock. He won't beat me. I won't give in. I won't be broken by him.

I've got a temperature, I feel sick.

Everything's against me, but I won't give in.

I've been lying on the bed with G.P.'s picture beside me. Holding the frame in one hand. Like a crucifix.

I will survive. I will escape. I will not give in.

I will not give in.

I hate God. I hate whatever made this world, I hate whatever made the human race, made men like Caliban possible and situations like this possible.

If there is a God he's a great loathsome spider in the darkness. He *cannot be good*.

This pain, this terrible seeing-through that is in me now. It wasn't necessary. It is all pain, and it buys nothing. Gives birth to nothing.

All in vain. All wasted.

The older the world becomes, the more obvious it is. The bomb and the tortures in Algeria and the starving babies in the Congo. It gets bigger and darker.

More and more suffering for more and more. And more and more in vain.

It's as if the lights have fused. I'm here in the black truth.

God is impotent. He can't love us. He hates us because he can't love us.

All the meanness and the selfishness and the lies.

People won't admit it, they're too busy grabbing to see that the lights have fused. They can't see the darkness and the spider-face beyond and the great web of it all. That there's always this if you scratch at the surface of happiness and goodness.

The black and the black and the black.

I've not only never felt like this before, I never imagined it possible. More than hatred, more than despair. You can't hate what you cannot touch, I can't even feel what most people think of as despair. It's beyond despair. It's as if I can't feel any more. I see, but I can't feel.

Oh God if there is a God.

I hate beyond hate.

He came down just now. I was asleep on top of the bed. Fever. The air so stuffy. It must be flu.

I felt so rotten I said nothing. No energy to say my hate.

The bed's damp. My chest hurts.

I didn't say a word to him. It's gone beyond words. I wish I was a Goya. Could draw the absolute hate I have in me for him.

I'm so frightened. I don't know what will happen if I'm really ill. I can't understand why my chest hurts. As if I've had bronchitis for days.

But he'd have to get a doctor. He might kill me, but he couldn't just let me die.

Oh, God, this is horrible.

(Evening.) He brought a thermometer. It was a 100 at lunch, and now it's a 101. I feel *terrible*.

I've been in bed all day.

He's not human.

Oh God I'm so lonely so utterly alone.

I can't write.

(Morning.) A really bad bronchial cold. Shivering.

I haven't slept properly. Horrid dreams. Weird, very vivid dreams. G.P. was in one. It made me cry. I feel so frightened.

I can't eat. There's a pain in my lung when I breathe, and I keep on thinking of pneumonia. But it can't be.

I won't die. I won't die. Not for Caliban.

Dream. Extraordinary.

Walking in the Ash Grove at L. I look up through the trees. I see an aeroplane in the blue sky. I know it will crash. Later I see where it has crashed. I am frightened to go on. A girl walks towards me. Minny? I can't see. She is in peculiar Greek clothes— drapery. White. Its sunshine through the still trees. Seems to know me but I do not know her (not Minny). Never close. I want to be close. With her. I wake up.

If I die, no one will ever know.

It puts me in a fever. I can't write.

(Night.) No pity. No God.

I shouted at him and he went mad. I was too weak to stop him. Bound and gagged me and took his beastly photographs.

I don't mind the pain. The humiliation.

I did what he wanted. To get it over.

I don't mind for myself any more.

But oh God the beastliness of it all.

I'm crying I'm crying I can't write.

I will not give in.

I will not give in.

I can't sleep. I'm going mad. Have to have the light on. Wild dreams. I think people are here. D. Minny.

It's pneumonia.

He must get a doctor.

It is murder.

I can't write it down. Words are useless.

(He's come.) He won't listen. I've begged him. I've said it's murder. So weak. Temperature 102. I've been sick.

Nothing about last night, him or me.

Did it happen? Fever. I get delirious.

If only I knew what I have done.

Useless useless.

I won't die I won't die.

Dear dear G.P., this

Oh God oh God do not let me die.
God do not let me die.
Do not let me die.

3

WHAT I AM TRYING TO SAY IS THAT IT ALL CAME UNEXpected.

It started off badly because when I went down at half past seven I saw her lying by the screen, she'd knocked it over in falling, and I knelt by her and her hands were like ice, but she was breathing, it was a kind of rasping sigh, very quick, and when I lifted her back to bed she came to, she must have fainted in the night when she'd gone behind the screen. She was cold all over, she began to shiver terribly, and then to sweat more and she was delirious, she kept on saying, get the doctor, get the doctor, please get the doctor (sometimes it was general practitioner— G.P., G.P. she kept on, over and over again, like a rhyme), it wasn't her ordinary voice but what they call sing-song, and she didn't seem to be able to fix her eyes on me. She was silent a while, and then it was "Yankee Doodle Dandy," only the words were all slurred like she was drunk and she stopped in the middle. Twice she called Minny Minny like she thought she was in the next room (it was her sister), and then she started to mumble a lot of names and words, all mixed up with bits of sentence. Then it was she wanted to get up and I had to stop her. She really struggled. I kept on talking to her and she would stop a minute, but so soon as I went away to look after the tea or something she was off again. Well, I held her up to try to help her to drink the tea but it made her cough, she turned her head away, she didn't want it. I forgot to say she had nasty yellow pimples one corner of her lips. And she didn't smell fresh and clean like before.

In the end I got her to take a double dose of the pills, it said on the packet not to exceed the stated dose, but I heard once you ought to take twice what they said, they were scared to make it too strong for legal reasons.

I must have gone down four or five times that morning, I was that worried. She was awake but said she wanted nothing, she knew what was what, she shook her head anyhow. At lunch she drank a little tea and then went off to sleep and I sat out in the outer room. Well, the next time I switched on her light it was about five she was awake. She looked weak, very flushed, but she seemed to know where she was all right and who I was, her eyes followed me quite normally and I thought she was past the worse, the crisis as they call it.

She had a bit more tea and then she made me help her behind the screen, she could just about walk and so I left her a few minutes and came back and helped her back. She lay awhile in bed with her eyes open, staring at the ceiling, she had difficulty in getting her breath as usual and I was going to go away, but she made me stop.

She started to talk in a low hoarse voice, quite normal mentally, though. She said, "I've got pneumonia. You must get a doctor."

I said, you're over the worse, you look much better.

"I must have penicillin or something." Then she began to cough, and she couldn't breathe and she certainly sweated terribly.

Then she wanted to know what had happened in the night and the morning and I told her.

"Terrible nightmares," she said. Well, I said I'd stay with her all night and that she looked better and she asked me if I was sure she looked better and I said she was. I wanted her to be better by then, so I suppose I was seeing things.

I promised that if she wasn't well the next day I would carry her upstairs and get a doctor to come. So then she wanted to go up at once, she even wanted to know the time and when I told her, not thinking, she pointed out it was night and no one would see. But I said none of the rooms or beds was aired.

Then she changed, she said, "I feel so afraid. I'm going to die." She didn't speak quickly, there were pauses.

She said, "I've tried to help you. You must try to help me now." I said of course I would, I sponged her face again and she seemed to be dropping off, which was what I wanted, but she spoke up again.

She said in a loud voice, "Daddy? Daddy?"

Go to sleep, I said. You'll be recovered tomorrow.

She began to cry again. It wasn't like ordinary crying, she just lay there with the tears around her eyes as if she didn't know she was crying. Then suddenly she said, "What will you do if I die?"

I said, you're not going to die, don't be silly.

"Will you tell anyone?"

I'm not going to talk about it, I said.

"I don't want to die," she said. And then, "I don't want to die," again. And a third time, and each time I said don't talk about it, but she didn't seem to hear.

"Would you go away? If I died?"

I said, you're daft.

"What would you do with your money?"

I said, please let's talk about something else, but she insisted, after a pause, she was speaking normally, but there were funny gaps and then she'd suddenly say something again.

I said I didn't know, I hadn't thought. I was just humouring her.

"Leave it to the children."

I said, what children, and she said, "We collected money for them last term, they eat earth," and then a bit later, "We're all such pigs, we deserve to die," so I reckon they pinched the money they should have given in. Well, the next thing was she went to sleep for it must have been ten minutes. I didn't move, I thought she was well asleep but suddenly she said, "Would you?" again, as if we hadn't stopped talking. Then, "Are you there?" and she even tried to sit up to see me. Of course I calmed her down but she was awake again and she would go on about this fund she had collected for.

I gave up trying to say it was all silly, she wasn't going to die, so I said, yes, I would, but she wasn't, and so on.

"You promise?"

Yes.

Then she said, "Promises." Then some time after, "They eat earth." And she said that two or three times while I tried to pat her calm, it seemed it really distressed her.

The last thing she said was, "I forgive you."

She was delirious of course, but I said I was sorry again.

You might say things were different from this time. I forgot all she did in the past and I was sorry for her, I was truly sorry for what I did that other evening, but I wasn't to know she was really ill. It was spilt milk; it was done and there was an end to it.

It was really funny, though, how just when I thought I was really fed up with her all the old feelings came back. I kept on thinking of nice things, how sometimes we got on well and all the things she meant to me back home when I had nothing else. All the part from when she took off her clothes and I no longer respected her, that seemed to be unreal, like we both lost our minds. I mean, her being ill and me nursing seemed more real.

I stayed in the outer room like the night before. She was quiet half an hour or so, but then she began talking to herself, I said are you all right, and she stopped, but then later on she began talking again, or rather muttering and then she called my name out really loud, she said she couldn't breathe, and then she brought up a mass of phlegm. It was a funny dark brown, I didn't like the look of it at all, but I thought the pills might have coloured it. After that she must have dozed off for an hour or so, but suddenly she began to scream, she couldn't, but she was trying and when I rushed in she was half out of bed. I don't know what she was trying to do, but she didn't seem to know me and she fought like a tiger, in spite of being so weak. I really had to fight to lie her down again.

Then she was in a horrible sweat, her pyjamas were soaked, and when I tried to get the top off to put on new ones she started fighting, rolling about as if she was mad, and getting in a worse sweat. I never had a worse night, it was so terrible I can't describe it. She couldn't sleep, I gave her as many sleeping tablets as I dared but they seemed to have no effect, she would doze off a little while and then she would be in a state again, trying to get out of bed (once she did before I could get to her and fell to the floor). Sometimes she was in delirium, calling for a G.P. and talking to people who she'd known, I suppose. I didn't mind that so much, as long as she lay quiet. I took her temperature, it was over 104 degrees, and I knew she was ill, really ill.

Well, just about five the next morning I went up to have a breath of fresh air, it seemed another world out there, and I made up my mind that I would have to get her upstairs and ask a doctor in, I couldn't put it off any longer. I was there about ten minutes standing in the open door but then I heard her calling again, she brought up a bit more of the red-brown phlegm and then she was sick, so I had to get her out of bed and make it up again while she lay slopped in the chair. It was the way she breathed that was worst, it was so quick and gasping, as if she was panting all the time.

*   *   *

That morning (she seemed quieter) she was able to take in what I said, so I told her I was going for the doctor and she nodded, I consider she understood, though she didn't speak. That night seemed to take all her strength away, she just lay there still.

I know I could have gone to the village and phoned or got a doctor but for obvious reasons I never had dealings there, village gossip being what it is.

Anyhow I was so without sleep I didn't know what I was doing half the time. I was all on my own, as always. I had no one to turn to.

Well I went into Lewes and (it was just after nine) into the first chemist I saw open and asked for the nearest doctor, which the girl told me from a list she had. It was a house in a street I'd never been. I saw on the door surgery began at 8:30 and I ought to have guessed there would be a lot of people as usual, but for some reason I just saw myself going in and seeing the doctor straight off. I must have looked daft in the room, with all the people looking at me, all the seats were taken and another young man was standing up. Well, they all seemed to be looking at me, I hadn't the nerve to go straight through to the doctor so I stood by the wall. If only I could have gone straight in I'd have done it, everything would have been all right, it was having to be with all those other people in that room. I hadn't been in a room with other people for a long time, only in and out of shops, it felt strange, as I say, they all seemed to look at me, one old woman especially wouldn't take her eyes off me, I thought I must look peculiar in some way. I picked a magazine off the table, but of course I didn't read it.

Well, I began to think there all about what would happen, it would be all right for a day or two, the doctor and M perhaps wouldn't talk, but then . . . I knew what he would say, she must go into hospital, I couldn't look after her properly. And then I thought I might get a nurse in, but she wouldn't be long finding out what happened—Aunt Annie always said nurses were the nosiest parkers of them all, she never could abide people with long noses and nor could I. The doctor came out just then to call in the next patient, he was a tall man with a moustache, and he said, "Next" as if he was sick of seeing all these people. I mean, he sounded really irritated, I don't think it was my imagination, I saw a woman make a face at the one next to her when he went back in his room.

He came out again and I could see he was the officer type in the army, they've got no sympathy with you, they just give you orders, you're not their class and they treat everyone else as if they were dirt.

On top of that, this old woman started staring at me again and she made me hot under the collar, I hadn't slept all night and I was wrought up, I suppose. Anyhow, I knew I'd had enough. So I turned and walked out and went and sat in the van.

It was seeing all those people. It made me see Miranda was the only person in the world I wanted to live with. It made me sick of the whole damn lot.

What I did then was to go to a chemist and say I wanted something for very bad flu. It was a shop I hadn't been to before, luckily there was no one else there, so I could give my story. I said I had a friend who was a Peculiar Person (they don't believe in doctors) and he had very bad flu, perhaps pneumonia, and we had to give him something secretly. Well, the girl produced the same stuff as I'd bought before and I said I wanted penicillin or the other stuff, but she said it had to be on doctor's prescription. Unfortunately, the boss came out that moment, and she went and told him and he came up and said I must see a doctor and explain the case. I said I'd pay anything, but he just shook his head and said it was against the law. Then he wanted to know if my friend lived locally, and I left before he started nosing any further. I tried two other chemists, but they both said the same and I was scared to ask any more so I took some medicine they could sell, a different kind.

Then I went back. I could hardly drive, I was so tired.

Of course I went down as soon as I got back, and she was lying there breathing away. As soon as she saw me she began talking, she seemed to think I was someone else because she asked me if I'd seen Louise (I never heard her talk of her before)—luckily she didn't wait for an answer, she started talking about some modern painter, then she said she was thirsty. It wasn't sense, things seemed to come in her head and go. Well, I gave her a drink and she lay still a while and she suddenly seemed to get half back to normal (in mind, that is) because she said, when will Daddy come, you have been?

I lied, it was a white lie, I said he'd be here soon. She said, wash my face, and when I did, she said he must see some of that stuff I've brought up. I say she said, but it was all in a whisper.

She said she wished she could sleep.

It's the fever, I said, and she nodded, for a bit she quite understood all I was saying, and no one could believe it but I decided to go back to Lewes to get a doctor. I helped her behind the screen, she was so weak I knew she couldn't run away, so what I decided was I would go up and try and get two hours' sleep and then I'd carry her upstairs and I'd go down to Lewes and get another doctor out.

I don't know how it happened, I always get up as soon as the alarm sounds; I think I must have reached out and turned it off in my sleep, I don't remember waking up, once. Anyway it was four, not half past twelve when I woke up. Of course, I rushed down to see what had happened. She had pulled all the top clothes off her chest, but luckily it was warm enough. I don't think it mattered then anyway, she was in a terrible fever and she didn't know me, and when I lifted to take her upstairs she tried to struggle and scream, but she was so weak she couldn't. What's more her coughing stopped her screaming and seemed to make her realize where we were. I had a proper job getting her upstairs, but I managed it and put her in the bed in the spare room (I had got it all warmed), where she seemed happier. She didn't say anything, the cold air had made her cough and bring up, her face was the funny purplish colour, too. I said, the doctor's coming, which she seemed to understand.

I stayed a bit to see if she would be all right, I was afraid she might have just the strength to go to the window and attract the attention of anyone passing. I knew she couldn't really, but I seemed to find reasons not to go. I went several times to her open door, she was lying there in the darkness, I could hear her breathing, sometimes she was muttering, once she called for me and I went and stood beside her and all she could say was doctor, doctor, and I said he's coming, don't worry and I wiped her face, she couldn't stop sweating. I don't know why I didn't go then, I tried, but I couldn't, I couldn't face the idea of not knowing how she was, of not being able to see her whenever I wanted. I was just like in love with her all over again. And another thing, all those days I used to think, well, she'll be getting over it a long time, she'll need me, it will be very nice when she has turned the corner.

I don't know why, I also thought the new room might help. It would make a change.

It was like when I had to take Mabel out in her chair. I could always find a dozen reasons to put it off. You ought to be grateful you have legs to push, Aunt Annie used to say (they knew I didn't like being seen out pushing the chair). But it's in my character, it's how I was made. I can't help it.

Time passed, it must have been midnight or more and I went up to see how she was, to see if she'd drink a cup of tea, and I couldn't get her to answer me, she was breathing faster than ever, it was terrifying the way she panted, she seemed to catch at the air as if she could never get it fast enough. I shook her but she seemed asleep although her eyes were open, her face was very livid and she seemed to be staring at something on the ceiling. Well I felt really frightened, I thought, I'll give her half an hour and then I must go. I sat by her, I could see that things were definitely worse by the way she was sweating and her face was terrible. Another thing she did those days was picking at the sheets. Pimples had spread all over both corners of her mouth and lips.

Well at last having locked her door in case, I set off again to Lewes, I remember I got there just after 1:30, everything shut up, of course. I went straight to the street where the doctor lived and stopped a bit short of his house. I was just sitting there in the dark getting ready to go and ring the bell, getting my story straight and so on, when there was a tapping on the window. It was a policeman.

It was a very nasty shock. I lowered the window.

Just wondered what you were doing here, he said.

Don't tell me it's no parking.

Depends what your business is, he said. He had a look at my licence, and wrote down my number, very deliberate. He was an old man, he can't have been any good or he wouldn't have been a constable still.

Well, he said, do you live here?

No, I said.

I know you don't, he said. That's why I'm asking what you're doing here.

I haven't done anything, I said. Look in the back, I said, and he did, the old fool. Anyhow it gave me time to think up a story. I told him I couldn't sleep and I was driving around and then I got lost and I had stopped to look at a map. Well, he didn't believe me or he didn't look as if he did, he said I should get on home.

Well the result of it all was that I drove away, I couldn't get out with him watching and go to the doctor's door, he'd have smelt a rat at once. What I thought I would do was drive home and see if she was worse and if she was I'd drive her in to the hospital and give a false name and then drive away and then I'd have to run away and leave the country or something—I couldn't think beyond giving her up.

Well, she was on the floor again, she'd tried to get out of bed, I suppose to go to the bathroom or to try to escape. Anyway I lifted her back to bed, she seemed to be half in a coma, she said some words but I couldn't make them out and she didn't understand anything I said.

I sat by her almost all night, some of the time I slept off. Twice she struggled to get out of bed again, it was no good, she hadn't the strength of a flea. I said the same old things again, I said the doctor was coming and it seemed to calm her. Once she asked what day it was, and I lied, I said it was Monday (it was Wednesday) and she seemed a bit calmer then, too. She just said Monday, but you could tell it didn't mean anything. It was like her brain was affected, too.

I knew she was dying then, I knew all that night, I could have told anyone.

I just sat there, listening to her breathing and muttering (she never seemed to sleep properly) and thinking about the way things turned out. Thinking about my rotten life and her life, and everything else.

*   *   *

Anyone there would see what it was like. I was truly and really in despair, although I say it myself. I couldn't do anything, I wanted her to live so, and I couldn't risk getting help, I was beaten, anyone would have seen it. All those days I knew I would never love another the same. There was only Miranda for ever. I knew it then.

Another thing was, she was the only one who knew I loved her. She knew what I really was. Not like anyone else could ever understand.

Well, it dawned, the last day came. Strange, it was a beauty, I don't believe there was a cloud all day, one of those cold winter days when there's no wind and the sky is very blue. It seemed specially arranged, most appropriate, seeing she passed away so peaceful. The last words she spoke were about ten when she said (I think), "the sun" (it was coming in the window), and she tried to sit up but she could not manage it.

She never said another word to be understood, she lingered on all the morning and afternoon and went with the sun. Her breathing had got very faint and (just to show what I was like) I even thought she had gone into a sleep at last. I don't know exactly when she died, I know she was breathing about half past three when I went downstairs to do a bit of dusting and so on to take my mind off things, and when I came back about four, she was gone.

She was lying with her head to one side and it looked awful, her mouth was open and her eyes were staring white like she'd tried to see out of the window one last time. I felt her and she was cold, though her body was still warm. I ran and got a mirror. I knew that was the way and held it over her mouth but there was no mist. She was dead.

Well, I shut her mouth up and got the eyelids down. I didn't know what to do then, I went and made myself a cup of tea.

When it was dark I got her dead body and carried it down to the cellar. I know you're meant to wash dead bodies, but I didn't like to, it didn't seem right, so I put her on the bed and combed out her hair and cut a lock. I tried to arrange her face so it had a smile but I couldn't. Anyway she looked very peaceful. Then I knelt and said a prayer, the only one I knew was Our Father, so I said some of that and God rest her soul, not that I believe in religion, but it seemed right. Then I went upstairs.

I don't know why it was one little thing that did it; you'd think it would be seeing her dead or carrying her down the last time, but it wasn't; it was when I saw her slippers in the room where she was upstairs. I picked them up and suddenly I knew she wouldn't ever wear them again. I wouldn't ever go down and draw the bolts again (funny, I had still bolted her in, though), and none of it would ever happen again, the good or the bad. I suddenly knew she was dead and dead means gone for ever, for ever and ever.

Those last days I had to be sorry for her (as soon as I knew it wasn't acting), and I forgave her all the other business. Not while she was living, but when I knew she was dead, that was when I finally forgave her. All sorts of nice things came back. I remembered the beginning, the days in the Annexe just seeing her come out of the front door, or passing her the other side of the street, and I couldn't understand how it all happened so that she was there below, dead.

It was like a joke mousetrap I once saw, the mouse just went on and things moved, it couldn't ever turn back, but just on and on into cleverer and cleverer traps until the end.

I thought how happy I was, feelings I had those weeks I never had before and I wouldn't ever have again.

The more I thought about it, the worse it seemed.

It came to midnight and I couldn't sleep, I had to have all the lights on, I don't believe in spirits but it seemed better with the lights.

I kept on thinking of her, thinking perhaps it was my fault after all that she did what she did and lost my respect, then I thought it was her fault, she asked for everything she got. Then I didn't know what to think, my head seemed to go bang bang bang, and I knew I couldn't live at Fosters any more. I wanted to drive away and never come back.

I thought, I could sell up and go out to Australia. But then there was all the covering up to do first. It was too much. The next thing was I got the police on the brain. I decided the best thing was to go to the police and tell them the lot. I even got my coat on to drive down.

I thought I was going mad, I kept on looking in the mirror and trying to see it in my face. I had this horrible idea, I was mad, everyone else could see it, only I couldn't. I kept remembering how people in Lewes seemed to look at me sometimes, like the people in that doctor's waiting-room. They all knew I was mad.

It came to two o'clock. I don't know why, I began to think her being dead was all a mistake, perhaps she had just been asleep. So I had to go down to make sure. It was horrible. Soon as I went down in the outer cellar I started imagining things. Like she might step out of a corner with a hatchet. Or she would not be there—even though the door was bolted she would have vanished. Like in a horror-film.

She was there. Lying there, all in the silence. I touched her. She was so cold, so cold it gave me a shock. I still couldn't understand it was true, how she'd been living only a few hours before, and just a few days back walking about, drawing, doing her knitting. And now this.

Then something moved at the other end of the cellar, back by the door. It must have been a draught. Something broke in me, I lost my head, I rushed out and fell up the stair in the outer cellar and out. I locked the door down double quick and got into the house and locked that door and all the bolts home.

After a while the shaking stopped, I calmed down. But all I could think was how this was the end. I couldn't live with her down there like that.

It was then I got the idea. It kept on coming back, this feeling that she was lucky to be done with it all, no more worries, no more hiding, no more things you want to be and won't ever be. But finished, the lot.

All I had to do was kill myself, then the others could think what they liked. The people in the waiting-room, the Annexe people, Aunt Annie and Mabel, all of them. I would be out of it.

I started thinking how I could do it, how I could go into Lewes as soon as the shops opened and get a lot of aspros and some flowers, chrysanths were her favourite. Then take the aspros and go down with the flowers and lie beside her. Post a letter first to the police. So they would find us down there together. Together in the Great Beyond.

We would be buried together. Like Romeo and Juliet.

It would be a real tragedy. Not sordid.

I would get some proper respect if I did it. If I destroyed the photos, that was all there was, people would see I never did anything nasty to her, it would be truly tragic.

I thought it out, and then I went and got the photos and the negatives, all ready to burn first thing in the morning.

It was like I had to have some definite plan. Anything, so long as it was definite.

There was the money, but I didn't care any more. Aunt Annie and Mabel would get it. Miranda talked about the Save the Children fund, but she was already half off her rocker. All those charities are run by crooks. Save the Trustees, more like.

I wanted what money couldn't buy. If I really had got a nasty mind I would not have gone to all the trouble I did, I would have just visited the women you read about on the boards in Paddington and Soho and done what I wanted. You can't buy happiness. I must have heard Aunt Annie say that a hundred times. Ha ha, I always thought, just let's have a try first. Well, I had my try.

Because what it is, it's luck. It's like the pools—worse, there aren't even good teams and bad teams and likely draws. You can't ever tell how it will turn out. Just A versus B, C versus D, and nobody knows what A and B and C and D are. That's why I never believed in God. I think we are just insects, we live a bit and then die and that's the lot. There's no mercy in things. There's not even a Great Beyond. There's nothing.

About three o'clock I dozed off, so I went up to get a last sleep, I lay in bed seeing it all, the going into Lewes when I woke up, coming back, having a bonfire, locking up (one last look at my collection) and then going down. She was waiting for me down there. I would say we were in love, in the letter to the police. A suicide pact. It would be "The End."

4

A S IT HAPPENED, THINGS TURNED OUT RATHER DIFFERENT.
I didn't wake up till after ten, it was another nice day.
I had breakfast and then I went into Lewes and I got the
aspros and flowers and came back and went down and then I
thought I would just have a last look through her things. It was
lucky I did. I found her diary which shows she never loved me, she
only thought of herself and the other man all the time.

As it so happens, anyway, as soon as I woke up I began to have
more sensible ideas, it's just like me to see only the dark side last
thing at night and to wake up different.

These ideas came while I was having breakfast, not deliberate,
they just came. About how I could get rid of the body. I thought,
if I wasn't going to die in a few hours, I could do this and that. I
had a lot of ideas. I thought how I would like to prove it could be
done. Nobody finding out.

It was a lovely morning. The country round Lewes is very pretty.

I also thought that I was acting as if I killed her, but she died,
after all. A doctor probably could have done little good, in my
opinion. It was too far gone.

Another thing that morning in Lewes, it was a real coincidence,
I was just driving to the flower-shop when a girl in an overall
crossed the crossing where I stopped to let people over. For a moment it gave me a turn, I thought I was seeing a ghost, she had the
same hair, except it was not so long; I mean she had the same size
and the same way of walking as Miranda. I couldn't take my eyes
off her, and I just had to park the car and go back the way she was
where I had the good fortune to see her go into the Woolworth's.
Where I followed and found she works behind the sweet counter.

Well, I came back with the stuff and went down to see Miranda, to arrange the flowers really; I could see I wasn't in the mood for the other thing and I thought I had better think it over first and then in any case I found the diary.

The days passed, it is now three weeks since all that.

Of course I shall never have a guest again, although now Aunt Annie and Mabel have decided to stay Down Under, it would not be difficult.

Still as a matter of interest I have since been looking into the problems there would be with the girl in Woolworth's. She lives in a village the other side of Lewes from here, in a house a quarter mile or so from the bus-stop. You have to go along a country lane to get to it. As I say, it would be possible (if I hadn't learnt my lesson). She isn't as pretty as Miranda, of course, in fact she's only an ordinary common shop-girl, but that was my mistake before, aiming too high, I ought to have seen that I could never get what I wanted from someone like Miranda, with all her la-di-da ideas and clever tricks. I ought to have got someone who would respect me more. Someone ordinary I could teach.

She is in the box I made, under the appletrees. It took me three days to dig the hole. I thought I would go mad the night I did it (went down and got her in the box I made and outside). I don't think many could have done it. I did it scientific. I planned what had to be done and ignored my natural feelings. I couldn't stand the idea of having to look at her again, I once heard they go green and purple in patches, so I went in with a cheap blanket I bought in front of me and held it out till I was by the bed and then threw it over the deceased. I rolled it up and all the bedclothes into the box and soon had the lid screwed on. I got round the smell with fumigator and the fan.

The room's cleaned out now and good as new.

I shall put what she wrote and her hair up in the loft in the deed-box which will not be opened till my death, so I don't expect for forty or fifty years. I have not made up my mind about Marian (another M! I heard the supervisor call her name), this time it won't be love, it would just be for the interest of the thing and to compare them and also the other thing, which as I say I would like to go into in more detail and I could teach her how. And the clothes would fit. Of course I would make it clear from the start who's boss and what I expect.

But it is still just an idea. I only put the stove down there today because the room needs drying out anyway.

ABOUT THE AUTHOR

JOHN FOWLES (1926–) was born in southeast England and taught school for years before the publication of his debut novel, *The Collector*. His subsequent works of fiction include *The Magus, The French Lieutenant's Woman, The Ebony Tower, Daniel Martin,* and *Mantissa*. Fowles has also written literary criticism and books about the seaside town of Lyme Regis where he lives.